TRUTHS *that* SAINTS BELIEVE

THE *Klutch* DUET

ANNE MALCOM

Cover Design: Simply Defined Art
Editing: Kim BookJunkie
Formatting: TRC Designs

TRUTHS *that* SAINTS

BELIEVE

THE *Klutch* DUET

CHAPTER ONE

Jay

"**B**lack dress, black hair, fake tits, drinking a cosmo by the bar."

Jay leaned back and watched his security guard walk through the throngs on the dance floor, toward the woman he'd described.

He hated the ghost that haunted him in this moment. The déjà vu. He had spent far too much time ruminating over what he'd lost. What'd he'd thrown away. Even though he'd never *had* her. Not really. She'd loved an idea of him, not his true self. He'd shown her glimpses of who he truly was, the wickedness inside of him. And she'd loved those parts. Because she could love wicked things. Or at least, she'd thought she could. Jay was an intelligent man … he was smart enough to know that Stella would never be able to love the core of him.

He'd been reckless, selfish and dangerous even thinking that he could've made it happen. That he could have merged the cold, calculated, powerful and deadly life he'd created with the warmth and light Stella brought.

She would have hated him.

Eventually.

He would have hated himself for not letting her go. For tearing apart all of the dreams she'd had, for treading on all of the futures she may have had with another man.

Jay's fist clenched. The mere thought of another man touching skin he'd marked, skin he *owned*, turned his blood hot. The need to hurt—to end—any man who thought he had the right to what was his was overwhelming.

The entire point of him letting her go was for her to find someone capable of giving her what she deserved, but Jay could not be sure if she found someone else that he wouldn't kill the man. He sought control in every facet of his life, but he could not control himself when it came to Stella.

He could control himself even less in her absence.

He knew that people were talking. That his employees from both his legitimate and illegitimate businesses feared him even more than they had before.

Jay wasn't sleeping. As soon as he left his offices downtown, he came here until closing. Then, when night held the deepest shadows, he went to do things that could only be done in the dark. Things that he'd hid from Stella. Things that would've eaten away at her love for him like erosion on rock.

The soft whirr of the elevator doors opening and the click of heels on the floor interrupted Jay's thoughts. Well, not completely. He was always thinking of Stella. Her absence was a black hole in his mind. Left him distracted. Which was dangerous, especially with the stirrings in his territories. This was not the time to be distracted.

Which was why the knockout with the fake tits was sauntering into his office. He hadn't touched another woman in months. The only woman he wanted to touch was across the fucking world and out of his reach.

"Mr. Helmick," the woman in front of him purred.

And it was a *purr*. She was like a cat. Eyes sharp. Cunning. Knowing.

This woman was not ignorant to what he was. What this was. She knew the score. Had heard the rumors. She likely wore the dress that molded over her tits like a second skin precisely to try and lure in a big fish tonight. If not him precisely, then someone with a lofty bank account who was either deluded enough to think she liked him for his personality or smart enough to know that he was getting laid no matter her true feelings.

Those were the kind of women he had gravitated toward before Stella. The predictable, hungry and shallow ones. The ones after money and willing to do whatever and whoever it took to get there. Jay did not judge or blame those women; he appreciated them and enjoyed them. Because their motives were clear and simple, they were easy. They were willing to submit to his every whim, ready to mold themselves in to whatever shape they thought he'd like most.

"Take off your clothes," he demanded, still sitting in the chair, still seeing Stella standing there, talking about her cat and forgetting people's birthdays.

The woman did not hesitate. She smiled in a practiced way that made most men's cocks twitch and shimmied out of her dress.

She wasn't wearing anything underneath.

There was no fight in her. No battle. No anger. No outrage. Only hunger. And not for him. For what she could get from him.

Stella had obeyed him when he'd uttered this command at his home office. But she'd done it with fury. She'd done it despite all of her best instincts, and she'd done it because she'd had no choice. Like him, she was trapped in the connection between the two of them

The red string of fate.

"It will twist and tangle through the course of time, of life, circumstances. But it will never break. The red string will always keep them connected."

The memory caused physical agony, and Jay had to clench his fists on top of his desk so he didn't throw his glass of whiskey at the wall just so he could watch something shatter. Break.

Jay's eyes flickered upward at the movement in front of him. He'd forgotten the naked woman was even there. She was walking toward him. Sauntering with a practiced sway of her hips.

"Did I tell you to move?"

She stopped immediately, a sly grin teasing the corners of her artificially plumped mouth.

No fear.

Jay ached to create it. To use this woman and her body to sate the hunger that had been burning inside of him for months.

He wanted to break something.

He wanted to break her.

Just because he could. Because if he did that, then there would be no way back.

No way back to *her.*

"Leave," Jay bit out, barely able to move his mouth.

She blinked, the smile still frozen on her face. What she didn't do was move.

Jay remained still. "Get out. Now."

She flinched at his tone, and he was glad.

He didn't watch her redress, didn't watch her give him one last look, didn't revel in the shame on her face. No, he pretended to work. Pretended he wasn't longing for the one thing he couldn't have.

Then, once the lights had been turned on, the club emptied, he stalked in to the night to sate the one need he could sate: the need to create pain.

"You've been skimming, Jacob," Jay said, voice flat. He was staring at his accountant in his bespoke suit with his Rolex and diamond cufflinks, all bought with Jay's money.

Jacob blinked rapidly. He was already afraid. The man knew a meeting at three in the morning in a warehouse in a desolate part of the city did not mean good things. Especially when you were guilty.

Which Jacob was.

Jay had his accounts audited by a totally separate accountant once every six months. He usually did it himself every three as well. But he'd been ... distracted, so Jacob had managed to embezzle from under his nose. Three million fucking dollars.

Jay fingered the knife on the tray in front of him.

"It's impressive," Jay continued, already bored of this. "That you're brave enough to steal." He looked up at the man who was sweating through his shirt even though it was a cold night. "From me."

"Mr. Helmick—"

Jay held up his hand. "I did not tell you to speak. And right now, Jacob, you really want to listen to me."

Jacob's eyes squeezed shut, and he began crying. It disgusted Jay, this show of weakness, the lack of spine. This man knew he had broken the rules. Jacob knew what kind of man Jay was when he started this job two years ago. Jay had made sure of that. He had also made sure that he hired the best. Men without wives, children, without anyone who would miss them, could possibly become complications. If his accountants did fall in love, got married, Jay dismissed them with severance pay and assurances that their mouths would stay shut about the nature of their work for him.

Each and every one of them knew that they would die if they crossed him. So Jay felt no sympathy or remorse for what he was about to do to this man. He'd had a choice. Jay paid him a fuck of a lot of money, and he could've quit at any time if he'd so wished.

He hadn't.

Instead, he'd gambled with his life for a fucking watch and a nice car.

"You're greedy, Jacob," Jay announced, assessing the scalpel he held up.

It was at that point when Jacob tried to flee. They all did at some point. A survival instinct that didn't know logic kicking in. Karson, who was standing behind him, grabbed him by the shoulders and put him back down on the chair. Not gently.

"Please—"

"I told you not to speak," Jay clipped, feeling frustrated. He put down the scalpel, suddenly feeling tired, exhausted. He took the gun from his shoulder holster and shot Jacob point blank. The body slumped and slipped down from the seat. Jay wiped the blood from his face before sliding the gun back into his jacket.

He barely glanced at the corpse. "We need a new accountant," he said to Karson.

Karson nodded. "I've already vetted three."

"Make sure they're not cowards," Jay instructed. "I can deal with criminals, but I cannot deal with men pathetic enough not to accept the fate they choose."

Jay walked away, wondering if he was talking about himself.

Stella

"It's knock off time, so I'm gonna ask you the same thing I ask you every night ... come to the pub for a drink?"

I smiled at Brent, grasping the keys to my rental from my purse.

The creases around his ocean blue eyes deepened with his cheeky grin, one that was entirely white and straight except for one crooked tooth which made the grin and his rugged face all the more handsome.

His voice was smooth, light, teasing, and made infinitely more sexy by his accent, one that I was surrounded by daily and one that never got old.

Brent was the stuntman for the show we were working on. A local from 'down South' and the epitome of a rugged mountain man. I didn't know if he was actually *from* the mountains, but he was the guy who came to mind when I thought of such men. He was criminally attractive with dirty blond hair, a permanent tan and muscles bulging from the sleeves of his tee that was so faded there was no logo on it anymore. He smiled easily and had an air about him that he could fix anything that broke down in the vicinity. Which he had done many times on set. His hands were callused, tanned and always stained with oil or dirt.

They couldn't have been further from the hands that were neatly manicured, smooth, tanned and were more likely to be stained with blood than any kind of oil or dirt.

So theoretically, Brent was the healthiest and safest option for a rebound. Shit, Brent was *husband* material. The me before the arrangement, before *him*, wouldn't have let Brent ask me out more than once. This was a man who you moved across oceans for.

In another life, at least.

"Raincheck," I replied with a smile. The expression was forced, stretched and painful.

His brows furrowed ever so slightly. "You're not gonna be able to say no to me forever, darlin.'" His tone was still teasing, but there was a roughness to it. A sexual undertone that had grown these past months. It started subtle, a glint in his eye when he spoke to me, the casual touches, the way he looked at me. It had gotten more intense lately, with the wrap of the show looming.

It wasn't uncomfortable, his attention. Wasn't lecherous or sleazy. It would've been comforting if it hadn't reminded me of everything I'd lost. Of what I'd never have again. That my ability to love a decent and kind man was fucked.

I smiled sadly. "Maybe not," I agreed. "But tonight, I still can." I winked at him and walked to my car.

His eyes burned into my back as I did so.

I breathed a sigh of relief when I pulled into the small space under the shade of a eucalyptus tree with lush green bushes to my left and a garden complete with a fountain and various stone statues on my right. I considered the limestone fairy I parked beside, with greenery crawling up her wings, as my friend. My guardian. Maybe I was going a bit insane? Then again, she hadn't started talking to me or anything, so it wasn't full-fledged lunacy. Not yet at least.

After the slam of my car door, there were no sounds aside from the low rumble of the waves. No roar of cars, no sirens, no neighbors. Sure, I was thirty minutes from town—town being the small metropolis of Killsmore that consisted of three great coffee shops, one supermarket and three pubs—and where most of the crew was staying, but I was right on the ocean. The small 'bach' I'd found online had somehow been vacant for the exact amount of time I needed it for. The closest neighbor was ten minutes down the dirt road I drove in on.

When I'd first followed my GPS here, I'd frowned at the dust rising from the tires of my car, at the farmland around me, thinking I'd really fucked up and that I'd been catfished.

But then I'd pulled past the gates, ornate iron gates with plants curling around them. Drove down the winding drive edged with trees, carefully planted to hide the cottage away from the world, feeling like my private sanctuary.

Then the small house came into view. With a red corrugated roof and a porch that had grapevines climbing up it, making it look as if nature was taking over the house. Roses of every color were planted along the front with a porch swing to the right of the red front door. Large windows everywhere.

The front door opened right onto the ocean. Or that's what it seemed like. The windows along the living room were floor to ceiling, barely any walls to obstruct the view of the beach and water beyond. Sapphire and aquamarine ... a different ocean than the one I'd looked upon on another continent. In another lifetime.

A different ocean that carried the same memories.

If I was a smart woman, one who wanted to heal, to forget, I would've left this beautiful paradise that reminded me of my wretched, painful past and found something else. Something that looked upon the hills, the landscape of New Zealand, something closer to town, closer to distraction. But I hadn't. I'd closed the front door, walked across the tastefully decorated living room and opened the sliding doors, stepping onto the balcony and breathing in the salty sea air.

It was somewhat of a ritual now. After saying hello to my resident fairy. After making sure that there were no flowers I'd forgotten to water, no packages that I'd ordered at two in the morning after a bottle of wine.

Then I'd step inside, inhale the smells of this new place that was becoming home to me, opening those doors, inhaling the air that was all too familiar. That reminded me of a man who was a stranger yet knew me better than anyone.

Then, I'd make something for dinner, depending on my mood, my energy levels or whether I'd remembered to go to the store that day. Janet, the woman who rented the cottage for me, would sometimes 'pop by' with a basket of muffins, a lasagna, homemade granola, cherries, her favorite wine. Pretty much anything and everything. She had wild, bright red curls, creased tanned skin and had a penchant for the color purple. Her voice was thick, husky and evidence of a smoking habit she'd kicked five years ago. Her husband died six years ago, and she swore she would never marry again, but she'd surely have a lot of boyfriends. I knew all of this because she told me. On my second night here, she'd arrived with two bottles of red, dinner and an evening's worth of stories about her life.

She had no children, and I thought that a waste since there were plenty of women who would've benefitted from having a mother like her. Warm, confident, unapologetic about who she was. It was ugly and cruel of me to wish she had been my own mother. To wish my biological mother out of my life and out of existence for my own selfish reasons, so that I didn't have a darkness inside of me. So I didn't fear my own mind. Wasn't terrified of my own memories.

But wishing wouldn't do me any good. And if my mother hadn't been my mother, I probably wouldn't have been fucked up enough to find myself in Jay's office that night, or in his bed all the nights after.

And despite how much pain those nights had caused me, despite how much he'd ruined me, I didn't want anything or anyone to be the reason I didn't have the memory of him. The ghost of him.

I allowed myself to enjoy having dinner with Janet one night a week. A Sunday afternoon with her in the garden. Opening up the fridge to an eggplant dish she'd cooked for me along with more wine because she was starting to know me too well.

The air was colder now. Summer was creeping away, giving way to fall, even up here up at the top of the North Island where the weather was warmer than the rest of the country. My arms prickled from the chill. Not just because of the bite to the air but from the impending wrap of the show. It had been months. An uncommonly warm summer which meant I'd never felt a chill, leaving my skin as tan as it had ever been despite how religious I was with my SPF. There was a hole in the ozone layer here, apparently. Made the sun harsher. Causing me to burn that much quicker.

I'd already been burned, so the fire of a different kind felt nice. It was turning me in to something else. Or at least someone who looked different. My skin was no longer peaches and cream but a milky caramel. My hair was longer, bleached by that harsh sun, barely any strawberry left in my blonde. I'd put on weight where I'd needed it. If it was up to me, I would've forgone food except for when it was absolutely necessary and existed off coffee and wine. But there was Janet. And there was Brent on lunch breaks, bringing me a plate piled high with his crooked smile and easy conversation. I'd eat the whole plate without even realizing it, just so I could listen to him talk while making sure my mouth was full so I never had to offer any information about myself.

The food was fresher here. Purer. I could taste it. But I couldn't enjoy it. I couldn't enjoy much, really. Even the company of a good man, a strong, comforting woman, some of the most beautiful landscape in the world, the kindness of the people of this country.

Oh, yes, I was the definition of a cliché. Living and working in paradise, eating excellent food, being asked out by ruggedly handsome men yet not enjoying a single bit of it.

I looked good, though. With my permanent tan, with my long hair, with my new curves. But I was all sharp angles on the inside. Even breathing cut me open all over again. The pain hadn't dulled. Not one single bit.

I grabbed a glass from where it had been drying on the rack beside the sink. My eyes focused on the single plate, the mug—I was a tea drinker now—the single set of cutlery.

It was the ordinary things that hurt me now. The evidence of me living my life alone. Spinsterhood.

"Jesus Christ, I sound like Bridget fucking Jones," I muttered to myself, opening a bottle of red and filling the glass up, right to the top. I didn't fuck around with the half empty bullshit.

The native birds sang as I walked out the sliding doors off the living room, breathing in the salty air that rubbed in all of my open wounds. It was cold, cold enough that I should've gone back in to grab a sweater, but I kept walking down the sun-bleached wooden steps that travelled down to a sandy path which led to the beach beyond.

My beach.

My ocean, it seemed.

This little cottage—*bach* as it was fondly called in New Zealand—was nestled between acres of farmland that the owner refused to sell despite lucrative offers. This meant that the only resident of this beach for many miles was me. It was rather breathtaking, looking at the way the land bent in front of me, mountains looming in the distance, seeming to plunge into the turquoise sea. The last of the sun pressed down on me just as hard as the ocean breeze.

I sipped my wine, walking slowly, looking at nothing and trying very hard to think about nothing.

"I'm a sinner, pet. You know this. My job is lies. My very existence, inhaling and exhaling, are a series of mistruths, secrets and betrayals. There was no way I could admit to you, or myself, that I was capable of loving. Because I knew I was, and I knew that my love would be your curse. Knew that it was an inevitability to fall for you. Knew I'd ruin your life loving you. So I lied. Like only a sinner can."

The memory burned hot, even as the air chilled my exposed skin.

He was right. His love was a curse.

"Nice night for it."

I jumped, twisting around in the direction of the voice that just spoke.

Standing in front of me was a man. A man holding a gun.

CHAPTER TWO

Jay

J ay was staring at his computer screen when the elevator doors opened.

His hand automatically went to the gun he had sitting in the open drawer to his left.

"You're still here," an irritated female voice declared.

Jay let go of his gun and settled his gaze on the irritated female in question. Though he'd never met her in person, he recognized Wren Whitney from the intelligence he'd had done and from the photographs of her on Stella's social media.

She was more beautiful in person, which was saying something since she photographed incredibly well. Short, petite, angled cheekbones. Good hair. Eyes that held fire which made even Jay flinch internally.

He got why Karson was tangled up in this one.

"*Why* are you still here?" Wren demanded, storming up to his desk on six-inch heels before laying her palms flat on the surface in front of him. She leaned over to glare at him some more in a power move the head of the Italian Mafia wouldn't even be brave enough to pull off.

Jay was amused. Or he was *almost* amused. He was too fucking miserable to be anything else.

"I'm here because this is my office," Jay replied evenly. Normally, people who stormed into his office without an appointment and without respect pissed him off and were not long for this world. This was different, though. This was someone directly connected to Stella.

The elevator dinged. Karson strode in looking more flustered than Jay had ever seen the man look. His eyes narrowed on Wren's back, resting on her ass for a second because, despite the situation, Wren was his woman, and she had a nice ass.

Wren did not look back, her eyes were narrowed on Jay.

"I'm sorry sir," Karson uttered, walking hurriedly up to where Wren was hunched over, shooting Jay daggers. "I'll get rid of her."

Now Wren looked at Karson, her glare transitioning and one perfectly sculpted eyebrow raised. "Pray tell, Karson, honey, tell me how you plan on getting rid of me." There was a challenge there.

Yeah, Jay got why Karson was tangled up in that.

Because that challenge, that determination, that fire … that's what Jay had been tangled up in. That's what Jay had lost.

Jay almost wanted to grin, looking at the two of them. Almost. As much as he wanted Karson to have a good woman, the way he was feeling, Jay would be absolutely gleeful to see everyone else as fucking miserable as he was right now.

"It's okay, Karson," Jay stated, saving the man, an uncharacteristic mercy. But all he wanted was to get them out of his sight so he wasn't taunted with what he had thrown away.

Karson kept Wren's stare for a few beats more before he looked to Jay, nodded once and straightened. He stayed at Wren's side, coiled, tense and ready for attack.

She returned her gaze to Jay.

"You need to go to Stella," Wren ordered.

Jay was careful to keep his expression even as he heard her name out loud for the first time in months. If he hadn't trained himself better, he would've flinched.

He didn't answer because he didn't know what to say.

Wren continued to glare. "You know she's in the hospital, right?"

Jay's blood went cold, and there was suddenly a high-pitched ringing in his ears. He didn't remember getting out of his chair, nor rounding the desk. He wasn't sure what he would've done had Karson not stepped in front of him.

Karson's hand was flat on his chest, and his eyes were full of threat. Of danger.

"Stand down, Jay," Karson insisted, voice hostile.

Jay blinked. In all of the years Karson had worked for him, he'd never once been confrontational. He'd been steadfastly loyal, would take a bullet for him, would and had killed for him, Jay knew this. But right now, the closest thing he had to a friend looked like he was ready to kill him.

Jay's gaze flickered to Wren who he had been going to ... what? Grab her by the throat, shake her, hurt her for walking into the room, wasting his time, grandstanding instead of telling him Stella was in the fucking hospital.

Jay gritted his teeth. His blood burned. Karson's hand was still on his chest, holding him back. Jay was tempted, really fucking tempted to do something stupid. Do something like challenge the man he'd known for decades. And as capable as Jay was at handling himself, he didn't like his chances against Karson even under regular circumstances, and especially not when he was protecting his woman.

Wren, for her part, did not look like she needed protecting. She didn't even look rattled. In fact, she looked like she was amused. Fucking *amused*. While Stella was in the hospital. Jay clenched his fist and took three deep, long breaths before he stepped back.

Karson stayed in between himself and Wren, eyes homed in on Jay.

Jay didn't trust himself to speak, so instead, he walked around his desk, picked up his phone and dialed. He didn't even let his assistant finish her greeting.

"I need you to book me a flight to New Zealand. The next flight." Jay kept his eyes on Wren as he put the phone down.

It was his turn to put his hands flat on his desk, not as a power move but because suddenly, he wasn't sure if his legs would hold him.

"Tell me what you know," he gritted out. Black spots were dancing in his vision.

Wren slowly grinned, Jay having to blink multiple times to ensure he was seeing correctly. Jay may not know much about the woman, but he knew she cared about Stella fiercely and would not even smirk if Stella was in any kind of pain or danger.

"I *knew* you still loved her," she smirked in satisfaction.

Jay stared at her. "What the fuck are you talking about?" He was struggling immensely, keeping his voice and stare even.

"I mean I knew that the second you thought Stella was hurt, you'd get your head out of your ass and go to her."

Karson had his thumb and forefinger on the bridge of his nose behind Wren.

"You mean she's fine?" Jay asked slowly, unable to slow his heart, quiet the roar.

Wren's eyes narrowed. "Of course she's not fucking fine. You shattered her heart into a million pieces, and she's run off to the middle of nowhere New Zealand, not a Sephora or Nordstrom to be seen. She's nowhere near fucking fine."

"But she's not in the hospital?" Jay asked slowly.

Karson was on alert now. He clocked Jay's tone, realizing just how dangerous Wren's stunt was.

To be fair, Jay was very fucking tempted to do something. He didn't hit women, of course, but he was tempted to shake the shit out of this bitch.

"Settle down," Wren addressed Karson. "He's not going to hurt me."

"How can you be so sure?" Jay asked quietly.

"Because you know how much I mean to Stella, and you wouldn't hurt her. Not beyond what you've already done. And you most likely did that trying to be noble or some shit. Trying to protect her." She rolled her eyes, looking at the back of Karson's head. "I swear, you fucking badass alpha male types are so hell bent on being noble, on protecting us from the world, from yourselves, you're blind to the fact that your toxic masculinity is the thing that fucks us up most." Her gaze darted back to Jay. "If you'd thought the unthinkable, to... I don't know, speak to Stella honestly, lay it all out and let her make her own decisions about what's good for her and what's not, we probably wouldn't be in this fucking predicament. Nonetheless, we are. So you're going to New Zealand."

Jay measured her words. Chewed them. Let them sink in. There was no option but to listen to a woman like Wren. Jay had never encountered a woman—or a man for that matter—like her. She commanded attention, showed no fear and seemed ready for a fight.

She also wasn't as obtuse or superficial as an uneducated observer first might think. Not by a long shot.

"No," Jay finally said. "I am not going to New Zealand." He looked to Karson. "We are."

Stella

I was frozen, still standing stationary, holding my glass of wine. I was sure that wasn't what I was meant to do when faced with a man holding a gun. Run, fight, blind him with the aforementioned wine … any or all of these might have worked. Not just standing there like some dumb horror movie heroine. Then again, he wasn't pointing the gun *at* me, it was pointed down at the sand, held casually in his arms like it was a French baguette.

He was smiling with friendly eyes, but then again, I'd heard that Ted Bundy had friendly eyes. He was also wearing camo. An orange, long sleeved camo top and tan cargo style pants. They clashed terribly.

"Sorry if I startled you," he said, voice thick with the trademark New Zealand twang. "I'm shooting rabbits along the fence line." He moved his gun to one hand so he could point with the other, toward the rolling and rugged farmland that bordered the beach.

I did not follow his hand. I thought it best to keep my eye on the man with the gun if I wasn't going to run from him or blind him with wine.

"I've already got twenty this evening," he shared proudly, grinning wide to reveal gleaming, straight white teeth.

I felt guilty for expecting them to be yellowed and crooked with at least one missing. The rest of him was scruffy, unkempt, a beard that seriously needed a trim, salt and pepper hair and a weather-beaten face with rosy cheeks. He wasn't tall or muscled, not overly imposing— well, unless you counted the gun, then he was slightly more imposing.

"Saw you walking and wanted to come to warn you not to get a fright if ya heard a coupla shots here and there," he continued, seemingly not bothered by the fact I had yet to speak.

"That's much appreciated," I nodded slowly, my mouth dry.

"You're the Yank stayin' at Janet's place?" he asked.

I nodded again, unsure if I should be telling the man with the gun where I was staying. Alone. Unarmed.

"I'll be sure to steer clear, don't want to hit you with a rogue bullet while you're out enjoying your brew." He nodded to the wine in my hand, chuckling, deep and throaty. "Imagine that, come from the land of mass shootings and gun violence to little ol' New Zealand and get hit with a bullet meant for a rabbit."

I swallowed, pasting on a tight smile. "Imagine that."

The sound of the waves was the only thing punctuating the silence for a while.

"Better get goin'," the man finally said, tipping an imaginary hat.

I didn't speak, only nodded again and waved lamely. I watched him trudge from the sand back up into the farmland until he disappeared, my heart thundering in my chest.

It hadn't beat so loud and fast for a long time.

Not since *him*.

Janet arrived at my door within a few minutes of me getting back. The walk took twice as long since I kept stopping and turning, making sure that I wasn't being followed, or squinting into the fields, hoping I wasn't in anyone's crosshairs.

I let out a little yelp when she knocked at the door, I was wound that tight.

"Heard Stanley gave you a bit of a scare," Janet chirped when I was brave enough to open the door. Her hair was a mess of red ringlets, her eyes magnified by the large, round, purple rimmed spectacles she was wearing. Janet rarely wore makeup, apart from a smear of bright lipstick. Today it was pink. Her skin was tanned and creased from the sun, yet somehow still smooth and youthful.

She was wearing paint splattered overalls with a long-sleeved band tee underneath, a collection of gold and silver necklaces and bright purple Chuck Taylors.

"Stanley?" I repeated, stepping back to let her inside.

She went straight to the kitchen, grabbing the kettle and taking it to the sink to fill it.

"Yes, Stanley, the man with the 22 you encountered earlier?" she clarified over the sound of the water.

"His name is Stanley?" I asked, frowning and moving to sit at the breakfast bar.

"Sure is," she replied, switching on the kettle. "Why do you sound surprised?"

I shrugged, sitting on a barstool, relieved for her company. "Not what I expected a man like him to be called."

She laughed throatily. "Stanley is never what anyone expects." She grabbed two mugs from where they were hanging on hooks beside the kettle. She took two teabags out of the cannister, putting them in, her jewelry clanging as she moved.

"How did you know I encountered Stanley?" I asked.

"He called me," she replied. "Said you looked a wee bit pale, maybe weren't expecting to see him on the beach. I thought I'd come over to make sure you're okay." She moved to the fridge, getting milk then commenced making tea, an almost sacred tradition to New Zealanders, I was coming to learn.

It was almost meditative, watching her make the tea, listening to the clang of the spoons against the mugs. I watched in a trance, begging my mind to wander. Not from the events of this evening, but from *him*. Even a man with a gun—granted, a gun designed for rabbits, not humans—could not sway my mind from its rumination over the past, over us, over what I might've been able to do differently.

"The surest remedy for anything from a headache to heartbreak is a strong cup of tea with three sugars," Janet announced with a grin, handing me a steaming mug.

I took it thankfully, placing my palms around the porcelain, letting it warm them. If only it could warm my insides, the places that were dead and cold since he walked away from me.

"Stanley is harmless," she told me, sipping her own tea.

I raised my brow at her.

"Unusual," she added at my brow raise. "But harmless. He's actually a very wealthy man with a Ferrari in his garage and properties all over the world. He was a private contractor, did a lot of work in Central Africa."

I gave her a look. "Is this meant to make me feel *better* about him roaming about the beach with a gun?"

She grinned. "I've lived next door to him for twenty years, and he hasn't killed me. That make you feel better?"

I rolled my eyes. "Sure, why not?"

We fell into a companionable silence, sipping our tea and listening to the swish of the waves through the open sliding door.

"So you going to go out with Brent?" Janet asked, not one to be content with silence.

I turned to gape at her. "How do *you* know Brent asked me out?"

She shrugged, eyes alight with mischief. "Small town. Everyone knows everything. I'm also nosy. And have coffee with his mother."

My eyes bugged out. "He told his *mother* about me?"

She laughed. "Of course not. He was talking about you down at the pub where John Aitkens overheard then mentioned it to his wife Selma who just so happens to go power walking with Jenny, Brent's mother."

"Jesus Christ," I muttered. "Small town New Zealand would give *TMZ* a run for its money."

"It sure would," Janet agreed. "Are you going to say yes? Jenny would absolutely love it. She's not the biggest fan of Brent's on again off again, Nikita—in other words, she fucking hates her. Plus, it'd give me more reasons to convince you to stay here."

"Stay here?" I repeated, swallowing my tea. "I can't stay here. I have a business, friends, family, an apartment and a..." I almost said, 'boyfriend', but that wasn't right. I didn't have anyone. And even if we were still together, *he* was never my boyfriend. "And a life in L.A. I couldn't move here, that would be crazy," I continued.

Janet gave me a knowing look. "Love makes you do some fuckin' crazy things, darlin.'"

Her words hit true as I gulped my tea, trying to hide my reaction while hoping that she had been right, that the sweet tea would help salve my wounds.

"Yes, but there's just one problem," I said, leaning forward to place my mug on the coffee table. "I'm not in love with Brent."

Janet dunked her cookie, otherwise known as a 'biscuit' here in NZ—a Gingernut, apparently the only cookie one could dunk in a cup of tea—in her tea before taking a bite. "Not yet," she said while chewing. "You're not in love with him *yet*. But you could get there. Brent is very loveable. And fuckable, for that matter."

I grinned, used to such statements from Janet. One thing I loved about the women here, they loved to swear. It sounded amazing in their accent, and something about it made me happy. Society made it 'unladylike' to swear because they wanted women to speak in soft tones, to not make waves or even ripples. I liked to surround myself with women who made tsunamis.

"Yes, he is fuckable and loveable," I agreed. "But not for me."

Her eyes narrowed as she chewed the other half of her biscuit. "And the man that is for you?"

It shouldn't have surprised me, how much she saw. I'd spent enough time with the woman—she'd had a front row seat to my heartbreak—even if I didn't speak of it.

"He's not for me. Not anymore," I said, staring out the window.

"Hmmm. I wouldn't be so sure. One thing about love … it's fucking crazy. Learn to expect anything and everything."

Saturdays were the worst. Well, the Saturdays that we were shooting were pretty great, but the ones that were empty, yawning and full of nothing were the worst. Sundays too. But Saturday was the harbinger of two desolate days where my paradise turned to hell. Every shadow resembled him, every moment without his scent, his touch, pure torture. Then I beat myself up for being such a pathetic female, mourning over a man who had dropped me without emotion and treated me coldly and cruelly for almost the entirety of our relationship.

It was an ugly, wretched and painful cycle. But I made it through, which was what truly mattered. I'd spent the day drinking coffee, half-assing an online Pilates workout, doing laundry and attempting to pull weeds in the garden. When I realized I'd accidently pulled out the flowers and left the weeds, I gave up, settling on the sofa to find some lifeless reality TV to get me through the day.

Tomorrow I'd do it all again, but hopefully I'd be hungover enough to sleep in, wasting away some of the day.

Yeah, I was pathetic.

I wondered what he was doing right now. Considering it was after midnight in L.A. right now, he might've been sleeping. Most likely not sleeping. It was Saturday morning there, which meant he was most likely with someone.

The thought scraped down my insides.

The crunch of wheels against gravel jerked me out of my pity party, my eyes narrowing toward the door I'd left open because I was planning on watering a couple of flowers at some point tonight.

Life was different here. It moved slower. People talked to strangers. No one locked their doors. As an L.A. girl, I'd scoffed at that and continued locking mine for at least the first month. Out of habit more than anything. I wasn't scared of being here in the middle of nowhere alone. I wasn't scared of much anymore. I'd forgotten, though. Gotten lazy here at the bottom of the world. However, this place that seemed so peaceful, so safe, was not immune to human wickedness. To danger. Nowhere was.

I highly doubted that the person pulling into my driveway was some assassin or serial killer coming to hurt me. No, that was not why my stomach dipped, not why my heart jumped up my throat or my hands started shaking.

It was because I thought of someone else who might be here. Someone who had already hurt me plenty and who I'd sell my soul to have back to hurt me some more. If he didn't already own it, that was.

It was a fool's hope. A little girl's hope. A fantasy that the man who broke my heart would come back with the pieces in his hands, intact and ready to put them back together. Put *me* back together.

It wasn't Janet. She drove a truck that roared and rumbled and sounded like thunder halfway down the drive.

I didn't move in the time it took for the stranger to park. To get out of their car and walk up the front steps and through the door. Because I was standing there, frozen with hope, not fear.

It wasn't a man in a ten-thousand-dollar suit standing in my door. No, life didn't work that way. Instead, it was a five-foot-five woman in six-inch heels wearing Chanel and a shit eating grin.

"I swear to *fuck* I thought I was going to arrive to find you in some kind of shack and would have to drug you with horse tranquilizer to get you out of here," she sassed, eyes flickering over me.

I crossed the living room at the same time as she did, meeting in the middle where we hugged like it had been half a lifetime since we'd seen one another. For us, it had. This was the longest I'd ever gone without seeing my girlfriends. I'd been too consumed by my heartbreak to realize how much I'd missed them all until this very moment. It wasn't just a single man who could ruin me, keep me together then blow me apart. No, a man didn't have that right. Not even *him*.

My girlfriends held valuable pieces of me, and Wren was bringing one tiny shred back. She held me tight, and I inhaled her perfume. The one that she'd had made especially for her. The one that was uniquely and perfectly Wren.

"Wren! Oh, my God, what are you doing here?" I asked, holding her much longer than our usual hugs.

Then again, there was nothing usual about this situation. About the fact that I'd never been farther from home as I had been these past months, had never been in a country where I didn't have a close friend, didn't have support, where I was entirely alone. Which, of course, had been the point. I'd had to get a world away from the man I loved, who broke my heart. But in doing so, I'd forgotten how important girlfriends were at helping to heal broken hearts. Or at least helping distract from the pain.

"Well, Karson is here with Jay because bad-asses cannot travel unless they are in pairs," she explained. "Or for 'business reasons,'" she air quoted. "That's the blanket term that Karson uses whenever he has to slink off into the night," she huffed. "As if I'm naïve enough to think he's sending fucking faxes." She shook her head. "Anyway, I actually think that's just an excuse. In my opinion, I think Jay is absolutely terrified of you rejecting him, and he needed some moral support in case he ends up flying home without you. Of course, he'd never admit that. I am quite certain he'd actually cut off a limb before admitting such a thing."

I blinked rapidly at her words. At the name she said, the one that I wasn't allowed to think. My heart thundered in my chest. *He* was here. In the same country as me. But he wasn't *here*. For whatever reason. It wasn't because he was afraid—that man wasn't afraid of anything. He was playing a game. That had to be it. Just another one.

Wren let me process the news for a hot second, maybe.

Her heels clicked on the hardwood floor as she explored my rental. "Cozy. Chic in a ... *rustic* kind of way." She looked out the window at the rolling waves. "Good view," she said in a tone that only a woman who had seen all of the world's most exquisite sights could produce. Appreciative in a vague, jaded kind of way.

She whirled around, back to the view, eyes on me. "The most important question for the topic we're going to be exploring—that is, whether you are going to reject Jay or not—where's the alcohol? The stronger the better."

I was already on my way to the fridge, knowing my friend far too well. Plus, I needed a drink after this influx of information. "I have wine, from all of the best wineries around here. Not that I've had the time to explore them, but a guy in production hooked me up," I explained, pulling out a bottle from the fridge.

"Did you *hook up* with this guy from production?" Wren asked, grinning.

I got flutes from the cupboard. "No, considering he's incredibly gay. I do adore him, though, and I'd totally have his children if he was willing to turn straight for me," I joked, pouring each of us a glass of wine.

Wren took hers happily.

My throat burned ever so slightly from my joke. Children. Mine. *Ours.* Exactly what this whole thing had been about. Well, one of the things. I wasn't stupid enough to believe that one offhand comment was the sole reason why he'd torn us apart. Torn me apart.

"When did you arrive?" I asked, aching to ask everything I could about *him*. Where was he? How was he? What did he look like? Was he ruined, tortured, changed forever?

Then again, Wren couldn't give me that information because Wren had never met him. Not when we were together, at least. There was obviously a whole lot I'd missed out on if she was referring to him in a semi-familiar kind of way.

"Plane landed about two hours ago," she answered, glancing at her diamond watch. I knew for a fact that it didn't tell the right time because it never did. Wren was not a person who lived by a watch. She just liked things that glittered.

I glared at her. How is it you look like *that* after a fifteen-hour flight?" I waved my hand at her perfectly wavy hair, dewy skin and unwrinkled outfit—a white suit, tailored to perfection.

Wren unbuttoned her blazer, throwing it over the back of the sofa, revealing the tight tank she wore underneath. "Good drugs, endless amounts of water and the beds that fully recline in first class," she replied with a wink. "Plus, Karson got me off when everyone else was asleep. I would highly recommend midair orgasms; does absolute wonders for the skin."

I laughed, not doubting her for a moment. Then I looked at her closer. I'd yet to see Wren looking terrible. Even when she was the hottest of hot messes—which was often a couple of years ago considering she was a true party girl—she looked wonderful.

But there was something different about her now. Something about her eyes. They shone. Happiness radiated off her in a way that even that most expensive of skincare or injectables couldn't mimic.

"You're happy," I observed. "With Karson, you love him."

Wren stared at me for a moment, eyes wide and full of something resembling fear before she threw her head back and laughed. "Of course not, darling. I couldn't *possibly* love him. I love my girlfriends, fine wine, diamonds, private planes and Botox. Not men. Never men."

I regarded my friend, hearing the firmness in her words. She was trying very hard to convince me, much harder to convince herself. I was not about to crumble her house of cards, knowing how vulnerable and exposed it felt when they collapsed.

I nodded knowingly instead.

"Cheers, bitch!" Wren changed the subject, clinking her glass with mine and pasting on a smile. "To us. Because we're *fabulous*."

"Cheers," I replied with a smile.

We both sipped our wine, and I enjoyed the cool liquid sliding down my throat. Wren regarded me in much the same way I had done to her.

"You look good, honey. On the outside, at least. Tan. Skin looks better than ever. Your arms will rival Michelle Obama's. Your outfit is, of course, *to die for*. Yes, on the outside you look wonderful, as usual. You almost look as if you've moved on from the mess Jay made back stateside. But I know you a little too well to believe what I see on the surface."

I had to clench my fist not holding my glass in order to keep my lips pursed, open enough only to drink. Wren had said *his* name. She had said he was here. And she'd said it like it wasn't earth shattering, heart breaking.

I wanted to grab her by her skinny shoulders and shake the information out of her. The mere mention of his name had turned me feral, desperate, ravenous for more information.

But this was my friend. One of my very best friends. Who I loved dearly. Who I hadn't seen in months. So I locked my shit down.

Barely.

Her hand reached over to squeeze mine, all flippancy leaving her face. Wren did a very good job at appearing vain and shallow to those who only wanted to see that, or moreover, to those she wanted to see that. But she was exceptionally deep. Felt a lot. Felt too much, which was why she'd self-medicated with a life of excess for so long. Most of the trust fund babies in L.A. had very little emotional intelligence or empathy because they had the luxury of not having to develop it through any kind of struggle. Wren had her own struggles, her own past, and knowing that made her all the more impressive.

"How are you? Really?" she asked, her eyes scanning my face.

My fist was still clenched. As much as I wanted to ask about him, demand to know what he was doing here, why he wasn't *right here*, I also needed to talk. I'd left the country without telling anyone what happened. I'd avoided any and all phone calls, sent texts full of lies and remained tight lipped with anyone at work who had tried to ask about my personal life. I'd spoken carefully about myself, diverting with questions, and luckily, the set was so busy there wasn't much time for small talk.

I was a volcano, simmering, smoking for months, and my friend's kind face, gentle voice and mere presence was the cause for eruption. Everything had been about Jay for so long. His presence in my life.

His darkness casting a shadow over everything. My need for him. My love for him. His absence.

I hadn't stopped, hadn't even paused to think about me. Wren was giving me that. Forcing it on me, the conversation about me before him.

"I feel guilty," I whispered. "For hurting this much. For being this broken without him. Beyond the fact that I should be able to tell myself—and believe myself when I say it—that my worth, my entirety of self, is not made or ruined by a man. That I am in control of my happiness, that my life, full of all other kinds of love and abundance, should be enough."

I paused, biting my lip and looking out the window for a spell.

I looked back at Wren. "But I can't. I can't think that because it's utter bullshit. No matter how long it's been without him, despite how briefly he was even in my life, he awakened parts of me, then he scooped them up and took them when he left. I hate myself for mourning in such a self-indulgent way. There are women who have lost children. Who have been given terminal diagnoses, who have survived attacks—women who are dealing with real things that ruin their lives. Not a fucking breakup."

"Stop," Wren hissed. Her eyes were alight with anger that was not at all common on her face. "You do not get to belittle your pain or your heartbreak because other people in the world are suffering. You do not get to beat yourself up over the fact that you loved so deeply. That you took a chance on something. The bravest thing you can do isn't just to let someone love you but to let yourself love them right back with all that you are. And you're a fucking lot, babe."

She stared at me, making sure the words punctured, giving me ample time to take a large gulp of my wine.

"Of course you feel like your world is a wasteland," she continued. "Not because you made this man your world, but because you intertwined his with yours. He had roots in you, just like you had yours in him. Ripping something away like that is going to leave empty spaces that will never regrow again because you're never going to feel that again. Even if things happen the way I want them to—which is him crawling on his hands and knees, begging for your forgiveness, specifically with a diamond ring." She shrugged. "I'm open to other forms of apology, of course."

I smirked. "So generous of you."

She refilled my wine. "Even *if* things happen that way, even if everything I want for you comes to pass, it will never be the same. He won't fill all of the holes he left, he won't heal all of the wounds he inflicted. But something else will happen. Something beautiful. But right now, it's not about what the two of you may become. It's about the woman you've become now. Through all of this suffering and pain. Through all of the terrible lessons that heartbreak has to offer."

I blinked at her. "Jesus, Wren. You get a visit from Yoda while I was gone?"

She grinned. "No, I just watched a lot of Oprah reruns."

"You flew with ... him?" I asked. I had been planning on saying his name. Being stronger than all of that. But I couldn't do it. Apparently, I wasn't stronger. Not right now.

Wren's face gentled. "Yeah. He bought my tickets. Of course, I told him that I was a Whitney, that I could buy my own damn tickets.

I could've bought the entire damn *plane* if I so wished, but man is that motherfucker pushy." Her eyes twinkled with teasing. With knowing.

I found myself feeling jealous of her. My wonderful, loyal and kind friend. Wickedly jealous that she'd spoken to him. That she knew him at all. Months ago, I wanted her to know him. But as a man in my life. As my man. Not as ... whoever he was now. Whatever he was now. Anger bubbled in my stomach, outside of my control.

"I let him buy my tickets," she shrugged. "But then I bought every single other ticket in first class. Just to let him know his dick wasn't bigger than mine," she winked.

My mouth was dry. I wanted to smile at the image of Wren playing games with the man who was used to fear and submission. But I couldn't smile. I took a sip of my wine. A big one.

"Why did he want you to come?" I asked, my voice still rough.

Wren's face softened. "Because, honey, he knows you. Well. He knew that he was coming to fight for you. And a wise man doesn't enter a fight without a secret weapon." She pointed at her own chest. "Secret weapon. But he thinks I'm his. The thing is, babe, I'm yours. I'm not here to fight for him. I'll only ever be here to fight for *you*. So if you want to drink the rest of this wine, tell me you're completely over him and want to ruin his life for fucking with you, I'm totally down for that."

She got up from her barstool, never able to sit in one place for too long, and began to pace around the living room.

"You want to tell me you've fallen in love with a hunky Kiwi and are going to start your life over here, I'll argue with the location, but I'll plan your wedding," she told me as she picked up a paperweight in the shape of a naked woman and nodded appreciatively before putting it back down.

"And if, and this is the one I'm thinking you'll choose, you want to let him fight, you want to let him win, we'll sit here and drink. For now. I'm sure there's plenty to be said and done later."

I pursed my lips. I already knew what I wanted to do. Wren already knew too. Otherwise, she wouldn't be here. She would've planted drugs in Jay's suitcase and made sure he was either detained at the border or couldn't even leave the US.

So we drank.

CHAPTER THREE

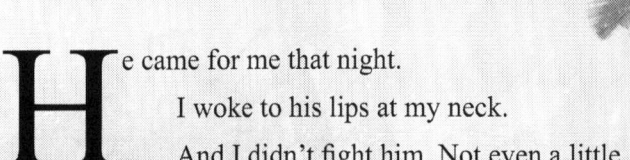

He came for me that night.

I woke to his lips at my neck.

And I didn't fight him. Not even a little.

Later, I would curse myself. Would chastise my traitorous body, my weak soul for letting him in without a fight. Without demanding reparations for what he took, exacting vengeance for what he broke.

But that was later.

There was a now to focus on.

I breathed in deeply. Inhaled the smell of musk, of leather, of *him*. It worked like a chemical. Like a drug, relaxing my entire body but setting it on fire at the same time. It worked like oxygen that I didn't know I'd been living without. My body came alive the second his lips touched my skin, the moment his scent invaded my senses.

He didn't speak, though I ached for his voice to vibrate my bones.

He knew I wanted that. Yearned for that. Needed it more than breath. But he kept it from me. Because he didn't want me breathing easy.

Hands went to my chest, but they didn't slip beneath the silk, didn't touch my skin. No. Instead, they *ripped* the delicate fabric. Right down the middle. Tore it from me.

I gasped at the violence of it. Sure, this kind of thing might've happened in the movies, in books, but not with *him*. He relished control. He'd never shown any outward signs of his hunger for me. Not beyond the way his hands and mouth moved against my body or the fire in his eyes—the ones I couldn't see this moonless night. I ached to lose myself in them, but I couldn't move to reach for the light. Yes, he'd shown how he wanted me in those ways, but he'd never strayed beyond the rules he'd set for himself. The rules I came to learn, to live by.

But there were no rules here. There was a hunger, a ravenous need from both of us, making the air too thick to speak through, breathe through. His lips were all over me. My hands tore at his hair. Lips on my nipple. Then teeth. I cried out, or I tried to. My throat was dry, parched, thirsting for more. Thirsting for *him*.

He moved to my other nipple, and I writhed against the bed, already close to breaking apart, already soaking wet, primed, ready, painfully empty without him. If I could've spoken, I would've begged him, would've pleaded for him to fill up all the empty places inside of me. But I couldn't speak. I just continued to feast on him, letting him take control.

I couldn't say his name. Couldn't even think it. I was afraid if I did, he might disappear. If I was finally and truly going crazy, imaging all of this, I'd relish insanity ... for a little while, at least.

It was dark. Pitch black. The window blinds were open because I liked to wake with the sun and look at the stars before I went to sleep. There were no stars tonight. No moon. Only darkness. He was the deepest shadow of them all, hanging over me. That was good. I didn't think I could handle seeing him—if he was real—at the same time as feeling him, smelling him. Tasting him.

His lips moved against mine as he lowered his body, giving me his weight. He was naked, his bare skin hot against mine.

I'd slept soundly in my bed while this man broke in—though I wasn't sure if it could be classified as a break-in when I'd kept the doors unlocked—and hadn't woken until his lips were on my skin. It was probably because I'd been dreaming of him, clinging to him in my sleep, so used to him being gone when I woke.

His lips moved down my stomach, and I breathed heavily, my body writhing underneath him as he worked his way down.

The next sound was the tearing of my underwear, his hands on my thighs, pressing them apart. Even though they opened for him without hesitation, I knew there would be bruises from his fingertips. The way he was pressing into my skin made me wonder if he needed the same kind of reassurance that I was real as I did.

There was no waiting, no buildup once he opened my legs, his mouth suddenly there. Right *there*, tongue gliding across my clit, moving expertly. My hands fisted the sheets of the bed, needing to tear the fabric apart while he was tearing me apart. Putting me back together.

His fingers entered me as the point my climax reached its peak, so

I clenched around him.

He made a sound then. A satisfied growl coming from the back of his throat, a hungry one. His mouth was gone, and his face was no longer in between my legs, his body moving until his lips were on mine, tasting of me, tasting of what he did to me.

He hovered there for just a moment, breath hot on my face, cock pressing up against my entrance, body bearing down on me. I held my breath, waiting for his voice. As much as I thought I thirsted for it, right now, I prayed he'd stay silent. This moment was far too full for words, the air still too thick.

But he didn't speak. Not one word.

I cried out as he surged inside, brutal, beautiful, filling up every inch of me, feeding everything inside of me that had been starving. It was at this point I could no longer keep clawing at the sheets, I needed his skin, needed to know he was real. So I let my hands move, raking my fingernails down his back in some kind of frenzy. I was mad from him. Maybe I had finally gone insane. At this moment, I didn't care. All I needed was more. More of him. More of his skin underneath my fingernails.

He moved slowly, but each thrust was hard, almost violent. I matched that violence, wrapping my legs around him as my nails scraped at his back—something I hadn't been allowed to do before. The thought was murky in my mad mind. It used to be forbidden, my hands on his back, my nails scoring his skin. But I no longer gave a fuck about what was forbidden. Not anymore.

He grunted in pain, or maybe pleasure—it didn't much matter at this moment—as I cried out with my climax, clenching around him, milking his release.

I didn't let him go. Couldn't.

What if I woke up?

What if he disappeared?

Seconds passed.

Minutes.

Nothing changed.

He was *here*. In my bed—or my rented bed. In the country I used as a refuge, as an escape, as a barrier against this man. The sounds of my rapid breathing seemed to fill up the room. I was sucking in air, gulping at it. Not just because of what had just happened. But because I hadn't breathed this deeply in months, with his arms tight around me, with his cum still inside me, with his scent enveloping me.

But parts of me were tensed, coiled too tight to fully relax in this moment, with this man. I was suddenly hyperaware of everything. Of just how loud I was breathing. Of all of my jellied limbs, tangled with his strong, muscled ones. What did I smell like? Sweat, desire? What did my skin feel like? Clammy? Too angular? Sharp? Too soft? I needed armor around him. My skin needed to be thick as marble.

It pissed me off, all of these thoughts. I was already preparing to shrink, to grow, to cut myself so I was the 'right' shape for him. My body tensed at the thought, my blood hot. No. I couldn't do that. Not now. Not again.

"Why are you here?" I rasped.

It hurt to speak. Was it because I'd been holding in my screams for so long? Or because I was afraid my words would shatter everything?

He didn't answer immediately. He waited. Kept his arms around me, tight. Too tight. But not tight enough. I needed bruises. Marks. Evidence. I needed pain. Because that was part of us. Because I couldn't be whole without it.

I moved because he moved, reaching to the side of the bed, the harsh click of the lamp puncturing the silence between us. The light was harsher still because I hadn't seen clearly in months.

It was shocking, seeing him after imaging him for so long. He looked the same. Better. Worse. All of his sharp angles were pointed blades. His jaw, still clean shaven, seemed to have more edges now. His cheekbones high, severe. The eyes. His fucking eyes. They weren't empty or guarded or cold. They burned like green fire, vibrant, electric, bursting with emotion.

Because I wasn't strong enough to maintain eye contact, to breathe underneath everything he gave with a single look, I moved my gaze to his hair. It was longer now, messier. I ached to tear my hands through it, but I was unsure now, even though I could still feel him inside me, even though I was naked—body and soul—I felt awkward. Scared that I might do something to shatter ... whatever this was. Breathing felt risky enough. Asking that question was reckless, stupid and necessary.

"I never told you what I was afraid of, though I suspect it had become rather painfully obvious over our time together," he said finally.

I sighed in relief when his voice hit the air. Caressed my skin. It was low. Throaty. Masculine. It was something else too. It was like his eyes, unguarded, full of things that I hadn't thought he was capable of.

His eyes kept mine prisoner. "I do not fear death, nor pain. I feared losing control. Only that. Because of my past. Because I lived a life where my body was not my own. Where my time was not my own. Where nothing belonged to me, not even my soul. I sold it in order to survive."

His hand moved up to cradle my jaw in a touch so gentle I barely believed it belonged to this man who I'd been sure only knew violence and pain.

"At least, I thought I'd sold my soul," he continued. "Thought there was nothing left inside of me for myself. Certainly not for anyone else. And then I saw you on that dance floor." His eyes ran over my face. "And you stole everything that was human inside of me. Gave me back things that I was sure couldn't survive inside of me. You took away my control. Gave me something new to fear." His thumb brushed over my bottom lip. "You, Stella. You are what I'm most afraid of. You terrify me, pet. You're my greatest fear. My only fear. And I've been a coward."

My body shook at the emotion in his voice. From the way he spoke to me. The naked honesty in it. The shame.

The *love*.

First, he'd spoken to me with his body, then with his soul, the one that he thought he didn't have. The one that he'd quite clearly just communicated belonged to me.

There was no apology. No, he'd never apologize for what he'd done. But it turned out I didn't need an apology. Didn't even *want* one. How could I expect him to apologize when he had been trying to do the right thing by letting me go? He was scarred, disfigured, broken and cruel. And he loved me. And he'd known what kind of sentence that love was. What kind of life. He'd been trying to save me from the punishment of his love.

He wasn't trying to save me anymore.

"We're also going to talk about the fact you were sleeping here, alone, unprotected and had the doors unlocked," he added, an undercurrent of anger to his tone.

It was small at first, the giggle that escaped me. Then it turned into something larger. Full on laughter. Body shaking laughter. The real kind. Not the stuff I'd forced and faked these past few months.

It felt nice.

"Of course you come and say all of that and have to end on something so utterly alpha male. So utterly *you*," I told him once I finally got control of myself.

"As beautiful as you are when you smile, when you laugh, it's not exactly the reaction I expected to all of this," Jay replied through gritted teeth.

There was unease in his voice. A lack of confidence that didn't suit him. Didn't suit the image I held of him. He was afraid. Afraid that he'd just crossed the world and laid his soul bare to someone who was going to reject him. Push him away or punish him for hurting me.

My hands went to his face, framing it. It was hard to believe I was touching him right now. That he was *letting* me touch him like this.

"I love you," I whispered. "I'll always love you. You hurt me.

You hurt us both. But I understand it. I'm not going to punish you for it. I'm definitely not going to hurt us both more just to prove something." I wrapped my legs around him, pressing his body to mine.

Jay's malachite eyes flared, and the veins in his neck protruded as he hardened against my entrance.

"I need you," I whispered. "In every way a woman needs a man. And then some more. You haven't lied about who you are. I'm a woman of sound mind. And I want you. There are things we need to talk about." I wrapped my hand around the back of his head and pulled down. His lips moved against mine, and I ran my tongue along his. "But right now, I really don't want to talk," I murmured against his lips.

I barely got my words out before he surged inside me, proving that he really didn't want to talk either.

Later, *much* later, we found ourselves in the kitchen. He'd taken me as many ways as a man could take a woman—or that's what it seemed like. We'd moved against each other until we were covered in sweat, until my muscles burned from exertion, until I'd had as many orgasms as any woman had ever had—or at least that's what it seemed like.

It was still dark. The night was still quiet, at its thickest, just past three. When all the ghosts and demons came out to play. All the sinners.

"The eggs here, they're something else," I proclaimed as I

spooned them onto the toast I had waiting on two plates.

Jay was leaning against the kitchen island, watching me work. I'd told him to sit at the breakfast bar, make himself comfortable, but he'd ignored my command. Of course he had. I was glad about it too. Even though the barstool was a mere few feet away, it seemed much too far. I needed him close, and he needed it, too, obviously. Because he swept my hair from my neck as I chopped tomatoes, kissing my bare skin. Ran his hand along the cleft of my bare ass—he'd made me cook naked, and I hadn't complained. He didn't help. He just stood there, watching. Sometimes touching. Not speaking. There would be words. Likely many. Later.

The way he looked at me made me want to peel the skin from my bones just so I could let him further inside me. I was ravenous for his gaze.

But something about it hurt. Something made me want to escape it. Him. This was a stranger, standing here without clothes on, regarding my naked skin, all of the exposed nerves inside of my soul. He was a figment of my imagination. The villain I'd come to escape. To forget.

But he was also too familiar. He knew me too well. Could see too far inside of me. There was no hiding from Jay. There was no way I could protect myself, try to do all of the things that I imagined I would do if I ever saw him again.

I was going to make him wait, or I'd planned to. Make him work. Torture him with the same cruelty and coldness he'd shown me. But that had been impossible. There was not one single part of my body or soul that was even chilly right now. Everything was on fire.

I had no resentment for this man. No need for payback. Because written there, right on his face, the one that had been closed and empty to me for the longest time, was open and naked just like he was. There was pain. There was agony. Regret. Most of all, there was love. Love that was tangled in pain and regret. Love that was ours.

My hands shook as I picked up the plates of eggs. I was glad I had something to do, but I worried that I couldn't handle the weight of the two plates as I struggled with the burden of Jay's stare.

He crossed the distance between us in two strides, taking the plates from me. Our fingers brushed ever so slightly, and I flinched at the effect such a simple, casual touch had on me. He'd had his hands all over me, there were bruises to prove that. The tenderness between my legs as I moved was evidence of his presence in my most intimate of places, but the way he brushed his fingers against mine ... that was something else. Something gentle. Something precious.

The moment hung between us for a lifetime before he broke our stare and turned to take the plates to the small table by the window. I watched him walk through the living room, his scars rippling against his muscled skin. He'd let me touch them, I remembered belatedly. Through the blur that was the clash of our bodies, the writhing climaxes I'd barely lived through, I remembered my hands on his back. My nails sinking into his skin with the animal need to draw blood in order to make sure he was real. And once I'd realized he was real, I'd needed to mark him. I'd needed to add scars of my own to his body ... just in case. Just in case something happened. Just in case he left me again. So then he'd wear the reminder of me on his skin.

Because I wore all of his scars, regularly cutting myself on the sharp edges he'd created.

Reluctantly, I stopped staring at him and followed him across the room to sit at the table. We sat close, too close, but not close enough. The scrape of knives and forks against plates the only sound. I didn't taste the food, ate it mindlessly, because my body needed it, because I needed to do something, needed to gather my thoughts.

Jay was here.

Sitting across from me eating eggs.

I'd imagined it so many times but it still seemed utterly surreal. There were many ways I'd imagined a reunion going, when I'd allowed myself to entertain fantasies I wasn't supposed to be thinking about. It had been hot sex, it had been his skin on mine, his scent, his presence. But none of the logistics, none of the realities. None of the questions answered.

Our problems hadn't started *that* morning. The morning he left me. It wasn't just about kids. Or even marriage. It was about the secrets he kept. The shadows he lived in. The laws he broke and the lives he took.

It was about my insecurities. My fears, my demons, my needs.

There were a million little details that went in to loving someone. To making it work. To repair the million little cuts that were still bleeding.

That's what the rational part of me was saying, at least. The irrational, crazy in love—pardon the Beyoncé reference—part of me was happy to keep bleeding as long as Jay was here.

Those two sides of myself fought while we ate, my hand shaking each time I brought the fork up to my mouth. Unfortunately, there was only so much food on my plate, eventually I had to finish. I had to break the spell.

My stomach was in knots as I carefully placed my knife and fork close together on my plate, pressing a napkin to my mouth. My hands were still shaking. When I finally found the courage to lift my eyes, I found him already staring. He had been the entire time. I knew that. His gaze was a physical thing, peeling back the layers of my skin, brushing against every exposed nerve. Every wound.

You can do this, I said to myself.

"I need more," I whispered, my voice rough. "I understand that you're giving me a piece of you that no one else has seen, that you're trying to make me understand your coldness, your cruelty, the pain you've caused me. I also understand that not all of that pain came from you, it purely came from loving you."

I raked my gaze over this man, naked in front of me, his skin like marble, his scars only making him more attractive. He was hanging on my every word.

"I've figured out that I'll never be able to truly love someone without pain," I continued, my voice still low, raspy. "And as a woman who has been with you, I know that I'll never love any other man as completely and wretchedly as I love you. You're a poison. One I'll never be rid of. One I don't want to be rid of. But I cannot survive this with only a piece of you. If we are going to do this, if I am going to do this, I need everything. I need all of you."

I sucked in a ragged breath when I was done, feeling like I'd run a marathon, or what I imagined running a marathon might be like. I wasn't crazy enough to run one, just crazy enough to love this dark, twisted man.

Fear clutched at my throat as I second guessed myself, worrying over every word I'd said, what I'd demanded. I hated that as a woman, I felt guilty and sick for asking for what I deserved, hated that it was some part of my DNA to be quiet. To submit.

I'd submitted to Jay in many ways. Almost every way. But I couldn't do it this way. I'd hate myself for it in the end.

He placed his knife and fork together on his plate before pushing it away so he could focus on me. As if he hadn't been before.

"You know about my parents," he said.

I nodded, thinking about the cold, emotionless way he'd spoken of them months ago. Thinking about how many of the scars on his body belonged to them. And the ones on his soul, for that matter. Yes, I knew about his parents. And if they were put in front of me right now, I'd be sorely tempted to cut them to pieces with a butter knife.

"I won't go into any more detail about my time with them," he continued, his eyes dark. "They are not worth the air it takes to speak of them. I won't give that to them. Suffice it to say, what they did to me when I was a child laid the groundwork for the man I am today." He made it clear by his tone that he found that man lacking.

I gritted my teeth and wished I could tell him how wrong he was. That he was magnificent, in his own warped and twisted way. That I'd fallen in love with him for the man he was, not whoever he thought he should've been. But I couldn't speak. It wasn't time for that. I needed to listen instead, despite how hard it was to hear what Jay thought of himself.

"And as soon as I considered myself a man, I left," Jay continued.

He reached forward to grasp my hand, as if he couldn't help himself.

I was glad for the contact, and my body relaxed ever so slightly.

"Sure, I could've fought back. Could've killed them. They deserved it, of course. It wasn't humanity, love or a conscience that stopped me." He rubbed my hand with his thumb. "I was capable of taking their lives, of living with myself afterward. But leaving them trapped in their miserable lives, inside of themselves, seemed to be more of a punishment than the mercy that death offered."

My breathing was shallow and rapid, listening to Jay speak, his thumb rubbing rhythmically. I was hanging on his words, soaking them up. His tone was flat, cold, but his eyes were still on fire.

He stood then, letting me go, and I couldn't help but let out a little mewl of protest, losing his contact and proximity. Jay's face softened at the sound that humiliated me. He leaned forward to stroke my jaw before straightening and walking away. I had to steel myself from getting up, following him like a desperate shadow. I did check out his ass as he moved, then the streaks of blood mingled with the scars on his back.

Jay had gone over to the bar cart, the clink of glasses telling me he was pouring drinks. I watched the muscles in his back move, rippling in the shadows and the dim light coming from the kitchen.

He came back, two glasses in his hands, eyes on me. I thankfully took the glass he extended. I definitely needed it, even though I wasn't a whisky girl. Whisky was the only thing you could drink at three in the morning when the love of your love was telling you about his bloodstained past.

Jay sat down, took a sip of his whisky, placed it down on the table and reached for my hand. I sighed in relief.

"I was homeless at fifteen," he continued. "I didn't have friends or family to take me in. No one wanted to take in someone like me. I was dirty. Had something sinister about me, even then. I scared people. Scared my parents, which is partially why they did what they did to me. A very small part, to be sure. The rest of it was because they were pure fucking evil. Nothing else. No bad childhoods, traumas. They were just two rotten souls drawn to each other."

He took a drink while I stared at him in horror, knowing that this was the beginning, the prologue. We hadn't even gotten to chapter one yet.

"Had twenty-two dollars to my name," he said. "I already knew that I wouldn't be able to walk into a fucking McDonalds and get a job. Wouldn't get anything legitimate. As fucked up as I was, I was still a dumb kid. As evil as my parents were, I wasn't prepared for the world. Or maybe I thought it couldn't possibly be as cruel as the life I lived. Ignorance mixed with hope. Deadly cocktail."

He pulled his hand away. Something about his voice was different. There was something in it I'd never heard before. Fear. Unease. He was uncomfortable telling this story. He was scared to share this with me.

I wanted to touch him. Very, very badly. Wanted to initiate physical contact that would communicate to him that I was here for him. That it didn't matter what he shared, I would still want him. But I kept my lips pursed and my hand fisted on the table.

"I trusted the wrong people," he said. "I was desperate for a family. For love. So I fell in to a crowd that looked like they offered those things. Just as freely as the drugs. I didn't like the drugs. Didn't like being out of control. Didn't like how vulnerable they made me feel. That had been a vow I'd made for myself when I left. That I'd never be vulnerable again. Tricked myself in to thinking I could walk out of that house a victim and enter the world as a victor."

He took another drink, and I gulped in air, unaware I had been holding my breath the entire time he was speaking.

"Everything?" he asked me.

It seemed like he was trying to give me an escape hatch, a way out of the conversation that was only going to get worse. But I didn't want to escape him.

"Everything," I echoed, my voice small. Although I was resolute in my decision that I needed to know all of him, I feared I wouldn't be able to handle it. But wasn't that what bravery was? Feeling the fear and doing it anyway? And wasn't the bravest thing you could do love someone?

"They—the street rats who I thought were family—fed me enough drugs to be able to sell me, and I was too fucked up to fight. They turned me into their whore. For a time." He drained his drink. "Then someone pulled me out. Whether he saw something in me, was feeling charitable or was just looking for someone disposable, it didn't matter. He got me off the drugs long enough to see straight. Gave me the discipline I needed to kill every last one of the cretins who thought they owned me. Thought they could sell me."

I no longer tasted whisky on my tongue. I tasted bile. The innards of my stomach trying to rid themselves of the air I'd just swallowed. Not because Jay was telling me about the people he'd murdered, but because I wished I could've done it myself.

In all of my imaginings about what could've made Jay ... Jay, nothing like this had ever entered my mind. He was so strong, so unyielding, the prospect that anyone had ever taken advantage of him—especially like that—was barely believable.

But it was impossible not to believe it. The truth was venom in the air.

"Duncan Heller ran a stable of girls and a big part of the gun trade in the city," Jay continued. He wasn't looking at me anymore. "He used me as his rabid dog. After what had happened, I was ready and willing to hurt everyone he told me to. Without remorse, without reason and without mercy."

He drained his drink, stood up and walked to refill his glass.

"I was happy to do that, for a time," he added with his back to me. "But then I got hungry for more. To be the man with all of the control. To be the one giving orders, not taking them."

Instead of sitting back down with me, Jay walked toward the open doors, standing in the doorway.

I got up and followed him outside where he was leaning against the porch railing. I ached to come up behind him, circle his body with my arms, press my breasts against his back, give him something. But the air around him was too thick, too impenetrable. He had to go somewhere inside himself to tell this story, somewhere away from me. In order to know him, I had to understand that his cruelty had a purpose. His coldness was a shield.

Instead of touching him, I stood beside him and waited.

"Though I was impatient, I waited," he said to the night.

"Watched Duncan work, saw where his weaknesses were. I made connections with his competitors. With people in his employ who were dissatisfied with how they were treated. There were many. A lesson I learned, in our business, you employed killers and thieves. Killers and thieves were ready to kill and steal from whoever paid them more or scared them the most."

Jay's form seemed darker than the night that surrounded it, despite the fact that wasn't possible. I hung on his every word, though I began to shiver with the breeze.

Jay noticed it. He grasped my wrist and pulled me inside, closing the door behind us. He sat me back down at the table, snatching the blanket hanging off the back of the sofa and wrapping it around me, then he sat back down.

Although the blanket was cozy, warm and expensive, I still felt chilled to my bones, though I restrained from shivering, because I needed Jay to finish his story.

"I killed him," Jay said. "Duncan. The man who saved me. Who gave me somewhere to live, people to kill, who taught me everything he knew. I killed him even though he gave me all of that because I wanted to take everything from him."

One of Jay's hands was wrapped around his whisky tumbler, the other was fisted on top of the table. He would not look at me.

"The rest contains just as much death and crime," he continued. "I only got worse as I got older, richer, more powerful. There is no redemption in my story. Redemption would've been letting you dance in Klutch and never speaking to you. But bringing you in to my life, that is my most damnable act."

I stared at him. He truly believed that. That his biggest sin was loving me.

The silence rang proceeding his story—his hideous, heartbreaking story—rang loud and unyielding. Jay stared at me, his face inscrutable now. I figured it had cost him a lot to venture back in to his past, to dredge up memories he had spent his adult life trying to bury.

I got it, now. His business. Handling the women, the sex workers, keeping them safe, making sure they were in control of their own destinies—he was doing for them what no one had done for him. The homeless shelters, the ones that he paid for completely, the ones that were touted as some of the best in the nation—those were a safe option for people who had nowhere else to go. What he had never had. His life was packaged in sins, but twirled around inside of those sins was some kind of saint. A dark one to be sure, a flawed, dangerous and cruel one. But to me, a saint.

"Let's go to bed," I whispered, now brave enough to reach out and touch his hand.

Jay blinked at me, shocked. He had been expecting something different. He'd come knowing he'd have to tell this story, that he'd have to perform an autopsy on his wretched past, lay it bare for me. He'd expected it to scare me. Disgust me.

It all clicked now. The way he'd touched me, the way he'd watched me, it was not his version of a new beginning, it was him saying goodbye. It was him trying to sear me into his memory.

"Take me to bed, Jay," I repeated.

I could've tried to say a lot more. Tried to find the words to comfort him, to express my horror and sorrow at what he'd been through. But nothing would measure up. Nothing was right.

I stood, our hands intertwined, pulling him slightly. He stood up, yanking me into his body as soon as he was vertical. I gasped at the impact of his body on mine. "Stella," he murmured.

"Take me to bed," I repeated for the third time, putting my finger to his lips to stop him from saying more.

It was then he took me to bed.

CHAPTER FOUR

We slept late. We'd exhausted ourselves with our bodies, with our confessions, with our mutual pain. In all the mornings I'd spent with Jay, I'd never seen him sleep later than precisely six thirty. He was usually up by five, and before he got out of bed, he fucked me. Or went down on me.

He did both at ten in the morning. After two orgasms and a shower—with Jay—I was still waiting for the moment when this was all stolen away. It was utterly surreal to see Jay in the daylight, in this little cottage in New Zealand.

We were naked, except for my panties and his underwear, eating breakfast. I sipped my coffee, staring at him with the ocean in the background, the sea air blowing from the open doors. The salty air mixed with Jay's scent.

"I still want children," I exclaimed suddenly, putting down my

coffee cup. "At least one. Even though I know the risks. Of turning into my mother. Even if I don't, I know that I may pass something on. I know it's a risk. And maybe it's selfish of me to want that. But I do. I want to be the mother mine wasn't. And I want you to be able to love a child like your parents didn't."

I didn't know why I'd blurted this out on what could've been a perfect morning. But I found I wasn't looking for perfection. Perfection was empty, fickle. It was in the difficult, in the painful, that I was going to be most satisfied.

Jay stared at me for a long time. I felt sick for making a demand that sounded dangerously like an ultimatum. Here was the man who stalked my dreams, the one who owned my heart, who had marked my soul, coming back to me and giving me everything I wanted, yet I was demanding more.

Because I deserved more.

"I won't be a good father," he proclaimed, putting down his fork.

"I disagree," I argued.

He narrowed his eyes ever so slightly. I was pissing him off, and that was turning me on.

"It's something that I will have to come to terms with," he said. "But I want you. There is no way I can let you go. No way I can let you live a life without me."

I bit my lip. There was pain in his voice. It was palpable, and it was uncomfortable to hear it, to feel it. I was struggling to breathe underneath the weight of everything he was giving me. He was giving me everything that I'd craved, wished for when we were together, parts of himself he had been holding back.

The time we spent apart had stripped something from him. Not all of his shields, not all of his coldness, but there was something raw about him now.

Yes, this was what I wanted. But it was really fucking hard going from a famine to a feast.

Jay didn't wait to drop another bombshell, it was at our next meal. Lunch, prepared in our underwear after we'd gone back to bed.

His presence itself was a crater in the fragile house of cards I'd tried to build in his absence, the life that I'd constructed without him.

Then there was the fact that he was suddenly going to 'come to terms' with having children with me. Which wasn't exactly what a girl wanted to hear. I didn't want him to have to *come to terms* with having a child with me, but I knew that for him, with what he'd been through, it was a lot. It wasn't romantic by any means, but it was a huge gesture. A forever kind of promise. Not empty. Jay wouldn't make that kind of statement just to get me back and then go back on his word. Through all my ruminations these past few months, I realized I truly knew little about the man who I'd let ruin my life with his love. But I knew that Jay wouldn't tell me pretty lies to get me back. He'd tell me ugly truths as some kind of challenge, on purpose, as if he was hoping he'd scare me off. Even now, after crossing an ocean for me in the kind of grand gesture he'd promised me a lifetime ago he wasn't capable of, I sensed that he was clutching on to me with both hands while simultaneously daring me to push him away.

To escape him.

I wasn't sure when I'd made the decision to clutch on to him right back. He hadn't exactly given me time to do that since he'd arrived in the darkness. But then again, it wasn't throughout the night when I'd battled with the decision to fight or stay. The decision was already made, the second I felt his lips on my neck.

Whether or not it was weak of me to welcome him back into my life without a battle, I didn't quite care. Beyond that, I also knew Jay well enough to know that this had already been a battle for him. I could see it all over his face. He was ravaged by this, by me. My absence. It satisfied me to see that our separation hadn't just caused pain. It had hurt him deeply enough that even he couldn't hide the emotional scars from it all.

Which is what I'd needed all along, proof that he hurt too. That loving me had caused him the same pain that loving him had caused me. I didn't want smiles, soft words, loving promises. I wanted to see the agony of it all, wanted to make sure that I left the same marks on him that he left on me.

Now that I saw that, I was done. I wasn't going to tell him what he'd done to me, curse him for being so cold, so cruel. I'd known he was a cold and cruel man when I'd fallen in love with him, and I'd stayed anyway, despite the strong premonition that he'd hurt me.

That didn't mean that I wasn't still processing the statement he'd made about children, chewing on it as I ate the eggs I'd made us.

Jay had been sitting across from me, watching, food untouched in front of him, silent.

That was, until the bombshell.

"We're going to get married." He spoke as if he were saying 'we're going to go to the store tomorrow.' No inflection. His voice was devoid of emotion. His mossy green eyes were not. The way his Adam's apple moved when he swallowed heavily after speaking was another signal of something below his granite façade.

I blinked at him across the table, my fork midair. "Is that a proposal?" I asked once I figured out how to collect myself. This man sitting across from me, naked, statuesque, beautifully brutal, was real. And he'd just opened his mouth, the word 'marriage' coming out of it.

"No, I do not do proposals," he replied. "I will not pretend that I am capable of any kind of toxic romance that women have come to expect." His eyes flickered down to his hands for a moment. A small moment, but the gesture was huge.

Jay kept eye contact. Always. No matter how hard it was to speak, no matter what he was speaking about. But he broke it with me now, in the moment I needed it the most.

My throat burned with the need for him to look at me once more.

After what felt like an eternity, he looked up and continued speaking as if he hadn't just paused in what was most likely one of the most important conversations of my life.

"I do not think you hold such stock in traditional farces, but I will apologize if you expected romance or if this has disappointed you somehow," he stated, hands fisted on top of the table. "Even marriage as an institution and the fanfare of it all rather sickens me. But I much like the idea of making you mine. In as many ways as I can. And since I plan on having you as mine for the rest of the time I draw breath on this earth, I think marriage is a great idea."

I blinked at him again, fork still in the same place it was when he started speaking. I glanced at it then quietly set it down onto my plate before returning my gaze to Jay.

"You are aware that we have only recently gotten back together, and prior to us breaking up, we had only been together for *six months*. The majority of that time being involved in a rather businesslike arrangement that consisted of sex and not much else." I pointed out, a slight bite to my voice.

I didn't consider myself a hopeless romantic. Almost a decade of dating in L.A. had quashed any notions that romance existed beyond a guy paying for your Uber home or getting you an expensive dinner while flirting with the waitress the entire time. Yes, I was not a romantic, but it was a little jarring to have the man I loved approach marriage in such a cold way.

Then again, why was I surprised? The man I loved was cold. Didn't I love him despite that? Or because of it? And wading through everything he'd just said, one could find a few romantic statements.

I plan on having you as mine for the rest of the time I draw breath on this earth.

Yeah, who needed cheap flowers or music or fanfare? That statement right there was the only thing my hungry heart wanted. It was an oath. One that Jay would not break.

Jay was staring at me, too, of course. I didn't think there had been a moment since our reconciliation—apart from that chasm of a pause—when he had stopped looking at me. It was intense, unyielding, and I wasn't sure if I would want to survive without it.

"You've been quiet for too long, Stella," he rasped, his voice husky.

I blinked again. Jay's hands were still fisted on top on the table. Veins in his neck were protruding, evidence of the force he was using to hold himself still, as if he was bracing for a blow. As if he was expecting a refusal.

It hit me then. Jay knew me. He knew a lot of things about me. Most likely more things than I knew about him, but he did not know my thoughts. *I* didn't just make a grand statement about wanting to be with him until my dying breath.

Not out loud, at least.

Jay was scared.

Terrified, actually, if appearances were to be believed. This was a man who worked in certainties. Who made sure he could control everything around him so he could know the outcome, chase away any uncertainty like what he'd been forced to endure early in his life. That was what the arrangement was all about.

But we weren't in an arrangement anymore. He didn't get any reassurances, any promises when he got on that plane, when he broke into my rental last night.

This was the first time since I'd met him where he'd said more than I had.

My chair screeched against the hardwood floor as I stood, moving quickly toward him. Jay was standing by the time I got there.

It was hard not to stop to marvel at what he looked like, towering over me wearing nothing but his scars, but I managed.

I lifted my hands so I gripped either side of his neck, needing to touch him, needing our naked bodies to brush. My stomach dipped as he hardened against me, and need coursed through my veins.

"Jay Helmick," I whispered, momentarily losing myself in his green irises. "I cannot explain it, I will never be able to understand it, but since the moment I met you, I have not been able to take a breath without your name on my lips. I have not been able to close my eyes without your face haunting me. And any future without you in it seems cold and abysmal. There is no way I could say no to forever with you." A tear trailed down my cheek when I finished speaking, emotion filling me up to the point where it was impossible not to let it out somewhere. Hope, fear, happiness, love and pain mingled in my body, filling me up from my fingertips to my toes.

It was a liberation. These truths, the ones spoken to me by my sinner who only specialized in lies. And the truths from my own tongue tasted so much sweeter than any of the lies I'd told myself for comfort or survival.

Sweeter still was the taste of Jay as he let me pull him down to meet my lips so that I could gently, slowly, lovingly kiss him.

It was a kiss unlike any we'd ever shared. Soft. Tender. One that was controlled by me.

My control was short-lived, which I was glad for since my body coiled up with need once more, desperate for a release, desperate to make up for all the nights I'd spent without Jay.

I lost purchase on his neck because his hands gripped my hair, fisting it to expose my neck. He grazed it with his teeth then bit down, soft first then harder. Enough to leave a mark.

"Fuck, Stella," he grated out, his voice rough, almost animal. "I don't know how to get enough of you. Don't know how to stop being so hungry for you." His eyes flared, and his other hand went down, between my legs then inside.

I gasped as his fingers moved expertly inside of me. Then they were gone. He lifted them up to his mouth, tasting me. "Starving," he murmured.

"I don't ever want you to stop being hungry for me," I whispered, knees shaking. "I want you to spend the rest of your life famished, just like me. I want us to starve and to feast together."

He grinned wickedly, showing all of his teeth.

There was the sound of clattering forks, plates shattering against hardwood, then my back was on the table. A screech of the chair as Jay pulled it in front of me, his hands wrenching my legs to dangle over his shoulders. His eyes glittered as he looked up at me from between my legs.

"It's time to feast," he growled.

Growled.

Then he feasted.

Later, when I regained used of my limbs, I did too.

We were back in bed.

The sun was rising. Soft morning light bathed the room that smelled of Jay, of me, of sex. At some point, he'd carried me from the living room to put me back in the bed, to make love to me slowly, gently. Something told me it was the first and last time he'd touch me this way. That there was no way to reproduce everything we were both feeling right now, the circumstances that pulled down every single one of his guards and exposed him fully to me. That was okay. I wasn't sure if I could survive the gentle, loving touch from the man I loved so violently.

I wasn't thinking of anything in particular. My thoughts were fleeting, soft around the edges, light enough to float past the backs of my eyes. It was unfamiliar, this feeling. These past few months, it was integral to avoid moments like this. Soft mornings in bed where my mind could wander. Before this, my thoughts had been anvils, black, all encompassing, prickly, dangerous things that did more damage the longer I let myself be idle and invite them in.

The man whose chest I was currently buried in had everything to do with both the former and the latter thoughts. But to feel so carefree, so light, was again unfamiliar. I didn't remember a moment like this with Jay.

"I'll do without the romantic proposal, if you'll indulge me when I embellish the details ever so slightly to my girlfriends," I mumbled into his chest.

"By saying that I put the ring into a glass of champagne or something?" he asked.

I moved up so I could scowl at him—my fiancé. My future husband. The man who knew how to make me fall in love with him and how to break my heart. Who knew my body. My fears. The man, for better or for worse, whose roots were intertwined with mine.

"That's an insult to both of us, to think you would do something that cheesy and tacky and that I wouldn't lie about it if it happened," I countered. "What am I supposed to do? Fish a diamond ring out of a champagne flute with my fingers? Get them wet? Or drain the glass and then have to spit the ring out to put it on my finger?" I shook my head. "Yuck."

Jay watched me in that very certain way of his that showed he was amused by me without his mouth moving. It was a very intimate thing to see that look, know it. I suspected I was the only person on this planet who could decipher Jay's looks, and I adored that. I felt very greedy over it too. As much as I should want Jay to open himself up to people, to friends, to let people know him, I also didn't *want* people to know him. Didn't want him to feel fond or close to anyone but me. It was an ugly and selfish thought, but that's what his love made me. Ugly. Selfish. Greedy.

"I'm going to say that there was music on, Debussy," I whispered. "That you waited for the sun to set. That you slid a diamond onto my finger, that you didn't kneel. Instead, you pulled me out of my seat so I could stand beside you, and you asked me to stand beside you, to walk beside you for the rest of your life." My voice was thin and wispy. I feared I sounded pathetic.

Something moved in Jay's eyes. Something soft and tender. All the muscles of his face were relaxed, he wasn't holding himself taut, wasn't bracing for attack. He threaded his fingers with mine, his large and lithe, mine delicate and breakable in his grasp. He rubbed the naked area of my ring finger.

"We'll get you the diamond," he stated. "One of a kind." He kept grip of my finger but looked me in the eye now. "And we'll play Debussy every single night in our home. I'll alter my proposal just a little, to remind you that although I think you aren't just my equal but are superior to me in every single way, that I'm honored to have you at my side, but I'll always be in front of you, protecting you from everything in this world..." he trailed off. "Except me."

"Don't you get it, Jay?" I whispered back. "The last thing in the world I want is for you to protect me from yourself."

His eyes shimmered with something I couldn't catch. "Wren."

I blinked. "Wren?" I repeated.

"She said something of the same variety."

I stared at him for a beat then grinned. "She's a smart woman."

Jay leaned forward and kissed my head gently. "Yes she is."

"Soooo…" I made the single syllable word drag into many so I wouldn't have to carry on with the sentence.

I was wearing a white bikini that tied up at the sides. Well, it was *supposed* to tie up at the sides. I had spent the majority of our beach day fighting Jay off. Though, I hadn't been fighting him that hard. The strings had only been not so securely refastened but five minutes ago. We were laying on the daybed that Jay had carried onto the private beach. Carried. While wearing a short sleeved linen shirt and white shorts. His tanned skin gleamed with the sunscreen I'd slathered on him even though his coloring meant he likely wouldn't burn. But I warned him of holes in the ozone layer here and skin cancer, and he'd relented.

My worries about skin cancer and holes in the ozone layer dissipated the second my hands started rubbing his naked skin. First the smooth, unblemished, magnificent skin of his arms. I moved rhythmically, slowly, eyes glued to Jay's skin, watching my hands rub the lotion into it. He was relaxed at first, apart from very clearly being turned on—as was I, despite the fact I'd only just cleaned up from him fucking me against the kitchen counter the second I came out in aforementioned bikini—but when I moved up his arms and onto his scarred back, he tightened. His jaw turned iron, veins in his neck pulsed and his previously liquid irises turned to stone. I bit my lip, considered stopping, but when he didn't tell me to, I continued. He had wanted to stop me. Wanted to cling to the rules of an arrangement that no longer existed. The arrangement that I had thought he created for pure control, but I was beginning to understand that the arrangement had existed primarily to protect him.

Without his strict rules, he had no defenses. He was laid bare to me. And the way he was gritting his teeth, holding his body, told me he was fighting to give me that. Give me him.

I moved slowly with the lotion over the marks in his skin, feeling the rough edges, hurting for the boy in the past who had just wanted his parents to love him.

I wanted to lay my lips on the marks of his body. Show them a tenderness that was decades too late. I wanted to take away Jay's pain, but if I did that, I'd take away the man he was. The man I'd fallen in love with.

I rubbed the lotion in. And he let me.

Then he carried the daybed onto the beach we had to ourselves. Then he untied the strings of my bikini.

Eventually, they were tied again. Eventually, he let me run up to the house and come back with cheeses and wine, which was what he was drinking while idly loosening the string at my hip once more. Eventually, I spoke, drawing out that single word because I feared what I was going to say afterward would tear through the perfection of the day.

"So?" Jay repeated after I'd been quiet for some time.

I looked from the sapphire ocean to Jay's mossy gaze. "So I have to go to work in the morning," I looked down at my hands, hating that reality loomed over us, hating that this perfect, almost summer day wasn't endless. Hating that I couldn't just live here, in this daybed, with Jay in his white linen looking every bit the handsome hero of some 1950s flick.

I'd expected Jay to stiffen, for his face to close down, his indifferent and cold posture to return. But it didn't. He continued playing with the tie on my bikini, took a sip of wine and waited for me to say more.

I bit my lip. "We're getting closer to wrap, so the days are longer," I explained.

The waves crashed softly in the background, native birds sang in the distance. Otherwise there was no other sound. No comment from Jay.

"I'm assuming you don't have business in New Zealand," I continued.

Now his face changed. Gone was the lazy satisfaction that had softened every one of his features. They were sharper now, eyes filled with intensity, his hand settled on my hip, pressing the pads of his fingers into my bone.

"The only business I have here is you," he murmured, voice low.

I swallowed, my stomach dipping at his words. The low, gravely tenor of his voice.

"And how long until you wrap up your business with me?" I asked shyly. I didn't know where my trepidation came from. No, I did. This weekend had been a whirlwind. Had been everything I hadn't let myself hope for. But it had not erased the months before. Had not filled in the holes left inside of me. Jay's absence, my heartbreak, was close enough to taste, to chill my bones despite the hole in the ozone layer. Large parts of me were choked with fear of Jay leaving again. Of not having his hands on me, not having his scent mingled with every breath I took.

Jay reached up to brush my hair from my face, cupping my jaw with his large hand. "Stella, I'm never going to be done with you," he said. "I won't leave this place until you're sitting beside me on the plane."

I blinked at his words. "You're going to stay here until I'm finished?" I clarified.

"Yes," Jay replied, kissing my neck.

I tried my best to focus. "But we don't wrap for another two and a half weeks," I countered.

Jay's deft fingers worked the tie at my neck so my top fell away. "I'm aware." His lips moved down the swell of my breast. I sucked in sharply at the way he made my pussy clench when he did that.

"And you are a very important businessman who is always working," I continued, voice breathy.

"Of that I am also aware."

Lips on my nipple now, his teeth grazing it with erotic warning.

"Well, I seem to recall you making a song and dance out of coming to Missouri with me, on Thanksgiving. For *three days*. Because '*you do not take vacations.*'" I had been planning on doing a whole deep menacing voice when I quoted him, but it didn't exactly work with Jay's lips where they were.

His teeth bit down to the point of sublime pain before he looked up at me. "I remember that, pet," he acknowledged. "But that was before. When I thought I could control you. Control us. Even then, I could not survive without you for those three days. I've existed without you for *months*. I shall not do it again. Wherever your work takes you, where mine takes me, we will be together. There won't be another night where you fall asleep without me. Without feeling my cock inside of you."

My stomach dipped delightfully at his words, my heart swelling so I was choking on it. Jay was not a man for empty placations. He was not hearts and flowers, saying anything he didn't intend on making good on.

It was not a practical promise to make, with our jobs, with life stretching out ahead of us, years promising all sorts of situations which would likely require us to part, situations beyond our control.

But that was the thing with Jay. Nothing was beyond his control when it came to us. I believed that he was promising me a lifetime together. And, despite the trials that I knew would come with it, I wanted it.

So I whispered, "Okay".

Then I lost myself in him again once more.

CHAPTER FIVE

"Is it safe to enter?" Wren called out with one hand over her eyes. The other was holding a bottle of wine.

I rolled my eyes from where I was sitting at the counter, watching Jay cook. I had been doing it ever since he started, and it was somewhat of a religious experience. Jay, my Jay, *my fiancé* in the kitchen. The same one I'd longed for him in. The same one, on a particularly bad night, I'd been curled up in a ball on the floor crying. Though to be fair, it was after almost two bottles of wine.

It was hard to tear my eyes from him for fear he might disappear, but I managed it.

Karson entered behind her, not covering his eyes which were focused on Wren in a way that communicated he was ready to jump in front of a bullet at any moment. Like she was his sun. Then they went to her ass because she had a great ass.

My heart warmed for my friend.

"You called me when you were leaving your house. Then you texted when you were ten minutes away, then five, then you texted as you pulled up in the driveway," I told her with a grin.

"Well, I know this is a reunion *for the ages,* and I also know you're a hot piece of ass. So I wouldn't be surprised if Jay caught you in this golden hour sunlight and totally forgot about his incoming dinner guests," she taunted, grinning at Jay.

He, of course, didn't grin back. He hadn't changed *that* much. But he did give her a mouth twitch that communicated he was not only amused by her but familiar with her. It warmed me more, to see that familiarity between two very important people in my life. But something bitter tainted it. A jealousy that was borne when Wren first arrived, talking about Jay with a familiarity that hadn't developed out of normal circumstances. That had been borne out of my heartbreak.

I quickly swallowed that bitterness. This was not the time to dwell on such things. This was a time to rejoice, to celebrate, to bask in the fact that despite the circumstances surrounding Jay's and my relationship, we were having a dinner. An *almost* normal dinner with my best friend and her boyfriend. Yes, her boyfriend was an ... enforcer? Hitman? For my fiancé—I still stumbled over that word, even thinking it. The fiancé who ran what I understood was the majority of the criminal underworld of L.A., whatever that meant. I knew it meant sex workers, murders and making enemies.

Mental note to get specifics on what the criminal underworld consisted of before I married the man who ruled it.

Wren kissed my cheek then perched herself on the barstool beside me. Karson did the masculine chin lift thing with Jay then set about to pouring Wren a glass of wine.

"This is exactly how it should be," Wren voiced with a playful smile aimed at the two men. "Men in the kitchen, waiting hand and foot on the women." She took the glass from Karson, and I clinked mine to hers.

"Amen," I concurred. But I wasn't looking at my friend, despite the fact I missed her and loved her dearly. My eyes were on the man in the kitchen who, incidentally, was staring right back at me.

"We're engaged," I blurted, still staring at Jay. His expression didn't change, but his eyes twinkled. Many would not say twinkled but glittered with murderous intensity, but potato, potahto.

Wren squealed with glee, clapping her hands together, slamming her glass down on the counter and jumping out of her seat. She snatched my hand, yanking it forward so quickly that she almost dislocated my shoulder, staring at the empty ring finger before glaring back up at Jay. "Where *the fuck* is the diamond?"

"Wren—" I muttered, immediately going to Jay's defense.

She held her hand up. "Nuh uh." Her eyes were still on Jay. "Jay is a big, bad boy, and he's adept at speaking for himself. He is also very wealthy and has good taste, therefore, there should be a four carat, oval cut, solitaire diamond sitting on *that* finger." She yanked my hand up in order to wave it in Jay's face.

I scowled at her and snatched my hand back. "We haven't had time for all that," I snapped.

Still, Wren didn't look at me. "Oh, you had time. Months and months. More than enough time to call the best jeweler in the city and get something custom made. Why in the fuck did you come over here if not to profess your undying love and demand forever out of *this* beautiful creature." She pointed at me aggressively.

I'd expected Jay to be pissed. Furious. This was a man who exuded power. He was used to people being afraid of him, treating him with respect. Wren was making it clear that she wasn't afraid of him and definitely wasn't afraid of a fight.

But Jay did not look pissed, not in the slightest. He looked ... amused? Cue the bitterness at the weird, positive and almost playful connection between the two of them.

"I came here for Stella," he responded simply.

Something about the way he said it sent soothing shivers up my spine, and my gaze went lazy toward Jay.

"Hmmm."

The sound came from Wren. I reluctantly looked at her.

"I guess I'll give you a break on the diamond since you've got my best friend looking like *that,*" she conceded, waving her hand up and down. "Looking like herself again." She pointed at Jay. "But upon arrival at LAX, there better be a fucking jeweler waiting with the most perfect ring to ever exist."

Jay nodded seriously.

I let out a snort.

Karson's mouth twitched.

All was well in the world.

I did not ask how Jay busied himself while I was working. I highly doubted he sat around watching Netflix all day or lounging on the beach. He set up a makeshift office in the second bedroom of the cottage, but he didn't spend any time in there when I was home. The second I walked through the door, his attention was on me. Wholly.

I did not complain.

Not in the slightest.

Though I didn't know exactly what he got up to, I figured being the CEO of all sorts of businesses—an organic food company and a solar power startup being two that surprised and amused me—he had a lot of work to get done, and the beauty of technology made it so he could do all that work at the bottom of the world.

His other work, the stuff we had not completely gotten in to—yet—I assumed it would be slightly more difficult to conduct over Zoom. I wanted to ask him who was running that side of things, especially while Karson was here but I wasn't ready for *that* yet. Now that I'd committed to forever with this man, I let myself put off such conversations. They'd come eventually. I just wanted to enjoy the time we had here.

But his midnight life always crept in.

To be fair, he didn't try to hide the gun. He had it resting behind the door in the second bedroom. I didn't have an occasion to go in there, except the day I was looking for a pair of tennis shoes I'd packed with the intention of taking up running while I was here. Needless to say, I hadn't worn them once. I was only searching for them because Jay wanted to go for a walk. A *walk*. It seemed so ordinary, so fucking vanilla, it excited me more than a simple walk should've. He'd read about a hike nearby. It was then that it had occurred to me in the months that I'd been here, I hadn't gone out of my way to explore this beautiful country. Sure, I worked six days a week more often than not, with long hours. But there were long weekends, sporadic days off. I just hadn't had the thirst to ... marvel at something. To seek out any beauty.

Until now.

Hence me all but skipping into the room in search of my tennis shoes. I found a gun instead.

I stared at it, resting right next to my Louis Vuitton suitcase. It looked ridiculous sitting there, like it was a prop for a photoshoot. I knew well enough it was no prop, it looked heavy, imposing, dangerous. Regardless of that, I moved forward to touch it, for what reason, I didn't know. Larger hands beat me to it.

I whirled to see Jay standing there, frowning at me. "What are you doing, Stella?"

I frowned back. "What am *I* doing?"

"Yes, what are you doing, trying to handle a gun?" he clipped.

"What is a *gun* doing here in the first place?" I snapped, putting my hands on his hips.

Jay's jaw clenched, but he didn't answer me.

Ah, so we were back to that. Silence when he didn't want to answer something.

"Where did you get a gun?" I asked, staring at the weapon in his hands. I was shocked, but also a little turned on. There was something so utterly masculine, dangerous and right about seeing something so powerful, so deadly, in Jay's hands. Something about the fact that I knew he wouldn't hesitate to use it on anyone who meant us harm.

I likely needed therapy being so turned on by the fact that my fiancé was brandishing a gun with familiarity and purpose, but I was going to need therapy for this whole damn thing.

"You think I'd spend time here with you—the single most precious thing in the world—without some kind of firepower to protect you?"

I blinked at him. "We're in New Zealand, Jay," I huffed out. "In small town New Zealand for that matter. There is nothing to protect me from." Beyond that, I knew this country had very strict laws when it came to guns which, of course, my crime lord fiancé had circumvented rather quickly.

"There is a man walking around the beach with a shotgun," Jay countered.

"Fuck," I muttered. "I *knew* I'd regret telling you that."

"This is my life Stella," Jay asserted. "This will be our life. There won't be a time when I'm not prepared, armed, ready for something to take you from me. At some point, someone is going to try to do that. It's the nature of my business. That's not going to change."

No apology. If anything, it was a challenge, another time where he was daring me to walk away, testing me to see if he'd scared me enough.

I didn't love guns. Didn't love violence. But I loved this man. And guns and violence were a huge part of his life. Of our life now.

And I'd lived without the violence and the guns. I hadn't liked it. So I stepped back, grabbed my tennis shoes and we went on a hike. A hike during which Jay pulled me over to the side of the trail and fucked me against a tree.

Yeah, life with Jay was so much fucking better.

CHAPTER SIX

New Zealand was special.

Beyond the obvious reasons why it was—the scenery, the people, the food, the absolute ... peacefulness of the country itself—it was special for Jay and me.

We'd never been with each other outside our normal environments. Outside of *his* environment. The city that he ... controlled? Owned? The underworld he commanded. The house with all of those memories. The terrible ones and the good ones.

There was a freedom in this little country at the bottom of the world. In the little house on the beach. In Jay.

Certainly, he still liked control in the bedroom. Or on the sofa. Or the balcony. Or the kitchen counter. Yes, he liked control in all of those areas. And in those areas, I liked giving it to him. No, I *loved* giving it to him.

Yet there were no other places he tried to take it.

Not here.

Not in our magical corner at the bottom of the world. He was still Jay, of course. Still shadows, angles, darkness. But there was something about him, away from his kingdom, his stomping ground, away from whatever it was he did back home, that made him lighter. Made that twinkle in his eye that much brighter. Made the corners of his mouth move upward in something almost resembling a smile.

The only hiccup we had was the wrap party he attended with me. Which itself was shocking. I'd mentioned it to him, told him that he could come in that offhand, casual kind of way that made it seem like I didn't mind one bit if he didn't—because that's what I was expecting—when really, I was desperate for it. For him to be that kind of ... fiancé—it still felt very weird thinking of him as that, calling him that—who could and would come to parties, events, shaking hands, making jokes, easing himself into the crowds.

But to have that kind of man, I'd have to abandon my life with Jay. Because Jay didn't ease into crowds, they parted for him. He didn't make jokes, didn't commence in meaningless small talk. He intimidated people without meaning to, he put them on guard. And then there was the matter of how protective he was over me. To say the least.

Yes, New Zealand was magical and special in many ways. It stripped away layers of Jay, showed me parts of him that I'd ached to uncover. But it did not change the core of him, nor did I want it to.

Even if he pissed me off *royally* at the wrap party.

Everyone was surprised to see me arrive at the party with a man.

Especially with a man like Jay. He was not wearing a ten-thousand-dollar suit. He was wearing jeans and a tee—what he'd been wearing for the entirety of the trip, and man, could he wear the absolute *shit* out of jeans and a tee. It was slightly off putting, seeing him without his protective clothing, but heartwarming to see him shed his armor, even if it was only for a short time.

Though I loved a cocktail party and a black-tie event as much as the next fashionista, I also enjoyed the informality of this country. The 'come as you are' mentality. Which was what the wrap party was. A barbeque. A lot of beer. Soft, reggae-type music filtering through the speakers. The party venue itself was nowhere near informal. It was in a large, sprawling house, open plan, with every single door and window open, a courtyard full of people and money leaking from every piece of furniture and décor.

The house was being rented by one of the stars of the mini-series, Avery Anderson. She was touted as a diva by the media because she talked back to producers and directors that talked down to her, and she'd refused to work on a movie until she was being paid equal to her male co-stars. There were also the regular rumors of her commanding crew not to look her in the eye and having assistants fired for not providing her with the right brand of designer water. Which couldn't be further from the truth. Avery Anderson was intelligent, soft spoken and one of the hardest workers on the set. She was nice to everyone from the sound guy to the director. Her and I might've gotten on better had I been more of a functioning human being, able to smile, joke and respond to her warm personality. Alas, I had not.

She'd had to fly out the second filming wrapped for a movie

but had offered her rental to the crew. People who'd worked with her before said that she did that kind of thing often, yet she was still hailed as a diva and a bitch in the media.

It was the way it was for women. Yet men like Jay were powerful, forces to be reckoned with, no matter what they did.

Despite my anger at such standards, something about walking into a room with Jay filled me with satisfaction. To be with someone like him, with that natural power, the vibrations that emanated from him. I didn't miss the stares, the widened eyes, the raised brows.

Although I hadn't exactly been a barrel of laughs during filming, I had still made friends with most of the people on the crew. It was impossible not to. Most were New Zealand natives, friendly by nature and virtually impossible not to like. There were many hellos, introductions and raised eyebrows at the title of fiancé that I used for Jay. The word was awkward coming out of my mouth. It felt sticky and thick and not quite right.

Husband would've worked much better. More permanent. No, I needed to tattoo myself on his fucking bones, wrap my veins around his so it was impossible for us to ever separate again.

Jay did do his best with the hurried introductions, the overly familiar handshakes with the accompanying back slaps. He tried. For me, he tried.

But he wasn't in a ten-thousand-dollar suit. He wasn't at a charity dinner where the entire purpose of his attendance was to intimidate, where every single person attending knew who he was, knew to be afraid of him and needed to impress him at the same time.

No, to everyone here, Jay was just the incredibly, devastatingly, heart wrenchingly handsome man who arrived at the party with the stylist. Nothing more than that. It unnerved him. I saw that. Normally, he'd cling to the mask he'd perfected over the years. Normally, he'd shut down, silence people with a mere look, do what he came here to do and leave.

But there was none of that here.

He was trying this for me.

"I love you," I breathed in his ear after one of the cameramen flung a beer at him.

His hand, the one at my waist, tightened. He didn't respond, but he didn't need to. His eyes said it all.

Then came Brent.

Well, it was after we'd been split up by a bathroom break and me getting caught in various conversations on my way back to Jay, who looked to be stuck in his own conversation with one of the production assistants. One of the very young, fresh faced, denim cutoff wearing production assistants. She was perky, from her tits to her toes. Perfectly nice.

But she was pressing her perky tits up at my man's face, and I swallowed acid. Jealousy did not become me. Nor should it overwhelm me. This man flew across the world for me. This man loved me entirely. I was certain of that. But that man was *mine*.

His eyes found me just as I extracted myself from a conversation. I knew they saw whatever toxic, possessive thoughts were floating through my brain because they twinkled with something resembling amusement.

I couldn't help but smile. Couldn't help but beam. We'd made it to that point ... somehow. That we could speak across a room with a mere look. That I could float around a party knowing that I was his and he was mine and that was the way it was going to be.

Forever.

"Stella!"

I was pulled into the crook of a very large arm. One that smelled of oil and *man*. Brent's azure eyes were soft and warm, focused completely on me.

"You're here," he smiled, squeezing my arm, pressing me farther into his broad and muscled torso.

I didn't look across the room. I didn't need to, the force of his stare was a physical thing. More physical than the large and impressive arm around me.

"I'm here," I agreed, smiling up at Brent while deftly stepping out from under his arm. Luckily, he let me do so ... after a moment of hesitation. I knew what Brent wanted from me. He hadn't exactly hidden his attraction for me. Hadn't pushed it either. Brent was a good man.

But my taste veered toward the wicked variety.

Brent's eyes flickered over me. I was wearing a loose cotton sundress with billowing sleeves and a short hemline. My legs—like the rest of me—were tanned, and I had on heeled wedges because even though New Zealand did 'come as you are casual', there was no way I could attend a party of any kind in *flats*.

My hair was wild and curly, and I wasn't wearing makeup except for a swipe of mascara. Lip gloss was impossible because Jay's mouth was on mine any chance he got. Because of that, my lips were pink, swollen, my cheeks in a permanent flush as I continued to relive his hands on me. My cheeks were not pink from the memory of pleasure. Not right now. They were flushed with dread.

"You look beautiful," Brent said, unaware of my panicked insides. The compliment was threaded with innuendo.

"Thank you," I replied, my smile polite and tight.

Still, I refused to look in Jay's direction. I'd never been in this situation with him before. He'd been very insistent about other men while in the arrangement, but I couldn't say how he'd react once we were out of it.

I got my answer when hands circled my hips. It seemed that Jay was not the man to watch from across the room as a muscled and rugged Kiwi hottie spoke to his woman.

Brent's eyes went to the hands on my hips, then the man they belonged to. Still, I didn't look up at Jay. His fury rippled off him, even though he wasn't technically entitled to any. I felt guilty even though there was absolutely no reason to. Even if I had, one night, taken Brent up on his offer for a drink, if I'd let him take me home to satisfy me with those callused hands, I would've done nothing wrong. In theory, at least.

But the mere act of smiling at him, of even considering letting that happen, felt like a betrayal.

"Jay," he introduced himself, holding out the hand that wasn't biting into my hip. His voice was even. Not quite pleasant. Not overly hostile either. But I was sure if I looked up, there would be some kind of challenge, some kind of ownership in his eyes.

I watched the soft, easy expression leave Brent's face. He shook hands with Jay, both men probably gripping with the intention to break a few fingers.

"Brent," he replied with some steel to his tone.

I barely restrained a snort at the blatant display of testosterone.

Brent's gaze flickered to me. "You never told me you had an old man, Stella," he stated this playfully, without any kind of accusation, but there was still an edge to his gaze.

I swallowed, still not looking up at Jay. "I..." I trailed off. What did I say? I had once been in a very strict sexual arrangement with this man, fell in love with him and then was cast out of his life when I wanted more than he could give? Then after months of pain and suffering, he made his way back to me with promises and a future?

Hmmm, no. A little wordy.

"I do, I have an old man," I quipped, grinning ever so slightly despite the situation.

"Come to take her back to America, mate?" Brent addressed Jay. "Good thing if you have because New Zealand is mighty fond of her."

Jay's hand at my hip gripped tighter. "I've come to take her back to where she belongs."

I was so fucked.

We stayed at the party for a couple more drinks—for me. Jay nursed his second beer—I'd never seen him drink beer in my life—and watched me talk and joke with the crew. He interacted when necessary, but he mostly observed. If anyone thought it was odd that I'd suddenly became a walking, talking, smiling human again accompanied by an unsmiling sex god, they didn't say it outright.

We left early because things were getting rowdy, and I was greedy for my time alone with Jay. Even though I felt an undercurrent, a tension, that had started building the second that Brent's arm went around me.

Especially then.

Because even though I did absolutely nothing wrong, I still wanted to be punished.

He was driving because I'd had more than a couple of wines, and also because he was the big alpha male here, and it was the alpha male's job to drive, apparently.

"Did you fuck him?"

I flinched at the cold emptiness of his voice. He hadn't spoken like that yet. Not since he got here. Silly of me to get complacent in this new dynamic between us. To think that it would be lasting.

"Who?" I asked, a slight edge to my tone. It took me a second to gather myself, to remember my backbone.

"The man with his hands all over you," Jay bit out.

I rolled my eyes. "He didn't have his hands *all over me*, Jay," I replied, eyeing his profile.

He was watching the road. "Did you fuck him?" he repeated. His knuckles were white.

I tilted my head and regarded him. The man I'd craved all these months. The one who'd said all those elegant things that first night, the one who had played with the tie on my bikini like he didn't have a care in the world. The man I'd agreed to marry.

The one who was seriously pissing me off right now.

"Did you bring anyone else up to your office in Klutch?" I asked him sharply. "Did you order some woman to take off her clothes, to open her legs and to not ask questions?"

My rage surprised me. I'd been so wrapped up in my utter relief at having Jay back in my life, I'd deluded myself in to thinking I wasn't just the least bit mad at him for leaving it in the first place. Yes, I understood why he left. I didn't blame him for it. But parts of me hated him just as much as they loved him.

I was under no illusions that Jay had stayed chaste for me like some hero in a Jane Austin novel. I knew that Jay would've done everything in his power to forget me, to be free of me. That would've included fucking other women.

It was lucky that he pulled the car over on the side of the dirt road leading toward the cottage because I would've flung myself out of it otherwise. I needed air that didn't smell like Jay. I needed to breathe.

He cursed as I stumbled out of the car before it had come to a complete stop. The gravel crunched against my feet, and I took hold of a metal fence, staring at the endless farmland, trying to get the image of Jay and some faceless woman out of my mind.

"Stella."

He was right behind me. But he wasn't touching me.

"We weren't together," I revealed, my voice low and raspy. "So neither of us can be mad or blame the other."
Still, he didn't talk. Didn't touch me.

"I didn't fuck him," I said after a handful of moments, staring out into nothingness. "There was no way I could let another man in.

The thought..." I trailed off, shuddering. Not at the thought of another man touching me but of another woman touching Jay. I tasted bile. "I wanted to," I continued. "Badly. To punish you. To punish myself for falling in love with you. I wanted so badly to forget you, but letting another man in would mean closing the door on us." I sucked in a ragged breath. "I didn't let another man touch what has been yours since that night at Klutch, though it would've served you right if I had. I wish I had. Wish I could've so the thought of you and another woman didn't tear out my insides quite so painfully. But I'm not that person. As much as I'd wished I could've been."

I clenched my fists at my sides, shaking with the force it took me to stand there, unmoving, unwilling to look at him as he lied, yet unable to survive him telling the truth.

Jay, of course, wasn't going to let me face away from him, even though he could hear the pain in my voice, even though he surely knew what this conversation was costing me.

His hand circled my wrist and he yanked me around, eyes dark, brows narrowed and mouth downturned.

"I brought a woman into my office."

I tried to yank my hand back, his skin too hot, my own too cold, but he only gripped tighter, pulled me closer.

"I told her to take her clothes off," he continued.

My stomach roiled, and I unwillingly let out a whimper of pain, unable to remain silent any longer. I tried to look away, but his other hand grabbed my chin, yanking it backward, forcing me to meet his eyes. They were tourmaline pools I was drowning in.

"I stared at her and stared at the kind of future I would have if I touched her," he went on, speaking quietly. "It was empty and cold, and I almost did it because that's what I deserved for hurting you like I did. But I didn't touch her. Because I knew that the second I did that, I'd never touch you again."

He loosened his grip on my chin to slowly brush the back of his hand against my jaw. "And, baby, not touching you ever again ... not a fucking option."

I sighed, my body relaxing ever so slightly, but my eyes narrowed on his handsome face. The handsome face of a practiced liar. Who'd once told me he lied as easy as breathing. Was he doing that now? To protect me from being hurt? No. Jay wasn't afraid to hurt me.

Still, it stung.

"Stella get in the car so I can drive you home and eat your cunt," he ordered without inflection.

The word coiled around his tongue and hit my lower stomach. My fingertips curled with need.

I got in the car.

CHAPTER SEVEN

Y ou can rewrite what you want out of life. With much pain. With much pleasure. With wounds, old and new, with bravery, and most of all, with love.

The story I thought I'd wanted was filled with fashion, friends and countless cocktails, to be sure. But that was just part of it. The rest was a home, eventually. A modest home with a not so modest closet. Warm, small, cozy. A love that was the same. A man who was safe, who was the hero of my story.

But then came Jay. Then came the villain.

And it turned out I didn't want warm, small, cozy. I needed an inferno, an all-encompassing, yawning, never-ending kind of love. Something that felt safe and wild at the same time. Dangerous and dark.

Wicked.

Yes, I did not want the happily ever after, did not want a Prince Charming. I wanted the uncertainty with the man on the dark horse.

My story was rewritten, not easily, not without pain, and I didn't quite know the ending yet, but it didn't matter.

Jay took me back to where I belonged. Home. L.A.

Malibu.

The house looked exactly the same, looming on the hill, a tomb of all of our memories, ghosts of who we once were. What we once were.

There was never a question about whether or not I was going back to my apartment. Just like there wasn't a question about Jay taking care of the flights home. First class. The kind of first class where we had our own fucking mini bedroom on the plane. Which, of course, we utilized.

There was a car waiting for us when we landed, and it wasn't until the house came into sight that I started to feel uncomfortable. Fearful. Of what had happened in the past. What was going to happen now. If Jay sensed my nerves, he didn't comment on them. He just kept his hand on my thigh and replied to emails on his phone.

Until we got to the front steps. He wouldn't let me take a single bag—of which I had many—not even my purse. When Jay gathered me up into his arms, I let out a little squeal of shock.

"What are you doing?" I snickered as he walked the last few steps.

"I'm carrying you over the threshold," he answered, as if it was the most natural and obvious thing in the world.

I stared up at him. "We're not married yet. It's something you're supposed to do when you're married."

"Stella, when have I been known to do anything I'm supposed to?" he asked, a smile in his voice. "I plan on doing this every time we walk through the door."

I giggled because he sounded serious and resolute. The walls moved past me in a blur. Jay wasn't moving that fast, but it I was busy focusing on his face.

His jaw was relaxed, his eyes soft around the edges. Something about him had relaxed when we walked in here. Our home.

He threw me on the bed when we entered his room—our room. It was going to be hard to think of everything that used to be his as ours. But he didn't let me consider that, not at all. Because he had taken off my shoes then my pants then my underwear. Then he had buried himself in my pussy, feasting, bringing me to climax in record time.

"Turn around," he ordered, lifting himself from between my legs.

On shaking knees, I turned on the bed.

His hands swept over my bare ass, caressing, kneading. I thought he was going to take my ass then. I was nervous, unsure if I was ready, yet hungry for him to take me in every way he could.

Jay moved, his hands on my hips, tilting them upward, then spreading my legs out farther.

"I'll be fucking your ass later," he read my mind, slipping his fingers inside me.

I gasped, fisting the sheets that were a thousand thread count and smelled of him.

"But I need inside your pussy," he continued, pressing against me. "I'll fuck you pussy hard and slow." His lips moved against my ears, sending shivers down my spine. "Then we'll shower. Then I'll cook you dinner. At some point, in the kitchen, you're going to bend over and give me your ass. And I'll take it."

Jay, a man of his word, did all of those things. And I did not think about any of the ugly, realistic things. Not for a long time.

I felt sick.

Nervous.

Very fucking nervous.

I supposed that wasn't a good thing, that I'd made myself sick with nerves over having to tell my very best friend I was engaged to be married.

I was surprised that Wren had kept this a secret for as long as she had; the woman was notorious for not being able to keep things to herself.

I'd already told Yasmin at lunch today, and she had been tentatively supportive, as she had been since I met Jay. I knew she didn't completely approve, but she kept quiet about her reservations.

Zoe would not.

We were at our favorite restaurant, the one where we'd spoken about Jay many moons ago, when I'd been worrying about being able to afford another cocktail. Now I could certainly afford another cocktail, I could afford more than I ever had before. Not because I was marrying Jay who had a lot of money—the actual number I could not even dream of—and who I had not yet spoken to about finances. His money didn't matter to me. I had enough for overpriced cocktails, the wardrobe of my dreams and being able to help my father put my mother into a care facility.

I did that all. Me. And I would have to tell my best friend I was getting married to the man who had broken my heart.

We did the obligatory hugging and the 'you look good'—which she fucking did—and asking about work—which was booming for her—ordering drinks and getting a bowl of fries delivered.

Zoe had raised a single brow when I asked the waiter—since we only ordered fries in times of crisis or PMS—but she did not ask. That wasn't her way. So she waited.

"Jay and I are back together," I blurted. "And we're getting married." I timed this to come out right when the waiter approached our table with fries, therefore she had a second to process while he put the fries down and topped up our waters.

She didn't speak until long after he'd walked away, and I'd started nervously shoving fries down my throat.

"This is intense, babe," Zoe frowned, leaning forward to grab a fry.

I popped a fry into my mouth. "Yes it is."

Her gaze was hard. "Intense works good in movies, books, Shakespearean plays. But not in the real world. In the real world, intense is synonymous with dangerous shit, with someone getting hurt, someone getting killed. Well, Shakespeare demonstrated that well, too, but the contemporary version of romance has not."

I sighed, mostly to hide the slight chill I got from her words. "You really are a cynic, my love."

She didn't smile. "No, I just love my friend. And I've seen you transform since this man came into your life. Not entirely for the worst, but not for the better. This love is going to make your life so much harder. I can see that already. I've seen that and heard it in your voice when you called me from the corner of the world—the one you crossed to try to escape him. He's going to hurt you. I do not want that for you."

I took another fry. "I don't particularly want to be hurt either. Furthermore, I wouldn't want my life any other way," I replied. "I know our story isn't likely going to be inspiring or heartwarming. If it was written down, it would likely tempt people to give up on love rather than believe in it."

I paused while the waiter offered us more drinks to which both of us replied with an enthusiastic yes before he'd even finished speaking.

"I'm happy," I continued, voice lower this time. "Maybe not in the way I thought I would be, maybe not in the way I thought happiness looked like. But I'm happy."

Zoe's face softened—just a tad. "Well, if you're happy, then I'll support you. Even if you were abjectly miserable, I would support you. Not because I wanted to, and I'd lecture you on what a stupid bitch you were being, but I'd support you, nonetheless. Because I love you." She sucked in her cheeks ever so slightly, telling me she had more to say and was trying to decide whether she was going to say it or not. This was not like my friend. If there was something that needed to be said, she said it.

Zoe's mantra was "*too many women, too many members of my culture have stayed silent because they were forced, because they had no choice. I have a choice. I'm never going to bite my tongue when generations before me never even got to use theirs."*

"Say it," I told her, grabbing my drink, figuring I'd need it.

She sighed, leaning back in her chair. "It's just ... do you really know this man, Stella? Like really *know* him? He seems like this ghost. This phantom. The mystery, the danger, it's one thing when you're in an ... arrangement. It's quite another when you're in love. When you're planning a future." She crossed her legs. "You want children. He doesn't."

I nodded. "Now he does."

"*Now* he does?" she parroted. "Just like that?"

I bit my lip. "Not just like that. Don't forget our long and painful separation."

Something moved across her face. "Oh, I remember because I didn't see my best friend for months, barely spoke to her, and when I did, it was like talking to a fucking zombie, trying their level best to act human. I remember it, Stella, because it was only a month ago."

She spoke softly, evenly, not raising her voice. But the words were sharp, full of emotion, anger.

And the worst thing was, she was right. I'd been little more than a zombie. I'd been weak. Been shattered. In the space of a month, everything had changed. I'd changed. Because of a man. I knew she was going to look at me differently now.

"I know you can't understand this," I began, voice low. "Because you are so strong. You would never be so stupid to attach everything you have and everything you are to a man, like a barnacle, unable to pry yourself away." It wasn't an accusation, though it came out as one.

She frowned at me. "No, Stella. I have," she shook her head, her words short. "I fell in to a love like that. Dark, unyielding. All encompassing. And I had to pick myself up out of the wreckage."

I stared at her. My beautiful, strong and badass friend. She had never spoken of this. Had never let me see the pain now obvious in her deep brown eyes. I shouldn't have been as shocked as I was. We all knew that Zoe had secrets. Wren, Yasmin and I had brainstormed many nights over bottles of wine. The more we drank, the more outlandish our theories had become. She'd been a spy for the CIA, now retired, living a quiet life, or that she was currently in the CIA, investigating corruption in Hollywood. That she was a time traveler, sent back to save humanity.

"I don't want to have to watch you survive that," she glowered, her voice husky.

My insides shook at her words, the icy chasm of pain in her tone.

I reached out and squeezed her hand, knowing that she'd locked up her hurt deep inside and wouldn't share it with me, not now. "I won't, I promise," I avowed, making a promise that wasn't mine to keep.

Jay was in the living room when I got home, Debussy playing. My heart melted. My entire body was relaxed, despite the humming of my martini buzz. Even though I was unsettled by my conversation with Zoe, unsettled by everything, my stomach in knots over the realities that I was facing with a life with Jay. But there was no life without Jay. I had to face those uncertainties head on.

With the help from a couple of strong martinis.

Jay was sitting in a big white armchair that was more than large enough for one person, even him with his length and generally overarching presence. There was a twin to this chair between a marble side table, but thus far, it had never been used. If Jay was sitting in his chair, I was too. Not that I was bothered by that. Not a single bit.

He put down his laptop in a dismissive way that only a very rich man would treat a very expensive piece of technology.

I climbed onto his lap without a word, my entire body relaxing even more as I did so. His arms went tight around me, and I wanted to stay there forever, burying my head in the proverbial sand that was literally my fiancé's rock hard, muscled chest.

But after an evening with Zoe, it was impossible to bury my head anywhere. After a delightful thirty seconds, I lifted my head.

"We haven't talked about finances," I spoke, staring at Jay.

He stared right back. "We have not," he agreed.

I jerked my foot up and down while I waited for him to say more. Though I knew Jay well enough to know he wasn't going say a word more. He just regarded me coolly, with that slight twinkle in his eye.

"I am going to live here," I said, moving my eyes around the lavish living room, not entirely sure how I would design it but knowing it would be remarkable. There was plenty of time to change things.

"Yes, you're going to live here," Jay affirmed. "Or, if you don't like it, we'll sell it and buy something else. Build somewhere else if you'd prefer that."

I stared at him. Not just at the blasé way he was talking about gaining and spending millions of dollars, but at how willing he was to change huge parts of his life for me. It was jarring to see him trying to be something he didn't know how to be—a partner, a lover, a husband.

"No," I replied quickly. "No, I like it here."

Although these walls held the cold memories of how Jay had been before, of the women who came before me, I loved his fortress on the hill. Our fortress on the hill. I loved that I could always smell the sea, loved that it was always mixed with Jay. Loved that I was watching this house evolve just like I was watching Jay evolve.

"Okay," Jay nodded once, moving his hand up my bare thigh.

My body responded immediately, as it had since the first time Jay touched me.

"No, not okay." I placed my hand on his, stopping its ascent.

His chin tilted down toward me in a way that told me he was irritated. Join the club.

"I need to contribute," I clarified.

"You do contribute," he argued, trying to move his hand.

I narrowed my eyes and squeezed his hand, using all of my strength to stop him. I knew if Jay really wanted to fight me on this, he would win in a heartbeat. And when his hand got to its intended destination, I wouldn't be fighting anymore.

"If you say that my contribution has anything to do with sex, you're really going to piss me off," I balked, trying not to think about how his hand would feel at its intended destination. "Because that is then basically describing a prolonged Julia Roberts and Richard Gere situation. Not okay."

Jay's brows furrowed ever so slightly. "How did Julia Roberts and

Richard Gere enter the situation?"

I hated that his voice bordered on playful. Hated how it turned me on further. But then again, I fucking loved that he was speaking in playful tones with a twinkle in his eye.

"Um *Pretty Woman*?" I huffed out. "Please don't tell me you haven't seen *Pretty Woman*, that's practically criminal."

The twinkle in his eyes brightened. "Oh, and I wouldn't want to be criminal," he teased.

I glared at him even more. "You can't get out of this by being cute."

Something moved in his face, then his hand on my thigh tightened. "You're really calling me *cute*?"

I rolled my eyes. "Stop. We need to talk about me contributing to this household. Taking over some of the bills."

His grip on my thigh was still tight, but all twinkle left his eye. His jaw hardened. "You're not taking over the fucking bills, Stella."

"Why not, *Jay*?" I scoffed, moving slightly so I could give him full view of the scowl on my face.

"Because it is my job to take care of you," he said.

I opened my mouth, ready to talk about the modern woman and how she could take care of herself.

He moved his finger to my lips. "I know you're successful, strong, independent," he said before I could speak. "I know you're capable. And, baby, I love that you want to contribute. Love that you're that kind of woman. But I'm trying to make you understand what you already give me." He rubbed his thumb over my bottom lip. "Stella, it feels fucking criminal to have you as mine. To have someone like you want to spend their life with me, knowing what I am. Knowing my past. It's a fucking gift. Every damn day. And I feel like a crook, a fucking demon for letting you give me so much Allowing you to give me everything without being able to do anything for you that measures up. Giving you this, a house that you turn into a home, clothes that I get to rip off, a bed that I get to fuck you in, that means something to me. It means a lot to me. I know it's not progressive, doesn't fit with the times or the fucking rules of how things are supposed to be these days. But in case you haven't noticed, I'm not a man who follows the rules."

I opened my mouth ever so slightly to let his thumb in so I could taste it, graze it with my teeth, feel him harden against me and watch desire cloud his eyes.

"Are you going to be okay with that, pet?" he grumbled, his voice thick.

I nodded very slowly, his thumb still in my mouth.

"Good," he growled.

Then we were up.

"Hands on the arms of the chair," he ordered.

I complied immediately, licking my lips that were now swollen from his thumb.

Jay's hands crept up my legs, under my skirt and to the sides of my panties, hooking his thumbs around them and pulling them down. I stepped out of them, my heels still on. My knees shook as his front pressed into my back, his fingers brushing my lips.

"Open your mouth," he demanded.

Again, I immediately complied.

Once his hands were out of my mouth, they went down, inside. I gasped, gripping the arms of the chair so hard my nails were digging into the fabric.

"This is what you give me, pet," he murmured in my ear, his fingers still working. "Your sweet pussy, always wet for me. Always hungry."

His fingers were gone, and I would've cried out in protest had I not heard the click of his belt. Jay surged inside without ceremony, filling me.

He didn't move, not immediately. "Stella, this is what you give me," he breathed his words into my ear, goosebumps peppering my skin. "You give me fucking heaven. You give me a home."

Then he moved.

And I did not argue with him about finances again.

Debussy was still playing when we were done. I was still clothed, right down to my shoes, except for my underwear. My body was beautifully spent, and I was sipping on the martini that Jay had made for me while I'd stumbled to and from the bathroom, cleaning myself up. He'd ordered me not to put on anymore panties, and I'd listened. The French doors were open, and the sea breeze mingled with Jay's scent, *our* scent.

My eyes were closed, head back against the chair, feeling calm, satisfied and utterly thankful for the risks I'd taken with Jay.

I kept my eyes closed, smiling lazily as a barely there touch brushed the back of my cheek. I froze when Jay lifted my left hand and slid something cold onto my fourth finger. Not letting go, he grasped my wrist and pulled me up gently.

My eyes were still closed.

"Open your eyes, Stella," he commanded, both hands on my neck now.

Shaking, I did so. I didn't look down at the ring that he'd put on my finger. Didn't want to or need to. Everything I needed was in his eyes.

"Even though I don't deserve to be the man standing beside you, I'll be in front of you my whole fucking life. I'll protect you from the world, Stella." He stroked my face again. "From everyone and everything except me. And I'll love you until my last fucking breath."

Tears ran down my face, and Jay wiped them with his thumb.

"You told me you didn't do romance," I whispered, my voice hoarse with tears.

He leaned in to kiss me gently. "I lied," he shrugged one shoulder. Just a tad.

Later, much, much later, I looked at my finger. Sitting on it was a perfect, oval cut, four carat, solitaire, gold diamond ring. Simple yet unlike anything I'd seen before.

"In my life, I haven't made it a habit to do what anyone says," Jay told me as I admired it in our bed, naked. "But I found it impossible not to listen to Wren, on this, because this is fucking perfect."

"Yeah," I whimpered through more tears. "It is."

And I definitely was not talking about the ring.

Three Days Later

"I was thinking..." I mumbled sleepily into Jay's chest, drawing circles on it lazily. The hand that felt gloriously heavy now. "Of going to see my mother."

"Okay," he replied. His hands were tight around me, his palm pressed against my ass.

I frowned into the darkness. "*Okay?*" I repeated. "That's all you've got to say?" The accusation and snark in my tone was unwarranted, but I couldn't help it. My mother was a vulnerable subject to me, and I was all open wounds whenever she was mentioned.

Jay's arms tightened around me as if he was expecting my escape. "What would you like me to say, Stella?" he asked evenly.

I blew air out between my lips in a huff. "I don't know. But you always have something to say. You always..." I trailed off.

He always saw clearer in to myself than I did in times like these. I wanted him to tell me it was a great idea or warn me against making a big mistake. One that could potentially fuck me up for the years to come.

I'd been managing my fears when it came to my mother, her illness, what could become *my* illness. First, because I was in so much pain over losing Jay that at one point, I'd thought some version of insanity might actually be welcome. Then because Jay was back in my life, swallowing up all my fears. For a while, at least.

Now we were back to normal. Or our new normal. My regular fears were coming back, and even with all of Jay's magic, he couldn't take them away from me. Only I could do that.

"If you want me to make the decision for you, Stella, I won't do that," Jay stated. "This is up to you. Whatever choice you make is what I will support."

I sighed. "Where has my alpha male dominant gone?" I moaned.

Suddenly, I was no longer on Jay's chest. I was on my stomach, arms above my head.

"Hold onto the headboard, Stella," he murmured in my ear.

Despite this evening's festivities, he was hard against me, pushing against the cleft of my ass.

"You feel that?" he asked against the back of my neck. "That's me, being that alpha male dominant. If you want some more of that, I'll spank your ass, then I'll fuck it."

I held my breath, unable to speak, my body thrumming with need. I had not thought I would be a woman who was in to ass play. Turned out I was. In a big fucking way.

"Yeah," he hissed. He pressed harder still, hard enough for me to sink my teeth into my lip, then he pulled away, his weight lifting from me.

I sighed in ... relief? Disappointment?

"I am willing to control many things about your life, Stella," he murmured. "Some areas you are more than okay with." He kneaded my ass. "Others, you are not. Others, you will fight me on, tooth and nail. Which is what infuriates me about you yet has me infatuated with you." He stroked my face. "But this is the one thing I won't control, won't take from you. This is your decision to make. I trust you to make the right decision."

I pursed my lips and did my best not to let the tears prickling the backs of my eyes fall. Although it didn't seem possible, I fell in love with this man more and more every day.

CHAPTER EIGHT

TWO WEEKS LATER

TWO WEEKS LATER

"Hey mom," I said while smiling weakly, my voice small and unfamiliar.

My stomach was in knots, and I hadn't been able to eat a single thing today. There was plenty of delicious food on board the private jet we'd taken to Missouri. The one that Jay had obviously hired to take me here when I'd made the decision to come. No way I could possibly fly coach in a plane without him.

He was in the car, outside of the new facility mom was in. I'd wished he'd come in with me, be the strong, comforting and unyielding presence at my side. He would've if I'd asked, in an instant. But this was something I needed to do on my own.

I walked through the doors. Signed in. Walked through more doors, these ones with locks on them and a burly security guard standing outside, nodding to me as I went past, looking bored and half asleep.

Beyond the locking doors, the place was nice. In the middle of nowhere, just an hour outside of St. Louis. My father had wanted mom in the same state, but in the best facility that was on offer. And this place was pretty good. There were fountains. Calming shades of white, tasteful artwork, comfortable looking chairs. But I couldn't get my mind off the security guard, the locking doors, and the smell of stale air that even the expensive oil diffusers couldn't mask.

People had been milling around the common area when I arrived. Most sitting, reading, staring out the window, playing board games and cards. I didn't know why I expected people talking to themselves in a corner or rocking imaginary babies, but I was angry at myself for doing so. I'd prepared for the worst.

My body was wound so tight during the walk to my mom's room, I thought I might snap.

It was big, her room. Had a wonderful view of a carefully tended garden, the blue, cloudless day. Her room was decorated in various patterns, colors and textures. A lot of purple. My mom loved purple. She had photos on the walls, of me when I was a teenager, graduation, very few of me and her because we didn't have that over the years. Because most of the time mom was convinced that cameras were trying to steal her soul.

"Pooh bear?" Mom asked, blinking at me.

She was wearing a purple velour sweat suit, her hair pulled back off her face. She looked young and vulnerable.

I smiled, tight, trying my best to swallow the nerves I was feeling, the awkwardness. I didn't quite know what to do with myself, where to stand, how to be. The last time I'd seen my mother was Thanksgiving before last, before Jay. She had been quiet, sullen, on medication that made her vacant and confused, which had also made her angry. She hated not being herself. Hated that the drugs made her numb to everything that made her *her*. Which was why she had so many episodes over the years, why she didn't get better or at least improve her quality of life like a large majority of people with the illnesses did. The dementia made everything worse.

She looked ten years older than she did when I saw her last and her eyes emptier than I'd ever seen them, even when she was on the strongest medications.

"Yeah, Mom, it's me," I said, trying my best to keep the shake out of my voice. Uncertain, I crossed the distance between us and pulled her into a hug. She smelled of Jasmine, like always, but she seemed so frail and small. I worried that hugging her too tight might break some of her bones.

When I let go of her, she cupped my face with her hands, her eyes lighting up in familiarity.

"Darling, you are beautiful," she said on a whisper. Her eyes—my eyes—searched my face. "And you're in love."

I blinked at her. "How do you know that?"

"A mother knows."

She let go of my face and smiled at me, open, loving—a kind of smile that made my heart long for the kind of mother she might've been. The kind of mother I knew she would've been if her illness hadn't stolen her from me. From us. Because she was beautiful, even with the years that had been added to her, even with the slightly gray pallor to her face. Even with all of that. There was something about her. Something that made me understand why my dad fell in love with her.

"Sit down," she urged, gesturing to the plush purple armchair in the middle of the room. "I'll make some tea."

I sat gingerly, putting my purse on the side table that held a framed photo of her and my dad on their wedding day. They were kissing, my dad holding her tight to him, white taffeta exploding around him. My heart clenched thinking of the happiness they must've been feeling on that day. The love. Things they thought would last forever.

My father had not stopped loving that version of my mother, I knew that. And I was sure that my mother loved him right back. Love had nothing to do with what separated them. Despite what popular culture liked to portray, there were a lot of things stronger than love. I felt sick at the feeling that all Jay and I might have one day are photos where our love was immortalized for how it was before life tore it apart.

"What's his name?" my mother asked, pouring tea into a flowery teacup with a matching saucer.

She didn't have a kettle or kitchenette in her small room, so she must've had it brought in before I'd arrived. Had two cups prepared. She must've been excited. I didn't think she'd had many visitors all the way out here, with my father still working full time. Guilt stabbed my stomach, realizing how little I'd been here to visit my mother.

"Jay," I answered her, watching as she crossed the small space. I wanted to stand up, help her. Carrying the two cups looked like it was too much work for the small woman.

"Jay," she repeated, handing me the cup and saucer.

I took it, thankful for something to do with my hands.

My mother's eyes went to the diamond on my left hand, then they went wide. "Oh, my God," she whispered. "You're getting married."

I nodded, smiling with uncertainty. "Yeah, we are."

The light in her eyes clouded over as her brows furrowed. "What does your father have to say about this?"

"He's happy, Mom," I replied, wishing that I had taken my father up on his offer to come here with me. I felt like a little girl all over again, old fears creeping in, visions of my mother pacing in front of me holding a knife.

She was sick then, I reminded myself. *I was too young to understand that. She wasn't going to hurt me.*

"He's happy?" she repeated, pacing. She was wearing slippers with bunnies all over them. "No, he cannot be happy about this. You're too young. You haven't finished high school." She stopped, pointing at me. "Just wait until he gets home. We'll be talking about this."

I stood up, moving toward Mom, even though old fears told me not to, even though they told me to run. This was my mother.

"Mom," I whispered, grabbing her hand. "We're not at home, remember? I graduated from high school. I'm almost thirty."

She stared at me, her eyes vacant and empty, terrifying for a handful of beats. Then they changed, sharpening with knowing and embarrassment. "Of course," she acknowledged quietly. "Of course you are, sweetheart." She pulled her hand away from mine, patting it gently. "Now tea. We'll talk about your man."

So we did. We drank tea. We talked about my fiancé. Like we were mother and daughter. Like we were not in a mental health facility with locks on the doors and security guards. Like the fiancé I was talking about was not a deadly crime boss. Like my moments, my seconds with my mother, were not dwindling with every day.

And Jay was there when I walked out on steady legs and a bruised heart. And although he was sure he was unable to be gentle or caring, he tended to that bruised heart, to my unsaid fears.

And it was okay.

For a while.

ONE MONTH LATER

My mind was on a lot of things while I was walking through the house. *Our house.* Mine and Jay's. Voldemort was happy in his new digs. More than happy. He barely hissed or scratched me at all. He lay in the various sun traps around the house, his favorite place being Jay's office. Especially if Jay was in there. The two of them had become fast friends, the two villains, apparently.

My photos were now scattered around the house, on side tables, on the walls, various surfaces. Wren had been sneaky enough to snap a photo of Jay and I at our dinner in New Zealand, just as the sun was setting. He was brushing a hair from my face, and I was laughing into my wine glass. He happened to be wearing a black tee, and I had on a yellow sundress, my hair long and wild. There were shadows behind me and sun rays behind him. It was striking and endearing. I'd had it blown up and framed, mounted in our bedroom, and I'd employed

Wren to be our personal stealth photographer, since Jay was not a man for selfies. Plus, the candid shots were so much better. It was my personal mission to fill the house with warmth, memories, love. My mind was on filling the house with something else as I walked down the hallway.

We hadn't spoken on the topic of kids since New Zealand. Not once. My birth control injections had long run out, which Jay knew since I was now getting periods again. Not that that stopped Jay from doing *anything*.

Every man I'd ever dated had been nervous, awkward or weird about women on their periods. Somehow, a menstruating woman was something to be scared of, the topic to be avoided and sex obviously out of the question for one week out of the month. Sure, for the first couple of days the last thing in the world I wanted was anyone touching me when I felt swollen, pissed off and crampy. But after the wretched two days, my sex drive was usually back with a vengeance. Which meant I was either frustrated for the rest of the week or my vibrator got a healthy amount of use. As much as men wanted to be seen as progressive feminists with healthy sex drives, they were just scared little boys when it came to menstruation.

Jay was not one of those little boys. He was *all man*. He was not scared or grossed out by a little blood. Not by a long shot. And I thought I would feel uncomfortable or gross about it—because that's how society wanted us to feel—but I fucking loved it.

So yes, Jay had to know that I was no longer on the injection because Jay definitely noticed the changes, but he did not say a single word. Nor did he stop finishing inside of me. It had been months of that and ... nothing. Sure, a baby wouldn't be ideal right now, not with a wedding to plan, being busy at work, Jay and me settling in to a new normal. Oh, and Jay's mysterious, definitely illegal business of running the underworld of L.A.

Yeah, I should probably get more details about that before I worried about getting impregnated by this man. But I couldn't get my mind off a little dark-haired baby with Jay's eyes, in his muscled arms ... yeah, that made my womb clench.

I was trying not to worry about the fact my aforementioned womb may or may not be barren after all the sex we'd had without protection. As if I didn't have enough to worry about.

It was in the midst of all that that I realized that I was not alone in the house.

"Oh, I'm sorry!" I shrieked when I walked into the kitchen, seeing a woman in the fridge, her back to me.

I had no idea why I was apologizing to the strange woman who was in Jay's—actually mine now too, I guessed—house. But I did, out of instinct, shock, whatever.

Felicity, it must've been. I was surprised that I'd lived here for two months and hadn't run into her. Her presence was everywhere, in the immaculately clean house, the laundry that was done, the freshly ironed sheets. The woman ironed fucking sheets. The illusive woman who seemed to be the only permanent female fixture in Jay's life, the woman who cooked for him, cleaned for him and as it seemed, shopped for him. It made sense. I couldn't exactly see Jay in a Whole Foods. It hit me then that the two of us had never even been in a supermarket together. And we *were engaged to be married.*

A seemingly benign chore for most couples, the norm, yet something completely foreign to us.

But that was not something to dwell on, not with *Felicity* standing in the kitchen, in the flesh, at last.

I'd imagined her to be an older, round Italian woman for some reason. Not a woman wearing expensive tailored pants that showed off an extremely perky ass and a tiny waist.

Her dark hair was in curls down her back, and the arm that was depositing almond milk—my favorite brand—into the fridge was sculpted and tanned.

"Felicity, right?" I asked, moving forward, my voice warm despite feeling unsteady at the fact that Felicity seemed to be smokin' hot. "I've been so looking forward to meeting you," I continued, forcing warmth into my voice, hating the acrid taste of jealousy crawling up my throat.

It was far too cliché to be threatened by an attractive woman in the employ of my soon to be husband. I trusted Jay, didn't I? Knew that he loved me beyond measure, that he could be cruel and ugly, but he'd never be a man who cheated. If he didn't want me, he'd end things.

Though that didn't make me feel much better.

It all got worse when the woman turned. It all came crashing down.

I stopped in my tracks as *Felicity* turned on her red soled heel. Her face was guarded, expression tentative but not threatening. Sad, almost. Just like it had been that night. The first night out with Jay. The woman in the red dress, the one who had most certainly been one of

Jay's women, who he had touched, owned. Whose heart and soul he had stolen.

And he had not discarded her. No. She was here. In his house. *Stocking his fucking fridge.* My blood was cold, and I was frozen in place, blinking rapidly at the gorgeous woman in front of me.

"Stella," she said, her voice low, throaty. "I'm so sorry, I didn't realize you'd be here, otherwise—"

"It's fine," I waved my hand, forcing a smile onto my face. "I had a client, and they cancelled last minute, so I decided to come home early, take a bath. I have a big stack of books that's only growing since I keep buying new ones without reading the old ones," I babbled. "I've decided to make it a goal to put time aside every single day to read a little since it's meant to be good for you. And I need to just slow down, you know?"

Oh. My. God. Why was I still speaking? Still babbling about fucking books in the beautiful face of Jay's ex ... whatever. The one who had meant enough to him to let in to his life. The fortress he'd kept so tight even I hadn't explored the entirety of it.

"Anyway," I paused, taking a long breath, waving my hand. "It's not a big deal that you're here. In fact, I'm glad you are. We never met properly." My smile was so tight it felt like my face might split open.

I was determined not to spew any of my toxic thoughts on to this woman. None of this was her fault. She didn't have obligations, commitments to me. She wasn't the one keeping secrets. She was just a woman who had fallen in love with the wrong man. The one who she hungered for. Starved for. And was living off the crumbs he had continued to give her. I shuddered to think how easily I could've become this woman.

"Me too," she smiled with uncertainty. "I know Mr. Helmick would've preferred to ... coordinate our meeting himself, but I am so glad you're back." Her eyes twinkled with warmth.

Sincerity? Surely not. It had been as plain as day that night at the benefit that she was in love with Jay. No woman who fell in love with Jay was pure and kind enough to be genuinely happy to see him doing the one thing he'd promised he'd never do: love someone else.

But I couldn't find anything dark or ugly on her face. Perhaps she was just a great actress. Or a better woman than me.

"I'm glad I'm back too," I gushed, injecting faux cheer into my voice like I was being graded for it. "For good, I'm back for good." I didn't know why I added that. It was catty and unnecessary, but I couldn't help myself. "You don't have to do that anymore either," I continued, hating myself, nodding to the fridge. "I can buy groceries. I know what Jay likes." There was no bite to my voice. There didn't need to be. What I was saying was as plain as day.

Jay is mine.

I never thought I'd be this woman. This petty, territorial woman, rubbing her victory in the face of the wounded, like salt in a wound. But here I was.

Felicity flinched. I hated myself some more for being responsible. Another sick, ugly part of me was satisfied, happy for causing that flinch, for hitting that mark.

She pursed her lips and nodded. "Of course," she replied in a small voice.

It was then that she moved her hand up to push her hair behind her ears, the sunlight streaming through the windows reflecting off her bracelet. Her diamond bracelet. Identical to the one that I wore on my wrist.

My heart thundered in my chest, and bile crawled up my throat. I did my best to swallow it. Did my best to keep that false smile on my face.

"You know, I completely forgot about an appointment I had downtown," I mused, snatching my purse from where I'd dropped it on the counter. "It's urgent, and the sooner I get there the better. It really was lovely to finally meet you, Felicity."

And then I ran out of the house.

Jay's house.

Because it certainly wasn't ours.

It struck me, right as I was storming past Jay's assistant and into his office, that I'd never been to Jay's offices downtown. The sleek, expensively appointed offices that likely housed all of his legitimate businesses. I hadn't met him here for lunch, hadn't met his assistants, had no clue about the specifics that went on here.

Jay had never even told me the location of this place.

His eyes widened ever so slightly when I stormed through the door. "Stella," he greeted, putting down the stack of papers he had been holding.

"Did you know that I had to Google the location of your offices?" I barked, storming forward.

He blinked once, face blank.

I didn't let him answer. "Yeah, I had to *Google* the location of my fiancé's place of work because he's never *fucking told me about it*!" I scolded, my voice raising to a shout. I had been planning on sitting in front of him at his desk, speaking calmly, eloquently, letting him explain.

Now that I was here, looking at his beautifully blank face, overcome with the feeling I had whenever Jay was near, fury was the only option. So I paced. And shouted.

"Another thing you didn't tell me about," I grated out. "Felicity. Sure, I knew of her existence, but I never knew her identity. But that was rectified today. When I went to your place—"

"Our home," Jay interrupted, voice cold.

I stopped in my tracks, narrowing my eyes at him. "No," I hissed. "Our home is a shared place. Somewhere free of secrets. With a fridge full of food that we buy together at fucking Whole Foods, not what your ex *fucking mistress* buys, stocks and cooks for you!"

I was aware that I was all but screaming in a very quiet, very upscale office, but I quite frankly did not give a shit about that right now. What made it even worse was Jay sitting there, calmly, with that perfect fucking face and that fucking twinkle in his eye. He did not seem rattled, pissed that I was pacing in his very fancy office causing a scene. He did not seem bothered by my obvious emotion, the emotion that was hiding beneath my fury. Jay was emotionally intelligent enough to know how much hurt was laying underneath all the yelling.

My fists were clenched at my sides, and it took a lot of effort not to hurl things at him. Not to think of ugly, cruel and bitter things to say. I wanted to hurt him, wanted to pierce deep enough to cause a reaction to get something from him. I wanted to hurt him like he had hurt me.

"She isn't my mistress, Stella," he replied.

The tenor of his voice only served to infuriate me further.

"She has the same fucking bracelet as me!" I screamed, shaking my wrist at him, suddenly unsure why in the fuck it was still around my wrist. I should've hurled it into the ocean or something equally dramatic before I'd arrived here for my tirade.

Too late now. "Did you or did you not give her that bracelet?" I demanded.

Jay was silent for a beat. His eyes were measuring. Assessing. He hadn't seen me like this before. This angry. I didn't think I'd ever been this angry in my entire life, and even if I had been before, I was never brave enough to unleash it on Jay lest I lost him. But I was starting to question whether I really ever had him in the first place.

"I did," he spoke finally, the words clipped.

My stomach dropped, and my mouth went dry even though I'd known that to be the truth before he spoke.

"And you've fucked her," I said, not a question, but I silently begged him to disagree.

"Yes."

I swallowed razors, nodding once. "You have a woman wearing diamonds you gave her—the exact same diamonds you gave me—minus the heart you took from her, in what is supposed to be *our* house?" I spoke slowly now. Quietly. There was no cause for screaming or shouting anymore.

"There's more to it to that, Stella," Jay said.

I nodded rapidly. "Oh, I'm sure there is, Jay. It's just a shame you didn't trust me enough to give me more."

It was then I turned around and walked out.

He didn't follow me.

CHAPTER NINE

"Dad." I nestled my phone in the crook of my shoulder as I carried a shit load of couture in my hands. I really, *really* needed an assistant. "I know I've been a terrible daughter, and I owe you about three phone calls, but I'm walking into a photoshoot, and I'm only on one coffee, so my braincells are sluggish. Can I call you back?"

All of this was true, of course. But I also really didn't want to talk to my dad because I didn't want him to hear anything in my voice that would cause him to ask questions. Like if I was okay, if things were alright with Jay.

I was most definitely not fucking okay, and things were not at all alright with Jay, but I did not want to tell my father that. Did not want to tell a single fucking soul about our fight. Even though it didn't feel as simple as a fight. It didn't feel fixable. The hurt inside me was a living, breathing thing that amplified every time I moved. I'd let him back in too quickly. Hadn't learned a fucking thing from last time. I'd put too much of myself in this relationship, so when it was splintering, it felt everything inside of me was breaking.

Fool me once and all that.

I didn't see a way out of this. Didn't know how I'd forgive him for this lie without wondering how many more he'd told me. And I couldn't talk to my girlfriends. Zoe because she was only just coming to terms with all of this, and I couldn't be sure that she wouldn't hire a hitman at this point. Yasmin would talk to me with calm reason, and calm reason would be to break up with the man who was deceiving me, who had already hurt me so completely before. The man whose life I didn't even know about.

Wren would be my best bet since she was the only one of my friends who was firmly Team Jay. But I wanted her to stay Team Jay.

And my father was not someone who I could tell because then I would have to explain the entirety of the 'arrangement' thing with him, and yeah, that wasn't exactly something a girl told her father. Especially since that father had come to terms with the idea of Jay being his son-in-law.

Jay had not called to ask for his permission first because he was Jay. My father was a progressive man, but I knew he was a little peeved about that whole thing. Luckily, my dad was not one to hold a grudge, and all he wanted was for his daughter to be happy. And luckily, he hadn't known that we broke up in the first place. I'd somehow managed to pretend we were still together for the entirety of my time in New Zealand thanks to the time difference and my dad's inability to read tone via text.

I was trying to digest this news, trying to heal this hurt on my own. Because even in my fury, I couldn't spend last night without Jay, was too weak to punish him. I'd slept with him last night. I'd let him touch me. Let him try to apologize with his hands, with his body. I hadn't said a word to him the entire time, but I'd responded, not vocally but with my own body. Because despite what he'd done to me, he still owned me.

I'd gotten out of bed this morning at the crack of dawn, showered and gotten ready all while ignoring him, leaving without even having a cup of coffee. Coffee that *she* had bought. Jay had watched me get ready, hadn't said a word. Hadn't tried to explain anything or mend anything. Maybe that's what hurt me more. I'd had expectations on what the man was meant to do after a betrayal of this magnitude. There were meant be apologies. Groveling. Flowers. Not that any of that would make a difference, but it was the effort.

Then again, I was expecting Jay to act like any other man. I'd fallen in love with him precisely because he was unlike any other man I'd ever met.

"Stella, honey."

Something about my father's voice gave me pause, my blood turning cold.

"I'm just going to say it because there's no way for me to break it to you gently. Your mother's dead," he told me, his voice uneven, shaky and not at all recognizable as belonging to my father.

I stared ahead at the set for the shoot I was on. It was Victorian England. Or it was meant to be. What it really was was someone who'd watched *Shakespeare in Love* and had no idea about Victorian England.

"But I just saw her," I rasped, blinking rapidly, trying to process what my father had just said. "She can't be dead. We had tea, with little flowery teacups. She was wearing slippers."

"She had a brain aneurism, Stella," Dad spoke slowly. "It was very sudden. Quick. She didn't suffer."

I tried as hard as I could to hold on to my father's words, his voice, but I couldn't. Everything was a dull roar, and my fingers turned numb.

"I, um, Dad, I'm at work. I have to ... deal with some corsets. I'll be home in ... soon. I'll be home soon. I love you."

Then I hung up. I hung up on my grieving, heartbroken father because I couldn't handle it. The weight of the phone was suddenly too much to hold up to my ear.

The couture and corsets I'd been holding tumbled to my feet, and I turned around and started walking. I had no idea where I was going. I'd told my father I was going home. I'd get to Missouri eventually, but for now, I didn't have a home. So I just walked.

Jay

"Dimitri, I've said it before, and I'll say it again, I do not want a partner," Jay kept his voice even, kept his face blank and kept his manner as friendly as could manner in the face of a murderous psychopath.

As important as this meeting was, Jay was thinking about Stella.

He needed to be focused on this, Dimitri was a slippery fucker, and Jay knew he would latch on to the slightest misstep and use it as a reason for retaliation—which was a euphemism for him trying to take over his business or assassinate his lieutenants. Jay did not misstep. Every word, every movement was so calculated it came easy to him now. Or it used to.

Before Stella.

Everything had been on unsteady ground since the second she walked into his office at Klutch that night. She had forced him to be human. Or as close to human as he was capable of. Which made being a monster an effort now. He couldn't hold on to it when he was concerned with her. Every beat of his heart was a thought of Stella. Even during the best of times between them, which they had not had many of. They were most certainly not in the best of times now. She was not speaking to him. He'd forced her to sleep in the same bed as him because he'd made a promise that they would never spend a night apart. She hadn't spoken to him, but she hadn't fought him either.

Nor had she fought him when he put his lips on hers, opened her legs and moved between them. She'd come for him, but she'd stifled every moan, hadn't spoken a single word. Not when he moved inside her, not when she clenched around his dick in release. Nothing. Afterward, she'd gotten up to clean up in the bathroom. Then she'd come back to bed, curled into a little ball and turned away from him. Jay hadn't allowed that, and she hadn't fought him when he'd yanked her across the chasm she'd put between them. She'd even relaxed into him, but she didn't speak.

It had killed him. Fucking killed him. He hadn't known how

to make it better. How to explain. Because there wasn't a sufficient explanation. And now he was sitting across from Dimitri, looking at the prospect of war that would put Stella in danger. It was a fucking bad day.

Jay ached to put a bullet in the square jawed asshole's brain, but it wasn't exactly that simple.

Dimitri leaned back in his chair, sighing audibly. "Ah, but *moy drug*, we are not asking if you want a partner. We are *telling* you you now have one." He grinned, showing straight, white teeth.

Jay's blood turned hot, his heart roaring in his ears as red crept to the edges of his vision. The second Dimitri turned up at Klutch two months ago, Jay knew that this wasn't going to end peacefully. He'd gone through the motions because he'd needed to be smart. Needed to make preparations. Needed to put protections in place for Stella. Before her, he would've been smart, yes. But he likely would've had this over and done with a lot sooner. His action would've been swift. Brutal. Effective, yes. But only effective because he'd had nothing to lose. There had been no way to hurt him.

Now there was Stella.

That was not only a way to hurt him. It was a way to *destroy* him.

He'd dragged this out. And now Dimitri was sitting in his office, making it clear that action was needed.

Blood would need to be spilled.

Leading right up to their fucking *wedding*.

If there was still going to be a wedding.

His office phone rang on that thought. "I've got to take this," he said to Dimitri. "Business doesn't stop."

Dimitri stood. "No it doesn't. We'll be in touch. Soon." There was threat in his voice, but Jay was not scared, therefore he nodded in dismissal.

"Jay Helmick," he answered, his mind still on Stella. Stuck on the one fear that he was nursing … that he'd lost her again. For good. He deserved to. But Stella wouldn't leave. They were tied together. For better or for fucking worse.

"Jay, it's Richard, Stella's dad."

Jay straightened immediately, Richard's tone making his blood turn cold.

"Is Stella with you?" Richard asked.

Jay was already tapping on his computer, locating her using the tracking software he'd put in her phone.

"No, but I know where she is," he said, standing up. "What's going on?"

"Her mother died suddenly," Richard told Jay in a hoarse voice. "I called her to tell her, and we got disconnected. I haven't been able to get hold of her since."

"I've got her," Jay assured him. "We'll fly there this afternoon."

"Thank you, Jay," Richard responded, the man's voice barely holding on to the even tone he was obviously forcing.

"We'll see you tonight," Jay said, then he paused at the elevator. "And, Richard, I'm sorry."

As Jay hung up, he found he was sorry. Because he'd heard it in the man's voice. What would be in Jay's if he ever lost Stella. And it scared the shit out of him.

He had to find her.

She was sitting on a bench in Santa Monica, staring out at the sea. The breeze was cold, and she was only wearing a camisole. Jay immediately took off his jacket and put it over her shoulders. Stella didn't even move as he did so. Didn't even look at him.

A tiny spark of fury ignited at her being so lost in herself. Regardless that she was quite obviously going through a lot, that was no excuse. How easily someone could mark her. Hurt her. Damage her in all sorts of ways. Jay had trouble enough not putting one of his men on her at all times—he knew she'd fight that—just so he could be sure that she was safe at any given moment.

Now was not the time to chastise her for being so flippant with her safety, though. It was a time to help her. Comfort her. Jay had no fucking clue how he was meant to do that.

It was a punch to Jay's stomach seeing her like that. She seemed so small. Tiny. Like she'd shrunk down in the space of a couple of hours. With one phone call. Stella, despite her physical characteristics, had always been so large to him. So strong. She took up every space in a room, and people couldn't help but notice her because she was fucking radiant. Stunning, charismatic, somehow managed to talk about her fucking cat or her favorite sci-fi television show with someone she'd just met, and they'd hang on her every word like she was giving them top secret information.

She was bigger than anything else in his life, her presence, her essence spreading to even the darkest of corners. Now it was as if this news had sucked all of the life out of her.

And if he hadn't fucked up with Felicity, Stella wouldn't have found herself sitting on a filthy park bench without a sweater, a prime target for anyone who wanted to take her. Stella would've gone to him. Because she'd gone to him with her pain, she'd trusted him with it.

Until he was the one who caused it. Until he was the one who broke her trust.

He'd punish himself for that later.

"Stella."

She blinked, still staring at the ocean, but he knew she'd heard him. Fuck, he wanted to touch her, but everything in her body language cautioned him from that. Ordinarily, Jay wouldn't have given a fuck about what Stella's body language cautioned. He'd spent long enough without her, being unable to touch her. If his woman was close enough, his hands were on her.

But he'd hurt her if he touched her. Something about the way she held herself made him afraid that she'd shatter the second he laid his hand on her.

"Stella," he repeated.

She looked at him with empty eyes. Jay restrained a flinch.

"Stella, we need to go." He wanted to add 'home', but that was a sore subject. That wasn't safety for her. Not anymore.

Because of *him*.

He held out his hand, and she looked at it with a blank stare.

Jay waited. She was well within her rights to ignore him, ignore his touch. He'd hurt her enough.

But after a few beats, she put her small hand in his.

Jay sighed inwardly in relief, even though he shouldn't have been so fucking satisfied that his woman was so willing to hold onto him, even after he'd hurt her so much.

But he was.

Stella

Jay packed for me. He put me in the shower, washed me and then picked out an outfit for me to wear. It was the first time ever that I'd been naked with his hands on me and it hadn't ended in an orgasm. Hadn't ended up with him inside me. Though there was a latent need hidden somewhere inside of me, it was buried deep below the layers of numbness I was currently hiding underneath.

Jay didn't try to touch me in that way, his brows furrowed in worry and his jaw hard throughout the process. But he took care of me. Gently. With patience. With love. With compassion I hadn't thought him capable of.

But there were a lot of things I hadn't thought him capable of.

I did manage to dress myself and brush my own hair. I gulped down the vodka he brought me, wincing at the sharp taste but thankful for the burn down my throat.

Then I got in the car, rode to the airport and got on the plane he'd organized. I didn't ask where we were going. Just like I didn't ask him how he'd found me or how he'd known what was going on. He was Jay.

It wasn't until we were thirty thousand feet in the air that he stopped being okay with my silence. Even though my mother had just died, parts of my brain were still stuck on what had happened before all of this.

Felicity.

What was wrong with me? Was I really that selfish?

All I wanted was to curl up into Jay, wanted to cling to him as the one safe, stable thing in all of this. But he wasn't. I couldn't cross the chasm between us because I hadn't forgiven him. Didn't trust that he was safe anymore.

"Stella," Jay kneeled in front of me, hands on my legs. His face was pinched, brows furrowed and voice clipped. He was worried, that much was clear.

"I need you to talk to me," he implored when I didn't answer.

"*You* need *me* to talk to you?" I repeated, my tone dead. "Why, because you're worried that I'm losing myself in sadness or despair over my mother being dead, or because you're worried about what your lies have done to us?"

He flinched. That should've been a victory, but it wasn't.

"Because going this long without hearing your voice is making me fucking crazy," he deadpanned. "I don't need you to forgive me. Don't expect you to. I fucked up. I fucking hate myself for hurting you. Hate myself for this bullshit coinciding with when you need me. And it's my fault."

It was then that he stood. I missed his hands on my thighs.

He ran his hand through his hair, the motion frantic, manic for a man like Jay. His brows were crumpled, mouth downturned. He'd taken off his suit jacket which was thrown haphazardly over one of the seats on the plane, his shirtsleeves shoved up messily, the veins in his sinewy forearms protruding.

"I don't know how to help you," he gritted out the words as if he was in pain. His eyes darted around the interior of the plane, looking anywhere but at me.

I watched in fascination as my man, my rock, my steel unraveled before me.

Irises like green marbles finally settled on me. "I can kill a man, Stella. Easily. Without mess. Without remorse. I can make it so he never fucking existed in the first place. I can ruin lives. Hurt anyone. I can make you come. Make you beg for me. Somehow, I've made you fall in love with me, but that isn't a skill, it was an accident of fate."

His hands settled on my hips, pulling me up from my seat onto his body. I was thankful for the contact, for the slight pain that came from the way he gripped me.

"I can be all of those things," he continued, inches from my face. "Because the world cut me when my skin was soft, and I scarred all over so no one would ever make me bleed again. I hardened against the world in order to never hurt, to make sure I was only ever the one who did the hurting." He lifted his hand to stroke my face. "But now I have you, and I need to be soft with you. And I don't know fucking *how.*"

The utter helplessness is his voice penetrated my layers. All of them. Hit the core of me, the part that was still bleeding from his betrayal, the part that was in pieces from my mother's death and everything left unresolved with my mother. As furious as I was with him, it wasn't as simple as holding on to my grudge and punishing him.

I moved my hand up to grip his neck, to press him even closer to me, to ensure he couldn't move away from me.

"You're doing it right now," I whispered. "You're being your own wonderful brand of soft. I don't need anything else but you."

"We need to talk about—"

I put my finger to his lips before he could say her name. I couldn't hear it right now.

"We do," I agreed, rage a simmering flame beneath it all. "But not now."

He searched my face. I knew that Jay was not the kind of person to put off difficult conversations. I also knew that Jay was not the kind of person to put off a difficult conversation just because someone else didn't want to have it.

But he nodded, leaning forward to kiss my head. "Not now," he agreed.

"Can you do something for me?" I whispered, clinging onto him.

"Anything."

I pulled back so I could stare at him. "Fuck me," I rasped.

His eyes turned dark. "I can do that, Stella."

And he did.

Twice.

ONE WEEK LATER

My mother's funeral was sparsely attended. Very fucking sparsely. Wren, Yasmin and Zoe had attended, of course. They'd arrived the same day I'd called them with the news, dropping everything without hesitation. Wren brought twenty-year-old scotch with her, my father's favorite. She got drunk with him the first night she arrived, tending to his emotional wounds in a way only Wren could. Zoe organized the entire funeral and wake, and Yasmin dealt with all of the legal stuff that came with death—apparently a lot. And all three of them packed up my mother's room in the facility with me, giving me shots of vodka as needed. So yeah, I had the best fucking friends.

Right now, I had the best fucking friends. But how long would they stay if my mind started fracturing, if I began to depart from who I used to be?

I suddenly had morbid thoughts about my own funeral, who would attend it, and hated that my mother hadn't had ride or die girlfriends to help her through the hard times in her life. Then I had the selfish, horrible thought of what my funeral would look like if I followed in her footsteps, losing myself and losing everything and everyone in my life.

I guessed it was a good thing that her funeral was so poorly attended, since my father refused to let me help pay for it, and he sure as shit wasn't going to let Jay spend a dime on it. It was a male pride thing, obviously, and as much as it pissed me off, it was my father. I'd tried to argue with him about it, but then he went and broke my heart.

"This is my job as her husband, Stells," he explained, eyes tired and full of sorrow. "Because that's what I have been all these years, that's what I still am. A husband takes care of his wife. Protects her. I couldn't protect her from the demons inside of her own head, couldn't fix her. But this, this is something I can do for my wife. This one of the last things I will do to take care of her, other than take care of you." He cupped my cheek and his eyes went to where Jay was standing outside with a phone at his ear. "I know there is another man whose job it is to do that now, but I'll always be there. No matter what.

"And I'll always need you, Dad," I croaked out. "Always."

He'd hugged me as I broke down in tears, furious at myself for not being able to hold it together in order for my dad to fall apart. But then again, Jay was always around—not that I was complaining—and my dad may have been grieving, may have been heartbroken, but he was also an alpha male, Midwestern man whose values were outdated but strong, which meant he wasn't about to let another man see him look weak.

"He's done good," Dad said once he'd finally let me go and wiped the tears from my eyes.

He was nodding at Jay who was leaning against the car, watching us. Jay, who had been here, non-stop. Who hadn't said a word during the service, had barely said a word the entire week, but that hadn't mattered. He had been t*here*.

Her name hadn't been mentioned, though my rage simmered just below my grief.

"He'll take care of you," Dad continued, looking back to me. He cupped my cheek again. "And I get the modern woman thing where you can take care of yourself," he added before I could interrupt. "You can take care of yourself, very well I should add. But it's nice to know you've got somewhere there, for when you don't feel like it. For when you've exhausted yourself trying to take care of your father, whose job it also is to take care of you."

There was a lump in my throat, one that was only partly due to seeing the man shoveling dirt on top of my mother's coffin, slightly more of it due to the sadness in my father's eyes, and unfortunately, most of it due to Jay.

Yes, here at my mother's grave—her fresh grave for that matter—the thing hurting my heart and soul the most was the man whose diamond I was wearing.

I was so fucked up.

But I couldn't help it. It didn't matter that he was always here, that I longed for him, that he'd made me come with his hand over my mouth at three in the morning, something rotted between us. Ate away at us.

And whatever was eating away at us was eating away at me because I'd fucked up. I'd intertwined myself in him so tightly that I didn't know where I ended and where we began. Which is something that every self-help book—and Zoe—would caution me against, but it was too fucking late.

So I was at my mother's funeral, in front of my grieving father, thinking about the way my fiancé had betrayed me by employing a woman he used to fuck.

"Yeah," I said to my dad. "He'll take care of me."

My dad hugged me, leaving me to wonder if I was lying or not.

Because that was another thing... I didn't know where the lies ended and the truth began.

There was only one day left in Vern before we went back to L.A. To Jay's house. The house that was meant to be ours. I knew that

I could not get on the plane without having *the* conversation. The one I'd been putting off all week because dealing with my mother's death was easier.

My father had gone back to work because a week off was about his maximum, even with me home. He'd busied himself with fixing things, mowing the grass, gardening and cooking, but my father needed to work, needed to keep busy, feel useful.

There was no excuse not to have this conversation. We couldn't have it at my dad's house, it was too small, stifling. I didn't know where else to go, so I'd made Jay drive us here, a place I hadn't been in decades.

We didn't speak during the ride. Jay's hand was on my thigh and my eyes were focused out the window. I'd sat in the car once we arrived, taking five minutes to find the strength to get out of the car. Jay waited next to me silently. Once I actually scrambled up the courage and got out of the car, Jay followed me.

"We used to come here and feed the ducks," I broke the silence, looking out to the pond that had existed clearly in my memories. The magical place with the lily pads, the animals and the trees that had fallen in to disarray. The water a murky green color now, trees yellowing and dying and not a duck or a lily pad to be seen. If that wasn't a metaphor for something, I didn't know what was.

"I'm glad," I said on a whisper, looking out at the water. "That's the terrible, horrible truth of it. I'm glad my mother is dead. I'm *relieved*. I'm relieved that she doesn't have to battle with herself daily. Relieved that my father isn't riddled by guilt, isn't putting himself in to debt, stealing away his retirement. Most of all, I'm glad I have no obligation to her anymore. I don't have to visit her. Don't have to pretend it doesn't chill my bones every time I see her, wondering if I have her fate. I'm relieved I don't have to look in the familiar eyes at the worst possible future."

That was when I finally found the strength to look at Jay. There was no judgement in his eyes, no revulsion. Of course there wasn't.

That was another thing I loved about Jay. I could tell him truths. The real ones. The dark ones, the ones most people lied to cover up. I could tell him anything, and he had thought worse, he'd done worse and he hadn't blinked.

He hadn't spoken yet. I knew this was not because he didn't have anything to say, but because he knew me well enough to know I wasn't done.

Fuck, maybe he already knew what I was going to say. He'd done all that research on me, back when we were just starting out. And what he hadn't found out, I'd told him. Everything. Except this. This secret that I'd held close to my chest, letting it rot, decompose and taint everything that lay inside of me.

"She tried to kill me," I confessed to his intense eyes.

Jay's face flickered with something, surprise maybe. Though I'd considered myself an expert on all things Jay, I didn't trust myself anymore. Didn't trust him anymore. I couldn't read whether or not this news was shocking to him. Though I'd been young at the time, I remembered my dad covering for her, promising not to call the police as long as she got help. That was it. The last straw that I'd glossed over when I'd told Jay about my mother. I hadn't even let myself think it. It was a prickly, dangerous memory that dragged me in to a dark place.

But this was my midnight man. He got me used to the darkness, made me less afraid of it.

"She was sick, really sick," I continued. "My dad didn't know how bad. Was working a lot, to support us. I don't remember much about that time. But I do remember that we were home one day. It was a bad day. I'd learned that on bad days, it was best to stay away from Mom. Hide sometimes. I didn't want to tell Dad because I knew he'd do something. Take her away. And my mom on good days was magic."

I smiled, looking at memories of the ducks that used to be here. My mom laughing as we fed them, as they chased her around. "I didn't tell him. It was our secret. Then one day she was really bad. My memory isn't that good, dark around the edges. But it was about demons. She was convinced that they were inside me. She had to cut them out to protect me. My dad came home before anything could happen. But I'd never seen him madder. At himself, mostly. For not seeing how bad it had gotten. It haunted him for years, what could've happened. It haunted her, too, I know. Which was why she stayed away."

I didn't look at Jay.

My mom had been a ghost in my life after that. Not just because of *the incident*. Not just because of her illness. She'd managed it well for a number of years. Well enough to have her independence, a semblance of self. But it was the guilt that kept her from me, the same guilt that ate away at her, that caused her to stop taking her medication because she couldn't stand the reality of what she'd almost done. I knew she pushed my father away. He'd wanted to reconcile, after everything, he was serious about vows of sickness and health. But my mother would not do it. Her intentions had been noble, to her, at least. She didn't want to hurt me, hurt either of us.

I had never entirely forgiven her for that. I could understand her illness, I could forgive everything it had taken from her, from our family, and I didn't blame her for any of it.

"I resented her," I admitted. "For her cowardice. For not being brave enough to face reality with us. It doesn't make sense, it may be ugly and cruel of me, but it's the truth of it."

Jay yanked me into his arms, and I went willingly, thankfully.

"Stella, you could never be ugly or cruel, even with your worst truth," he kissed my head, his words comforting me.

With all of that out in the universe, I took a deep breath. A deep breath of Jay, the stale water and the decaying plant life mingling in with everything else.

"I'm ready now," I declared, stepping out of his arms. "I'm ready to know why you didn't tell me about *her*. Why she was in your house this *entire time* and you didn't tell me. Why I ate her food, why she did my laundry."

It seemed that my anger hadn't dulled over this week, not a bit. If anything, it had been sharpened to a point, ready to do battle, cut anyone in the vicinity.

Jay's face shut down, his jaw turning hard. He grasped onto my elbow to stop me from retreating too far. I didn't want to be near him during this conversation, but I couldn't stand him being far either.

"I don't have an explanation that's going to suffice," Jay revealed, rubbing my arm with his thumb. "Which is why I kept it from you for so long."

I pursed my lips. "How about instead of keeping it from me, you just got rid of her?" I tried to keep my voice even but failed. "And by get rid of her, I do not mean kill her," I added, finding it insane that I had to say that and be half serious about it.

"That's a good question," Jay conceded. "But one I don't have an answer to. Simply, Felicity has been a part of my life for years, and I don't trust many people. I need someone in my employ in my home—our home—who I can trust. Who isn't a danger to my business, and most importantly a danger to you."

I stared at him. "You don't think *Felicity* is a danger to me?" I hated her name in my mouth. "To us?"

"Yes, I know that," Jay clipped. He was tense, coiled tight. I didn't know if it was from me calling him out or if he was angry with himself for what he'd done. I really fucking hoped it was the latter.

"So why, Jay?" I queried, my voice tiny this time, all of my hurt somehow packaged in to it.

He rubbed the back of his neck, visibly stressed in a way I hadn't seen before, except on the plane earlier.

"Do you..." I trailed off, sucking in an unsteady breath. "Do you love her?"

"No," he answered immediately and firmly. "Fuck no, Stella. I truly feel nothing for her."

"That's not true," I seethed.

"You think I'm lying?" he challenged.

"I don't know," I griped back.

He stepped forward, yanking me closer to him, eyes dangerous. "After everything, Stella, you think I'd lie to *you*, of all people?"

"After everything, Jay, after *Felicity*, I don't fucking know," I hissed in his face.

I was breathing heavily, glaring at Jay, my blood hot, but not entirely with fury. A dark, ugly and sick part of me wanted him. Wanted him right here on the fucking grass where I used to feed the ducks as a child.

His eyes told me he wanted the exact same thing. That he was restraining himself.

Swallowing my twisted desire, I leaned back ever so slightly, communicating that there was going to be no more of that until I got the truth, even though I was terrified of it. Even though I was secretly wishing for lies that would comfort me, heal what he had cut. But there were no lies capable of doing that.

Jay cleared his throat. "I don't have a noble reason for her being there, in *our house*." There was a bite to his voice, I knew that he was pissed off at me for abandoning the *our* in the wake of this, but I was too pissed off about *this* to care.

"The truth isn't going to fix this. Isn't going to make up for shit, and honestly, if I could think of a lie that would make what I did okay, I'd tell it," he proclaimed.

I pursed my lips. Had I expected anything less? Jay was standing stiffly, even though he was wearing his 'casual Jay' attire of faded jeans, a charcoal V-neck and expensive sneakers. His chest was broad and delicious, arms smooth and muscled and incredibly distracting.

He'd let his hair grow even longer because he'd noticed I liked running my hands through it, the inky black velvet curling softly around the harsh angles of his face. He was clean shaven because there was never a time when he wasn't, and his lips were pressed in a thin line.

He was pissed that I had put distance between us. I knew he wanted to touch me, I wanted it too. But I couldn't. Couldn't hear this with his hands on me. It would be too easy to forgive, to forget.

"She's a powerful woman," he continued. "A very rich woman. From a very old family. She was the first woman I had an ... arrangement with. In fact, she had enjoyed many such arrangements prior to ours."

My brain worked to process his words. She was his first. Beyond that, she was the one who taught him about arrangements. She was *special*. The thought was poison. My insides were melting, and I ached to scream at him to shut the fuck up. To never mention her again. But I kept my mouth shut, fisting my hands at my sides.

"I didn't love her," Jay went on, his voice hard and firm. "I need you to know that. Need you to stop with those toxic, destructive thoughts I know are tearing through your head." His eyes bore into me. "I appreciated her for what she gave me. But there was no love. Not on my side, at least." He paused, letting me digest everything.

Normally, if my fiancé was talking about the woman who taught him about his contemporary sex life, the woman who had been in our house for the entirety of our relationship... Oh wait, there was nothing fucking normal about this. But normally, if I was having an uncomfortable, hurtful conversation, I'd be fidgeting, pacing. But for this I was standing stock still, letting the hits land.

"She got attached to me," he shrugged ever so slightly. "Before her, I'd never let another woman close enough to love me. I was purposefully cruel and cold because I thought that there was no way someone could love me. I liked it. Liked that she loved me yet I didn't have any connection to her. When I broke it off, she wanted to stay in my life ... to serve me. Of course, I pay her."

"Of course," I sneered, not being able to help it.

Jay's jaw ticked, but he didn't comment on my snark. "It's wretched of me. After all these years, enjoying how she continues to want me, continues to accept working as my fucking housekeeper as ... something. But she's fucked up. Has her own shit that haunts her. This keeps the wolves from snapping at her toes. I was okay with that. There was no reason not to be, until you."

I folded my arms. "Until me," I mimicked. "But then you kept her doing ... whatever fucked up stuff she's been doing since we became us."

"I did," Jay agreed. "I was so fucking wrapped up in you, I forgot about her."

"She was cleaning your underwear and shopping for my almond milk. You're a criminal mastermind and read people like that guy off *The Mentalist*. There's no way you conveniently *forgot* about her," I jeered.

"The Mentalist?"

I levelled him with a steady gaze. "It's a great fucking show, and now is not the time to talk about the fact that you really need to start taking notice of popular culture, but you do," I sassed.

Jay nodded, his expression grim. "It's impossible to believe, and it sounds like a lie, but I'm telling the truth, Stella. She matters so little to me that she just disappeared. You're fucking everything. I can't go through a moment in the day without thinking about the way you smell, what your cunt feels like pulsing around my cock, the way your eyes twinkle when you're happy, how you seem to find a way to talk about a fucking television show when you're in the middle of a conversation I know is ripping you apart." Jay's eyes were so intense, my skin seemed to be melting from my bones.

"It's not healthy, my love for you, Stella. Because I'm not. I told you, I'm a wicked man. People are disposable to me. If they cease to be useful to me, they cease to exist. Except you. You're so fucking real to me that it hurts. That it terrifies me."

His fists were clenched at his sides. He wanted to touch me, the energy radiating between us was so thick that I could barely breathe.

"That's it," he stated. "That's the truth. That's all I have to offer. I fucking hate that I hurt you, but I told you I was going to do that. That I would protect you from the world, but I'd never be able to protect you from me."

He was done.

I could breathe.

Breath hurtled through my lungs, my beating, ruined heart sending blood rushing to my fingertips once more

Jay had told me he'd hurt me. There were no lies there. I'd known it, too, would've known it even if he hadn't said it. There was no way to hold on to a love like this without pain. Without agony.

Jay was much too complicated, damaged and cruel to love me gently or kindly. But he loved me with the ferocity of a thousand men. A million. He'd kill anyone who hurt me. And not in that figurative way that men spouted to sound alpha these days. He'd literally fucking kill anyone who caused me even the slightest discomfort. He'd get away with it and wouldn't lose a moment of sleep.

"Okay," I whispered, barely audible.

Jay's body twitched upon hearing my voice, his eyes opening a little wider, lips relaxing slightly from his grimace.

"Okay?" he repeated.

I nodded. "Yes. Okay. I don't forgive you, not entirely. But I understand. And as long as that woman never sets foot in our house again, I'll be okay. We'll be okay."

"Done," Jay said.

"And we're going to Whole Foods," I added.

"Also done," he deadpanned.

I swallowed thickly. The air was still electrified between us, with all the confessions we'd spilled into the air of my childhood paradise. The sun was hidden behind clouds, the air balmy, yet my bones felt cold, and my skin was on fire.

All the words had been said. We had none left.

"Take off your dress," he ordered, his pupils dilating.

My skin prickled. Okay, there were a few words left. "Right here?"

"You want me to tell you again?" Threat threaded through his tone, and my thighs clenched together.

I shook my head, slowly pulling my dress up over my head. Jay stared at me while I did so, staring at me in a way that made me feel vulnerable and powerful at the same time.

This area was relatively secluded, five minutes out of town and up a winding, poorly maintained road. The rogue beer bottles told me that this was more of a spot for bored teenagers than mothers pushing children in strollers. But it was still broad daylight, and there was nowhere to hide.

I still got naked in front of my fiancé.

Then with me naked and shaking—despite the warmth—Jay undressed. Completely.

"Hands and knees. On the ground, ass facing me," he commanded when he was magnificently naked and magnificently aroused.

I licked my lips and did as he said, the dirt soft and cool, my limbs thrumming with desire despite the fact that this felt animalistic and insane. Because it felt animalistic and insane.

Jay lowered himself behind me, his cock pressing into my entrance which was already soaking wet because he had me naked on my hands and knees in the dirt in the middle of the fucking day. Apparently, that turned me on. Big time.

He kissed the back of my neck. "I'm always going to hurt you, Stella," he murmured, teasing me with his cock rubbing against me. "But I'll never stop loving you, never stop breathing you, always fucking starve for you."

Then he was inside me, brutal, deep, magnificent.

I cried out. Loudly. My cry echoed off the trees.

Jay grasped a handful of my hair, yanking my head back, causing pain to explode in my scalp while pleasure coursed through my blood.

His other hand was biting into the flesh of my hip as he fucked me, a deep growl echoing from the back of his throat. That sound sent me over the edge, crying out once more, clenching around him. He pulled at my hair tighter and didn't stop. Didn't stop fucking me in the dirt. Not until I came again.

Yeah, it was incredibly fucked up and wrong that I felt healed from basically rutting in the dirt like an animal with my fiancé, but that was me. That was us.

CHAPTER TEN

ONE MONTH LATER

The death of my mother was a ripple in my life. In *our* lives. But it was not a tidal wave. Mostly, I was worried for my father, worried about the blame he'd place on himself. Males, especially alpha males who loved fiercely, tended to blame themselves for anything that happened to their women, even if it was outside of their control. Especially if it was outside of their control.

Jay watched me carefully, which was saying something since his attention had already been so focused and intense on me before. I wondered if he was waiting for me to crack, maybe for the illness that had killed my mother to slip through those cracks. For pieces of me to shatter and slowly grind down to dust until there was nothing left of who I was. Or maybe that was just me.

I had my moments, of course.

But there was always Wren with wine. Zoe with her firm reasons

whenever I started to spiral over myself having the same fate, and
Yasmin to listen, to pull up studies, medical journals, offers to set me
up with neurologists. Then there was Jay, there was always Jay.

We'd recovered from Felicity. I had taken a while to completely
forgive him, and I'd never understand why he'd had her in the house
for so long, but we got over it. Our relationship was not going to be
without bumps, without huge fucking valleys and mountains. I'd come
to terms with the fact that Jay was going to give me new scars while
he helped me come to terms with old ones. And I was okay with that.
Because of the live I had with him. The life that I loved.

And I truly loved what we had. Loved that I went to sleep with
him every single night, loved that no matter what, I came home to him.
Or he came home to me. But despite this—or maybe because of it—it
was hard leaving him. Even if it was for a dinner with Wren and the
girls which I was looking forward to because Wren was the only one
who even kind of understood what it was like, being in a relationship
with someone like Jay.

Even though there was no one even remotely like Jay.

Or Karson for that matter.

It was good to talk to her about the craziness of their lives. Of *our*
lives now. Craziness, which it seemed was only going to get crazier.

"I'm going to put someone on you from now on," Jay informed
me as I gathered my things and put them in my purse.

I glanced up at him from where he was watching me on the
bed. His laptop was perched on his lap, and he was still wearing his
shirt and pants. He hadn't taken them off when he'd fucked me on
my hands and knees in our closet. I'd had to change my outfit plans

since there were carpet burns on my knees now. I didn't mind one bit. He'd left me to get ready, only to grab the laptop from his office and work from bed. If we were both at home, we were close. Never in separate rooms. Jay only went behind closed doors when he got a phone call that made his face close off. When Karson entered the house looking grim—which was not much different from Karson's regular expression —or when he left our bed in the middle of the night without explanation as to where he was going.

Luckily, the latter was not something that happened often.

I didn't know what took him away from me in the middle of the night. I didn't know who was on the other side of those phone calls. I didn't know what made Karson so grim.

Still, even in my ignorance, I knew *something* was happening. Something bad.

"Excuse me?" I asked, narrowing my eyes at Jay.

"I am going to have a man in my employ, sometimes Karson, but not often since he's busy, travel with you wherever you go," Jay clarified.

Having someone follow me wasn't exactly a novel concept, but that was before. When things were different. Plus, I hadn't known they were following me at the time.

"*Why* is someone going to be following me, Jay?" I asked evenly, hands on my hips.

He closed his laptop. "Because I am in the middle of negotiations. They've turned hostile."

"Negotiations with whom?" I inquired, folding my arms.

"That's not important," he replied, brows dipping ever so slightly.

"If your negotiations are hostile enough for you to 'put someone on me', I disagree," I refuted sharply.

Jay pushed up from the bed, crossing the distance between us. I didn't like that. Distance made it easier to be pissed at him. When he got close, when he started touching me, things seemed less important.

"Don't come over here and try to distract me," I asserted, holding my hand up.

Jay did not stop his advance. He merely grabbed my wrist and pulled it into his chest, therefore pulling *me* into his chest.

My entire body relaxed and tightened at the same time. We were silent for a few breaths while he held me.

"Will these people—"

"The Russian Mob," Jay offered flatly, as if he were saying 'the people at the FedEx office.'

I sucked in a harsh breath. "Will the *Russian Mob* try to hurt me in the process of these negotiations?" I asked, trying to match Jay's flat tone and failing.

His grip on my wrist turned painful. "No, Stella. No one is going to touch you."

An oath.

I swallowed thickly. We were silent once more. I inhaled deeply. Leather. Sea salt. Jay. Home. Safety.

There were some questions one must ask when one's fiancé tells them they're going to need protection because the fiancé in question is having hostile negotiations with the Russian Mob.

Namely, *what in the fuck is it that you do in order to have any kind of contact let alone negotiations with the Russian Mob?*

And then a bunch of other questions about the level of danger he was in, how many years in jail would these negotiations buy him should the police ever find out. Was this going to be my life, worrying about the Russian Mob?

Stuff like that.

Instead of asking all of these questions, or even one, I stayed silent.

I arrived to dinner late with the man named Eric—who had driven me—sitting two tables over. Eric was African American, strong jawed, broad shouldered and had a 'do not fuck with me' vibe. Eric had also complimented my shoes.

Although I was forty minutes late to dinner, I was the first one to arrive. Wren rushing in less than a minute after the waitress had put down my dirty martini.

She drained it the second she sat her ass at the table.

"Two more please," she said to the waitress who was walking past the table. "Yasmin is still at the office, and Zoe is stuck in traffic," she said in greeting. Her cheeks were flushed, and her hair was a dazzling mess of curls. "I'm late for the same reason you probably were. Because I had a very dangerous man between my thighs," she winked.

I smiled back despite myself, despite my mood.

"Things are still going well with Karson?" I asked, even though I really didn't need to.

"*Well* would be an understatement."

"I'm happy for you, sweetheart," I meant it. I loved seeing my girl so happy.

Wren grinned. "I'm happy for me too. My vagina is even happier," she chuckled, wiggling her eyebrows.

"What about your heart?" I asked tentatively.

Wren had yet to admit that she actually loved Karson even though he was damn near living at her house, she hadn't even considering breaking up with him and it had been months. Almost a year.

An eternity for Wren.

She shuddered. "My heart belongs to Alexander McQueen," she said matter of fact.

"Alexander McQueen is dead," I pointed out.

"Which means my heart is too."

I narrowed my eyes, ready to call bullshit, but she glanced down at her phone which was buzzing on the table. "Fuck," she muttered. "Both Zoe and Yasmin bailed. Which sucks because we haven't all been together in forever but doesn't suck that bad because I kind of like you, and now we can have an entire baked camembert to ourselves." She grinned wickedly.

I shook my head, grinning back. "Let's do it."

"I don't know if I can do this," I whispered.

"What? Eat half of this baked camembert? Bitch you can, and you mother fucking will," Wren claimed after she swallowed a mouthful.

I rolled my eyes and dutifully dipped a slice of bread into the cheesy goodness.

Wren nodded in approval.

"I don't know if I can be her."

"*Her*?" she repeated, cocking her head as she scrutinized me. "Okay, let's pretend that we live in a world where you should ever try to be anyone but your own damn self. Who is *she*?"

"She's *me*," I replied. "Or who I figure I have to be in order to be with Jay. In order to be his wife."

I dipped more bread into the cheese because I really needed melted camembert and carbs with this conversation.

"He's some kind of organized crime lord," I added once I'd swallowed. "Yes, he wears a nice suit, goes to nice charity dinners and lives in a very nice house, but I'm aware that there are parts of his business that are..." I trailed off, unsure of what Karson had told Wren about the nature of Jay's business, unwillingly to betray Jay's secrets to Wren, even though she was one of my closest friends, and I trusted her with my life.

I didn't want to accidently spill something that would put her life in danger.

"Not so nice," I finished lamely. "Parts of his business require me to be strong, to be somewhat of a badass myself." My mind wandered. "To not blink when I'm woken up in the middle of the night to..." I trailed off again, not wanting to say something I was sure I shouldn't talk to Wren about. More secrets.

"Jay did not put that ring on your finger because you are some cold, hard, badass woman who can handle all that kind of shit and not even blink," Wren reassured me before I could figure out what I was going to say.

"Now, those women are most definitely awesome, but they are an acquired taste. Just like men like Jay are. He does not need or want a woman hardened to the ugliness of his world."

She reached out and squeezed my hand. The one that wasn't shoving cheese in my face like a wild animal.

"He needs *you*," she continued with a smile. "Someone kind. Someone who loves openly, unconditionally. Someone the total opposite of everything that he breathes every single day." She took her drink and sipped it. "This isn't a fairy tale. Not a fucking Disney movie. We are not riding off into the sunset with some handsome, two dimensional princes. We're with the villains, honey. And they're *much* better in bed. You think Prince Charming gave Cinderella multiple orgasms?" She shook her head. "Nuh uh, baby. We made the right choice."

I clinked my drink with hers. Yeah, we had made the right choice.

And this was confirmed when I got home and was given multiple orgasms which Cinderella definitely didn't get.

I quickly got used to doing my job with someone following me. With Jay checking in with me multiple times a day. I actually loved that, hearing his husky voice on the other end of the phone. Sometimes he was just asking me what I was doing, if I was good. Other times, he ordered me into the bathroom of whatever location I was working on, making me touch myself while he listened. So what if his potential beef with the Russian Mafia was the reason for the calls?

When he called earlier, I'd told him I had a celebrity job, that was in a gated community and there wouldn't be a way for a man in a dark sedan to follow me inside without raising a lot of questions.

"I don't give a fuck about questions," Jay retorted in a clipped tone.

I pinched the bridge of my nose, expecting such a reaction. "Well, I do because this is my job. These are my clients."

"Your job isn't important right now, Stella," Jay replied. "Your safety is what matters."

I gritted my teeth. "My job is important, Jay," I told him slowly.

"You don't need it," he said. "I can take care of you."

I took a deep breath, then another. "I'm going to ignore that statement because I know you're stressed out over everything going on. But you need to remember that you fell in love with me because I'm not some doormat whose only goal in life is to be taken care of by a man. I'm keeping my job. I let you put a fucking bodyguard on me without an argument."

I looked out my car window, waving at Eric with my fingers.

He nodded back once, far too badass and serious about his job to do the finger wave. But not too badass and serious to say no to me setting him up with a good friend of mine who would be perfect for him. Kieran liked bad boys, but not the good kind of bad boy.

Eric was the perfect kind of bad boy for Kieran. And Kieran was perfect for Eric. Sweet. Kind. Hot as balls. Had impeccable style. And Eric had made it clear through our time together that he loved fashion. We bonded regularly over footwear.

I turned my attention back to my conversation with Jay, the one I was trying not to let get out of hand.

"Look," I sighed. "I'm going to a movie star's home. Their security is top notch. I know that because Greenstone Security handled it, and they know their shit."

I waited for Jay to argue with me, but I knew that he wouldn't because I was right. Greenstone Security did Jay's house too. Keltan, the owner, had been out last week, checking up, doing updates, commencing in an alpha male huddle with Jay and Karson. Jay wouldn't employ anyone but the best.

"Eric can sit outside on the curb. I will text him every five minutes if that will appease you. But I'm going in there." My stance on this was clear from my tone. There were a lot of times when I'd let Jay tell me what to do. Most of them were in the bedroom, sure. But outside of it, I'd found safety in that. In him. But that did not mean I was a submissive. At least not entirely. My independence, my agency, was something I'd never give over to him.

He sighed on the other end of the phone. "You're getting punished when you get home, Stella." Though his voice was strained, there was no mistaking the erotic promise in it.

My hands gripped tightly on the steering wheel, and I pressed my thighs together.

"Well, if I'm going to get punished..." I hung up the phone with a smile.

I hadn't told Jay who my client was on purpose. It wasn't *technically* lying, but it was close. A dirty trick, considering what we'd gone through with Felicity. But I'd figured a genuine client who he was once unnecessarily jealous of compared to a woman who he actually used to fuck then had in our house weren't the same, like *at all*.

Ollie paid well, and he was great for my career. He'd recommended me to a bunch of his very rich and famous actor friends. Plus, I actually enjoyed his company.

Ollie pulled me in for a hug as soon as he opened the door. And it was Ollie who opened it, not an assistant or a housekeeper. Which was Ollie. Who was not thinking friend thoughts when he hugged me tight and a little too long for a friend.

Fuck.

"Stella! I cannot believe you disappeared across the world, leaving me to dress myself," he accused once he'd let me go, not before his eyes went up and down the tight t-shirt dress I was wearing with strappy Manolos.

"I went on Jimmy Kimmel, and I did not pull off the snakeskin loafers my publicist talked me in to." His eyes were warm and teasing.

"That I cannot be blamed for," I replied, walking inside his impressive foyer. My heels clicked against the marble floor. "You're a strong, intelligent adult man, you know better than snakeskin loafers."

I reached up to push my hair behind my ear, feeling slightly uncomfortable being alone in a house with a man who was making it clear that he wanted me. With his teasing eyes and lingering hugs. I didn't feel threatened or unsafe, but it felt weird and wrong now that I belonged to Jay.

Ollie stared at my hand. Specifically, the large diamond glittering on my left finger.

"Fuck," he muttered.

I raised my brow at him in question.

He nodded to my hand. "I'm too late. Should've asked you out the first time I met you. But I'm not very good at that shit. Thought I'd work up the courage next time I saw you." He ran his hand through his hair in what was most definitely a nervous gesture. "But then you go away for five months and come back belonging to someone else. I'm too late. So ... *fuck*."

He looked at me, rubbing the back of his neck, a shy smile on his very attractive, very famous face. It was slightly insecure. Which made it all the more endearing. Ollie radiated such confidence, he seemed so sure of himself, yet there was something boyish and genuine about him that set him apart from every other leading man with a square jaw and broad shoulders.

"If it makes you feel any better, I belonged to him the first time I met you," I told him, my mind wandering to a place where I hadn't met Jay, where I waited for Ollie to work up the courage to ask me on a date, where I said yes.

I'm sure he could've brought more sunshine out in me, made it so that the darkness inside of me was just a mere shadow that visited sometimes. Of course he could've been putting on an act this whole time, turning out to be a huge tool who was bad in bed, but I didn't think so.

Wondering didn't do much good. The same way that it hadn't

with Brent. My life was the way it was now. I wouldn't change it. Didn't want to, Even though it scared me sometimes. Even though Jay scared me sometimes, the way I felt for him. His life, the one that meant blood on his hands, that meant men with guns, that meant 'fighting for territory', that meant a bunch of different ways he could be stolen from me.

Ollie was tilting his head, looking at me. "It doesn't make me feel any better," he smirked. "But he's a lucky man."

"I'm a lucky woman," I countered.

He narrowed his eyes. "He ever fucks up, you call me."

I laughed. "He's not going to fuck up."

His face went serious. "I don't suspect he will, if he's smart."

Silence lingered, leaving me feeling slightly uncomfortable before he clapped his hands. "Well, if I can't marry you, I'll at least get you to make me look like a normal man so I can attract a normal, down to earth woman."

I smiled. "Well, you're never going to look like a normal man, since you're ... you. And you're in the wrong industry and city for that matter for a down to earth woman, but let's try our best."

And we did. Just like that, Ollie weathered the rejection. Did not sour or turn mean and dangerous. He accepted that he couldn't have me, accepted that I'd chosen my man and accepted we were going to be friends.

Yeah, luckily for me, he was a good guy. Pretty darn close to Prince Charming.

Which was great. If you are in to that kind of thing.

The punishment I was expecting when I arrived home did not come. Debussy was playing, Jay was in the kitchen, his shirt sleeves rolled up, still wearing the rest of his suit. It was postponed because after dinner, we were going to drinks that Wren was throwing. Drinks that were bound to be strong enough to fell a horse, which meant eating prior to consuming them was a must. I'd mentioned this to Jay as a joke last week when she told us about it, but I hadn't figured he'd take me so seriously.

It warmed my heart that he had.

My heart was warm right until I saw his face, sensing his energy when I came into the kitchen, depositing my purse on the counter.

He still kissed me hello, still squeezed me close, but something was off. Something that had me retreating to the other side of the kitchen counter, happy that there was a fresh martini there.

Jay did not speak. Nor did I. He wasn't exactly the guy to say, "hey honey, how was your day?" But he was the guy who had promised a punishment when I got home tonight. And Jay was a man who kept his promises, especially when it came to punishments. Punishments in the form of sex acts, punishments that included canes, blindfolds and extremely dirty sex. Yes, he kept those promises. Every. Time.

But not tonight.

Though I hadn't done a single thing wrong, anxiety ate at the pit of my stomach. This in itself was a punishment. The bitterness in the air, Jay's stiff jaw, his shuttered eyes.

"You're not to see him anymore," Jay finally spoke.

I blinked at the man in front of me. My future husband. The one who had uttered that sentence so mildly. Who said it and then returned to chopping mushrooms.

"Excuse me?"

My tone made him look up from the mushrooms. As it fucking should've.

"This Oliver Cummings. He wants you, Stella. And you're mine." He enunciated every word, speaking slowly. Purposefully. He'd put down the knife he had been using, palms now flat on the kitchen counter, giving me his full attention. "I do not want you spending time with a man who wants what's mine."

I took a deep breath. Then another. "Okay, so despite the fact that you're a very intelligent, street smart, master criminal, you obviously do not know to decipher the warning in those two words I just spoke, and you didn't decide to check yourself before you wreck yourself." I did not speak slowly. Nor did I speak evenly, like Jay had. My face was not carefully blank. I made sure to show just how pissed off I was with my tone, my expression and my body language.

"Don't try and cute your way out of this, Stella," Jay said, eyes glittering ever so slightly with amusement.

Which made all of this worse. "Don't try and fucking patronize me by insinuating my anger is 'cute' to you, therefore insignificant and not valid. Because when you're angry, God save the person who would describe you as *cute*," I hissed, leaning forward over the counter.

Jay's jaw went tight, and his brows puckered ever so slightly. "I did not mean to insult you, Stella."

I tilted my head. "No, you just meant to tell me who I can and can't work with because you seem to believe that they want to fuck me."

"He does." His stare unyielding and no longer glittering with any kind of amusement.

"Good for him," I replied sharply. "I'm hot. I think I'm somewhat of a catch. So throughout the remainder of my life, I'm going to hazard a guess that I'm going to encounter some men who may want to fuck me. But guess what? Wanting is as far as they'll get. Because I have no interest in letting another man touch me. I am committed to you. I think I've proven that well and truly. But my commitment does not mean you get a say over who I do and don't work with."

I got up out of my chair, snatching my martini off the counter and began to pace. It was either that or climb across the kitchen counter and slap Jay silly.

"No, Stella," he disagreed, watching me pace. "The ring on your finger means you're mine. Means that I won't have you around men, alone with men who want to fuck you. You may think he's a good man, but many men can turn bad, turn dangerous once they get rejected. Especially when they're used to getting what they want."

I blinked. "So now you're insinuating that Ollie is going to *force* himself on me?" I scowled.

Jay rounded the counter now, walking toward me. I stopped pacing because my body was still a fucking traitor that was hungry for him.

"I'm not putting you in a situation where that is ever going to happen again," he declared fiercely, coming to stand in front of me but not touching me.

Something cold moved at the bottom of my stomach at the

mention of the night that I still dreamed about sometimes. That woke me in the middle of the night in a cold sweat, my heart thundering in fear. Jay was always there for that.

"I rejected *you* at first, Jay," I reminded him, trying to hide my reaction. "Are you telling me that you would've turned dangerous because you wanted me and were used to getting what you want?"

He gripped my wrist. "Careful, Stella," he warned.

"No, you be fucking careful, Jay," I spat, yanking my wrist back and storming over to the counter where my phone vibrated.

I glanced down at my phone. We were late. "We have to go," I said flatly, trying to step around Jay.

He didn't let me do that. He continued to cage me in. "We are not going anywhere. We're not done." His eyes were granite, gemstones without the glitter. Resolute.

I met his stare, the one that used to terrify me so much more than it did now, and I jutted my chin up in defiance. "We are done for now," I retorted, done with this conversation.

"You're not leaving this house, Stella."

I titled my head at him. "What? You're going to physically restrain me? Chain me up?"

His hand trailed up to my throat, resting there without pressure. Nonetheless, my heart thundered against that hand, my body responding with a need that my angry mind was not in control of.

"I don't need to chain you up to make you stay," Jay murmured, his voice liquid now instead of iron, those gemstone eyes transforming into pools of desire.

I hated that he was right. That he could control me so easily.

Without force. Without restraints. Purely with the desire that I had for him. The need I had for him. The one that hadn't dampened since we got back, that hadn't plateaued, the one that grew with every passing day.

Every passing hour.

How was I going to survive a lifetime with this man?

"No, you don't need to chain me up to make me stay," I agreed. "But you're not going to make me stay. Because we're not in our arrangement. You don't get to win every time. You don't get to control me." I evened my gaze in challenge despite my racing heart, despite my need for him.

Jay met my stare, considering my words. I knew he was still contemplating making me stay despite what I'd said, that was just Jay.

When he stepped back, a victory, I hated myself for being disappointed.

We arrived at the party and put on the faces of a couple who were pretending they weren't in a fight, but everyone who knew them well spotted the tension the second they walked through the door.

My friends had spent enough time around Jay and I to understand our dynamic. They at least knew me well enough to understand my mood, to clock that something most definitely wasn't right. But apart from a couple of raised eyebrows, they said nothing. And we said nothing to each other.

I knew that Jay did not particularly want to be here, amongst all these people, amongst the craziness of Wren's party which included synchronized swimmers in her pool, a henna artist and some guy eating swords. I did not miss the men wearing expensive suits, skulking around the edges of the party, clinging to what little shadows there were.

Hmm.

Karson must've worked hard to get that to happen since the men definitely did not go with Wren's aesthetic. That would've pissed her off royally. I knew this because I knew Wren took her parties and her 'aesthetic' very seriously. I also knew this because she kept glaring at Karson across the room and muttering, "asshole" under her breath. As much as I really wanted to know the story behind that, I figured asking would be gasoline on a fire.

If I wasn't angry at Jay, I would've just asked him. But I was angry at Jay, so I treated him to some across the room glares and mutters of my own. I also stayed much longer than I would've had I not been pissed. I knew that this was not Jay's scene, not by a long shot. I also knew that he'd made the effort to come because of me. Which might've been sweet before all the alpha male possessive bullshit.

It wasn't right now.

I had two more martinis than I'd planned, threw myself in to conversations with old friends and did my best to look like I was having a fabulous time even though I wasn't. I was worried about Jay the entire time, which only served to piss me off more. He never strayed too far from me despite my glares and muttering. And when he wasn't on the fringes of whatever conversation I was having, he was in some kind of man huddle with Karson, his brows furled ever so slightly and his jaw hard.

It didn't help that he looked absolutely marvelous in his midnight suit and charcoal shirt, unbuttoned at the throat. His hair curled around the nape of his neck, and a few strands fell perfectly across his forehead, accentuating his glittering gaze and sculpted features. Too many women approached him. He needed a fucking wedding ring. Or a sign around his neck that said, "Property of Stella, fuck off." Wait, wasn't I mad about the whole jealous, possessive thing?

Not the same I decided.

It was the women, the knitted brows and the unsettled pit at the bottom of my stomach that eventually had me stomping toward Jay and grabbing his arm and whispering, "we're going home," in his ear.

He turned from Karson, raised a brow ever so slightly and set my panties on fire with his gaze.

I swallowed roughly. I'd never made such demands of him like this ... it felt foreign. And hot.

Despite this, we didn't speak on the ride home. Anger still burned through me. Anger at Jay, sure, but also at myself. At the wrong and warped parts of me that had been turned on by his jealousy, by his ownership. I fucking loved being owned by Jay. Parts of me hated myself for loving that.

We might've gotten over the whole Felicity thing, but there was no way I could ever forget it. There were also parts of me that loved this. Loved making him feel this way, even though he had no right to be pissed at me. I wanted him uncomfortable, envisioning me with another man, because despite all the healing I'd done, there were times

I still saw her. Still imagined her teaching Jay things he did to me.

So yes, I was still burning hot when I got out of the car—definitely not waiting for any man to open it for me—and stormed into our house. I might've also been the teensiest bit drunk. And a pissed off sober woman, more often than not, turned in to an absolutely fucking furious drunk woman.

I was taking off my makeup in the bathroom when he came. I'd been expecting it, hadn't I? Longing for it.

He wasn't wearing his suit. His shirt was unbuttoned, displaying his olive chest, his impossibly sculpted torso, the Apollo's belt all the more pronounced because his pants were also unbuttoned.

I steeled myself against all the feelings that came with seeing that and tried my very best to look in the mirror, focusing on the task at hand.

"Are you still angry with me?" he murmured in my ear. His hand brushed over my hip.

"Yes," I whispered, glaring at him in the mirror. "Furious."

"Good," he said. "Lift up your dress and put your hands on the table.

I really wanted to disobey him. I really wanted to walk away, run myself a bubble bath and lock Jay out. But there was no locking Jay out. No ignoring the way my pussy clenched at his tone, at the molten sin in his eyes.

I did as he instructed.

Something smooth and cold ran along my bare skin. My knees shook. I knew exactly what that was. The leather cane that Jay used on me. The one that left raised red welts on my ass and made it uncomfortable to sit for days. The one that I fucking loved.

"I know you like this, pet." He leaned forward so his breath was hot on my ear. He ran the cane up and down, teasing me.

I gripped the counter and watched him in the mirror. His gaze was wicked, evil. It set me on fire.

"You know I like it too." He kissed my neck. "I like seeing my marks on your impeccable pale skin." His hand bit into the skin of my thigh. "I like hurting you."

I gasped as his hand moved from my thigh to cup me over the top of my panties.

"You like me controlling you, Stella. That's what makes you so mad. You fucking love this."

His hand was gone from my panties, and he was no longer bent over me. He was standing to my left, watching me in the mirror. The cane moved in a flash and slapped against my skin. Burning pain spread from where it hit, my knees almost buckling. I kept my eyes on Jay, my body shaking with the desire that was painted on his face, that thrummed through my blood.

"You want it again?" he asked, moving the cane gently over my burning flesh.

I gritted my teeth and nodded.

"No, Stella," he scolded. "You do not get to continue the silent treatment. You want it again, you ask for it."

Rage mingled with my need. "Fuck you," I hissed, surprising myself.

Jay's jaw ticced, and his eyes flared with something. Not anger. No. Hunger.

"Oh, I will Stella, I will be fucking you so hard you'll be unable to sit down without thinking about my cock for the next week. But first, you need to ask." The cane moved across my skin. "Nicely."

My eyes were almost slits, they were narrowed that much, my breathing heavy and my heart a dull roar in my chest.

"Hit me again," I chided, hating him, loving him, needing him.

Jay tilted his head ever so slightly.

My teeth sunk into my lip in defiance, eyes never leaving his. He didn't move.

"Hit me again, sir," I relented, my tone animalistic.

He grinned, showing all of his teeth, all of his wickedness. "That's my pet."

Then he hit me again.

And again.

Until I was soaking wet, inches from climax, until my knees were quaking, barely able to hold myself up. Then he carried me to our bed, put me on my hands and knees and fucked me. Hard. Relentlessly. In a way that sutured his brand over every inch of my skin. His ownership.

And I fucking loved it.

Later—much, much later, when I'd regained the ability to speak, after Jay had gently, reverently, rubbed lotion onto my red, stinging skin, once I was splayed over his body because I was unable to stand even the thousand thread count Egyptian Cotton sheets on my bare skin—I spoke.

"I'm not dropping Ollie as a client." My soft voice cut through the night with the hard truth.

Jay stiffened underneath me, his arms tightening around me.

"I get it," I whispered, my hand cupping his cheek. "I get how much you want me because I want you just as much. I can't breathe thinking of another woman near you." Felicity simmered between us, and I pushed that aside—pushed her aside. "But I will not drop clients. I will not let you tell me who I can and can't spend time with. You have to trust that I'll remove myself from any situations that get too close to something you don't like."

"I don't like the thought of a man being close enough to fucking smell you, for your scent, your smile and your ass to harden his cock," Jay seethed.

I grinned despite myself, need overcoming me again despite how tender I was from Jay's love. From his brand.

"That's not realistic, Jay," I sighed.

Silence hung in the air for several long moments. "I know," he relented finally, his hand brushing against the sensitive skin that was deliciously swollen. "I'm not going to stop," he added. "I'll never stop wanting to kill any man who thinks that they have any kind of right to what's mine." He kissed me, teeth brushing against my lips. "But I'll try."

"Want to know the truth?" I whispered.

"Always."

"I never want you to stop."

His hands clenched around me. "I never fucking will."

CHAPTER ELEVEN

I t was a Saturday.

An unusual one where we were both free.

Now that I was here full time, there were no days that belonged purely to Jay. He had them all. But somehow, unfortunately, we were only spending slightly more time with each other than we had back then.

I was busier than ever with work, so more often than not, there was some event to go to. If not for something to do with my work, for Jay's. The more legitimate side of it, at least. The side with the parties, with the charitable donations, the Botoxed wives and the rich, old husbands.

Not the side with the blood, the weapons and whatever else. I didn't see that. Still, even now, Jay protected me from that side of his life with ruthless determination. As much as I didn't want to know

about it, I had to. I was *marrying* this man. If I was going to spend my life with him, have his children, there couldn't be pockets, chasms of his world that remained unknown to me. Even if the mere prospect of learning about them absolutely terrified me.

For now, though, we had a quiet Saturday night.

One with a roaring fire, one with a slight breeze coming in from an open window, because despite the chill, I liked to smell the ocean, hear the distant crash of the waves. I was curled up on the sofa. Debussy was playing. Jay was wearing jeans and a soft cotton tee. It was a little pocket of perfection. And I didn't plan on ruining it by demanding the truth.

"Wren is planning our wedding," I told Jay as he poured me a glass of wine. He did not let me pour my own. The second my glass was even close to empty, he was there, refilling it. I hadn't bothered to comment on how I could pour my own damn wine. Jay knew very well I could pour my wine. He wanted to do it. One of many small gestures that yes, may have spoken to his penchant for control, but it also communicated the way he wanted to take care of me. The small, intimate things he wanted to do.

Like fill my cup.

Which he did.

Every damn time I breathed him in, saw his verdant eyes watching me from across the room, every morning I woke up.

"I'm not surprised," he replied when he had finished pouring my wine and was moving on to his own.

Another thing, he always took care of me before he even thought about himself. Always. And not just in the bedroom—thought that in it of itself was somewhat of a rarity.

Though I hated sweeping generalizations about men and women, some unfortunately, for the most part, tended to exist because they were true. Women in love, women in lust, women in a committed relationships tended to go out of their way to care for men. In a hundred and one little ways, one hundred of which usually went unnoticed by men because they weren't exactly wired to notice the way their woman got them a beer before they finished theirs, the way they picked up their favorite brand of yogurt at the store, sucked their dicks not because they particularly liked the act but because they wanted to give them pleasure.

Men, as a rule, didn't exactly go out of their way to do the little things, because mostly they didn't notice them.

Jay noticed everything about me. Even things I hadn't noticed about myself. And the way he felt for me, how deep his commitment went, was becoming more and more clear since we'd gotten home.

"You have no issues with Wren planning our wedding," I clarified when he sat down beside me then proceeded to pull me so that I was practically sitting on his lap.

Jay liked me close.

Before the split, sure. But more so now. As if he thought I might run off and put an ocean between us again. As if he worried he might push me away again.

"Even if I did have an argument, I don't like my chances of winning it," Jay said, sipping his wine. There was a lightness to his words, to his voice, to his gaze that warmed my insides. "But no, I don't have objections to Wren doing it. Do you?"

I shook my head. "Of course not. I have no earthly choice in the matter, and if my super powerful, badass fiancé doesn't like his chances going up against Wren, I certainly wouldn't fare well."

Jay reached up to pull my hair out of the messy bun I'd piled it into earlier. He brushed out the strands with his fingers. "I think you doubt your own strength, pet," he murmured.

I smiled at him. "You know that a Wren wedding will have a lot of fanfare," I warned, going back to the subject at hand.

He nodded. "I've met Wren, so yes."

"The guest list will be monstrous," I continued.

"Again, not surprised." Jay spoke with ease, with no tightness to his jaw, no shuttered over his eyes. It was unnerving, seeing him like this.

Relaxed.

It was unnerving yet wonderful. I didn't want to wreck it, this comfortable, easy moment between us. Because I knew no matter how much it seemed like things had changed, how much Jay had changed, I knew that people, especially men—especially Jay—did not change *that* much.

This evening would not become the norm. I ached to hold on to it just as it was, not creating a single ripple.

But as much as I didn't want to yank apart our pockets of peace, I wanted to make sure nothing went unsaid between us. Relationships did not crumble because of things said in anger, words used as weapons. Sure, they made marks. But they did not cause irreparable damage.

It was what wasn't said. It was thoughts, feelings, fears,

reservations, swallowed because speaking them seemed too hard, too uncomfortable. They burrowed, those unsaid words, like termites, eating away at things under the surface.

"Jay," I said.

"Stella," he replied, still playing with my hair.

"Not long ago, mere *months* in fact, you told me in no uncertain terms that you would *never* marry." I forced a casual tone even though the mere memory of that conversation stung.

Some of that lightness left his eyes, and I hated myself for being the reason.

He didn't reply. Jay remembered that conversation. Of course he did. He knew that that wasn't all I had to say. So he waited.

"I know that the time we were apart changed a lot of things," I continued. "I know that it made things become clear. But I just want to make sure that you're not doing something that you don't want to do just to keep me. The reasons you have for not wanting to get married are valid. More than valid. And they were concrete until recently. Yet now you're agreeing not only to a wedding but one that will most likely have a long-retired pop group singing at the reception and will be attended by many, *many* people." I bit my lip. "It's ... a lot."

Jay leaned forward to put his wine glass on the coffee table in front of us, then he took mine from my hand and did the same. His hands found my neck, gripping it, forcing my attention to him—which was where it had been the entire time. He wasn't the only one who still felt the cold shadows of our separation.

"Stella." He voiced my name in a low rasp. "I get to stand in front of a crowd of people and vow that you will be mine until the day I die.

I could not give a fuck about the fanfare of it all." His eyes roved over my face as if it was the first and last time he was ever going to see me.

His intensity never dulled.

"As for what I said about marriage, that was in the midst of the lies I was telling myself." His thumb brushing against my jaw. "That was before I lived my life with the ghost of you in it. I'm not saying I'm going to be good at being a husband. I'm not saying I'm not going to fuck up. That my past won't negatively influence periods of our lives, that it won't be a battle against the uglier parts of me. But I'm making a promise that I won't let them win."

It wasn't hearts and flowers. It definitely wasn't Keats, but to me, Jay's words were poetry.

It took me another week to have the conversation that I should've had the night that Jay asked me to be his wife.

No, I should've had this conversation *much* earlier than that. But conversations like this one weren't allowed before.

He was cooking.

It was something he did often. Although my cooking skills were actually skills now, Jay liked feeding me. He liked serving me.

It was safe to say I liked it too

"You know, I agreed to be your wife before I actually really knew what your life entails," I told him, sipping my wine. Liquid courage was definitely needed for this conversation.

"I told you what my life entails," Jay replied, his drink untouched in front of him. It unnerved me, in the midst of serious conversations, his unwillingness to fidget. His emotional courage to stare unblinking at me. I, on the other hand, needed something. To fidget with the fabric of my pants. My hair. A drink containing alcohol.

"You told me in your vague, ominous, 'I'm not good for you, and I may or may not be a mob boss' kind of way," I refuted.

"I'm not a mob boss," Jay corrected.

I canted my head. "Okay, you're not a mob boss, but you manage a ... 'stable' of sex workers? And you *may* or *may not* have people killed? Even though I'm not educated on the complexities of life in the underworld, I know there's more than that."

His stare was inscrutable. "Yes, Stella, there's more than that."

I waited. He didn't speak. I waited some more. He still didn't speak. "Well," I snapped. "What else?"

Jay stared at me for a few beats more before he turned his head down to the cutting board and his onions. It was his nonverbal way of saying the conversation was over.

I leaned forward, snapping my fingers at him. "Nuh uh. You don't get to choose when the conversation finishes now. I'm your soon to be wife. I'm your equal. And I'm entitled to know what in the fuck my husband's life entails." I was getting pissed off now. And obviously, I was not hiding it.

"You are entitled," he concurred, still looking at the onions.

I gritted my teeth and waited for him to speak once more.

Thankfully, he did. But he may as well have stayed silent. "But I'm not going to tell you." He looked up in time to see my glare.

"More secrets," I fumed, anger a living beast in my gut. "Felicity wasn't the end of it, was it? Your world is built on lies, and I'm living in it, but as *your wife*, I'm not entitled to actually *be* in your life. Everything is still on your terms."

I pushed up from my seat, intending on storming off for effect and also because I did not want Jay to see my cry. It was something that really annoyed me about myself, my penchant for bursting into tears when I was angry or frustrated. It really didn't do much for the strong female image I was trying to portray, and I didn't want Jay to see that weakness in me.

Of course, I didn't manage to storm out. Jay moved quickly, leaving the kitchen in a handful of long strides so he was blocking my way with his body. I scowled up at him, hating that he was so fucking beautiful, that the power he had over me hadn't dulled. Not one bit.

"Okay," he said stepped forward, his hand cupping my cheek. "Okay, Stella. I don't keep things from you because I don't trust you, because I think you're weak. I keep certain things from you because I think so highly of you. Because you are the only thing in my life untouched, pure, good, right. Because I am a greedy man, because I want you to be the one pure thing in my love. Untainted by my life."

My heart broke for this man. This damaged, broken and complicated man. Who loved me more than I'd ever thought a human could be loved and hated himself in that same measure.

I made it my silent vow to figure out how to rid him of that hate, to see himself how I saw him. But that would take a lifetime, which was fine since that's how long I intended to be with him.

"I knew what I was getting in to with you," I choked out, staring up at him. "And I am not untainted or pure—that's one of the many

ANNE MALCOM

reasons I fell in love with you. Because you gave the dark parts of me a home." I took a deep breath. "After my childhood, what happened with my mom, I realized that something ugly existed inside of me. Something I'd tried to forget, bury." I paused. "Until you. I'm not afraid of anything inside of me now because of you, Jay. The more you hide from me, the more afraid I get."

He regarded me as if he were trying to peel me apart, see the insides of me. I wished he could, wished there was a way I could show him every single thing.

"My business is running the streets of L.A." he revealed finally. "The areas of the city are divided up into territories and controlled by different street gangs. Those gangs do not get along, for the most part. But they do not engage in war because they all answer to me. I do not control them, do not police their activities, I do not stop them from doing whatever horrible violent things they need to do to survive, it's important you know that."

Jay's hand moved from my cheek to my neck, spanning my collarbone, resting his palm above my thundering heart.

"I'm no Robin Hood," he continued. "There is no nobility in my job. There is money and there is power. Don't bother trying to make it right or okay in your mind. There's no way to justify what I do or who I am."

He sighed. I'd never heard Jay sigh before. The sound was innocuous, natural enough for most people, but not Jay.

I swallowed roughly. "Tell me the rest," I whispered.

"I control a lot of the arms and weapons coming in and out of the city. I own most of the police. My job is to make sure things don't get too loud, things don't make headlines. That the criminals stick to the shadows. I started at the bottom of the pile. The very fucking bottom. I've done things to get to the top. I've hurt people. Killed them."

I'd known all this, hadn't I? Not the specifics, of course, but I'd known Jay had killed people. I'd known he'd killed Heller to get to the top. Known he probably would in the future. That he'd come home with death on his hands, staining his soul. I'd never thought I'd live so closely to something like this, that I'd sleep next to man capable of this and love him with every fiber of my being.

But I did. And I would. Forever.

"That's the reason for the charity shit," Jay explained. "I'm belated trying to balance some scales. Trying to offset some of the things I've done in this world." He played with a tendril of my hair. "I know I'm going to hell for my sins. I know I'm going to the darkest corners of it for bringing you in to my world and refusing to let you go. But I'll serve an eternity in hell for one lifetime with you, Stella. It's heaven."

I blinked rapidly, tears filling my eyes at the power of his words. The worship in them. In Jay's eyes.

"If you'll still have me." His voice was low, as close to a whisper as I'd ever heard. "I know I should've told you this before I put a ring on your finger. Should've given you the choice. But I'm a sinner, pet. I've told you that before. I didn't give you a way out because I didn't *want* you to have a way out." His hand tightened around my neck with possession. With need.

A need of my own opened up at the bottom of my stomach.

"I don't know if I can let you go if this is too much for you," he continued.

That should've scared me. The intensity, the oath, the promise in his words. It didn't. "I'm not going anywhere, Jay," I promised on a rasp.

His eyes moved over my face slowly, as if he was searching for a sliver of indecision, the hint of a lie.

"I know you think I'm some kind of saint," I shook my head, trying to communicate with not only my words but my eyes. Hoping he knew these words were coming from my heart. My soul. "I definitely don't agree, but let's say I am a saint, I'm telling you the truth. Saints don't lie. I'm not going anywhere. I love you for exactly who you are, for all of your sins. Because right or wrong, they kept you alive, they kept you breathing." My eyes watered. "They brought you to me."

Now it finally clicked. It didn't matter what Jay had told me, what he'd done.

Even if what he'd done was worse than what he told me—my imagination wasn't that great, but I figured there was worse—it wouldn't have changed a thing.

"I have to hide it, pet, my love for you. My dedication for you. The fact that you are inside me, that you own me. I have to hide that you're my everything. Because the only reason I've been as successful as I have at my business, the only reason I've been able to hold on to power for so long is because I have nothing they can take from me. Nothing they can hurt me with." He rested his forehead against mine and closed his eyes, taking a long, deep inhale. It was at least a minute before he opened them and spoke again.

"They can hurt me with you, Stella," he confessed. "And that scares the shit out of me."

"No," I protested, shaking my head. "They can't. You won't let that happen. I won't let that happen."

I said this firmly, like it was something I could control. Like Jay's dark, dangerous, deadly life was something I could control.

I'd learn soon enough that it wasn't.

We were out for drinks.

Me, Wren, Zoe, Yasmin, Eric and Phillipe—Wren's security detail. Wren suddenly had her own shadow now, despite her calling me at three in the morning a month ago saying that she and Karson had broken up over him trying to 'put a man on her' like Jay had with me. To quote Wren, *"I got myself out of a Thai drug lord's mansion on his own private island wearing nothing but a bikini, I think I can take care of myself with some Russians."*

When I'd told her that it was the Russian Mob more precisely, she'd made a dismissive sound and muttered about "details".

Needless to say, Wren did not end up having a man on her nor did she end up breaking up with Karson. He had it bad for her. She had it bad for him but was still refusing to admit it was anything but hot sex. Which obviously meant Wren was in love with him. We all knew and were all madly happy about it. Even Zoe, despite knowing that he worked for Jay in the shadier side of his business. I hated that that pissed me off just a little, that Zoe was accepting of Karson and the danger he presented yet just tolerated Jay. Sure, she spoke to him. She even came over to our place for drinks, engaged with him and did her best to support me. But I knew Zoe had not let her guard down with him. Had not forgiven him for hurting me.

Which was why it made no sense for me to be jealous of the support that Zoe had for Wren's relationship. Zoe wasn't exactly worried about the 'breaking the law' part of Jay's life, but more about the lack of hurt he had inflicted upon her friend.

Still, it irked me.

Then again, I had a lifetime for them to like each other.

Hopefully.

Jay was worried enough about my life to have a man on me, and Karson was obviously worried enough to go up against Wren—and win.

It became apparent exactly *why* Karson was worried enough to go to battle with Wren as soon as we all sat down and had drinks in front of us.

"I'm pregnant," Wren blurted out.

She just happened to say it right as I was taking a large sip of the martini she had ordered for me. So instead of letting the smooth liquid slide down my throat, it felt like it turned solid, and I choked and spluttered it everywhere.

It took a few minutes to get myself under control and to wipe up the mess I'd made. I figured in that time that either Zoe or Yasmin might've had some kind of response, both of them were struck dumb. One of the best trial lawyers in the city—in the country if you asked me, but I might've been biased—and one of the most outspoken and eloquent women—make that *person*—I knew was speechless at the news our friend was *with child.*

Then again, the friend in question vowed that she would, "never reproduce when the world was already grossly overpopulated" and also admitted she, "loved her life too much to let a child ruin everything." I knew it was more than that. I knew that, as much as she adored her parents, she wanted to be nothing like them. Wren was raised mostly by nannies and sent away to boarding schools by age ten. It was the only way she knew, and she'd confessed to me that she would try her best to give her child a better life but would likely revert back to her parents' ways.

"The guilt would eat me alive," she admitted the night we'd gotten drunk on very expensive red wine and decided to have a sleepover. "I'd fuck them up. I know I would. I would try my best, and I'd fuck them up. And then my life would be miserable. I don't want a miserable life. I want a fabulous one."

"Someone has to say something," she snapped, glaring at all of us. "Because I cannot drink to calm my nerves." She was eyeing my martini longingly.

"Honey, this is ... great?" Yasmin tried to make it sound like a statement, but her voice went up at the end because Wren's fury was kind of scary and not at all indictive of this news being happy.

"It's great if you *want* it to be great," Zoe amended.

"Right," I agreed. "If you don't want it to be great, if you don't want it, then that's okay, too, babe. It's your body."

Yasmin nodded soberly, and I reached out to squeeze her hand, knowing that she'd had to make that terrible, life altering decision five years ago when she was still struggling in her job and had a one-night stand with a man who would not be there for her. She still labored over that decision.

"Of course I fucking want it," Wren practically shrieked, throwing up her hands. "I love the man and his stupid super sperm that apparently are resistant to birth control."

"You were on birth control?" I queried, my stomach swirling with something I didn't like.

Wren's eyes went wide. "Of course I was on birth control. All the sex I was having? You've gotta be on three different kinds with Jay, I bet."

It was offhand, a joke from my somewhat hysterical friend. *Pregnant friend.*

But it hit true.

Luckily, no one was waiting for me to answer that in the face of Wren's news.

"Wait," Yasmin chimed in, holding up her hand. "You love him?"

Wren narrowed her eyes. "Yes, I love him. Of course I love him. Have you *seen* the man? He's the only one who can go head to head with me without flinching. He fucks like a stallion, he never gets boring and he's got all of these delicious and dark corners to explore." She scowled. "What has become of me? I'm pregnant and in love before thirty. This is not what I wanted from my life. I was meant to be the eccentric, wealthy aunt to all of your brood, buying them booze and sleeping with their friends." She glanced around the table. "And I can't even *drink*!"

"Don't worry, I'll do the drinking for you," I quipped, holding up my martini.

It came out as a joke as we toasted to Wren, but I gulped it quickly, trying to salve the burn at the back of my throat, trying to fill the pit at the bottom of my stomach.

Jay was in his office at Klutch. He'd called me to let me know this and to tell me the VIP room was open for me and the girls.

"And you'll come up to my office when you're done so I can eat your pussy then fuck you against the glass," he added.

A blush had crept up my neck as I mumbled an agreement. Wren, of course, had caught the blush and then winked at me with a sly smile.

We didn't go to the VIP area because Wren got morning sickness at night, and Yasmin was going to hang out with her at her place ... along with Phillipe, of course. Zoe had a party to go to for work. We'd all parted with hugs, congratulations and plans to go shopping for 'therapy' the next day.

As much as it made me a horrible person, I was glad I didn't have to hang out with my friends for the rest of the night.

Unlike what normally happened, my body did not relax as I stepped off the elevator and walked into Jay's office at Klutch. Instead, I found myself feeling more uneasy.

As he always did, Jay noticed that something off with me the second my heels began to click on the hardwood floor.

"Come here," he demanded instead of asking me what was

wrong.

I did as I was told, moving slower than I would've under normal circumstances, and in normal circumstances, I would've damn near sprinted onto his lap. Jay noticed this, too, his eyes following my entire journey.

As soon as I was within touching distance, Jay grabbed me by the wrist and dragged me onto his lap. One arm circled my hip while the other moved in between my thighs, brushing the edge of my panties.

Despite everything that was going on, my body tingled with need for him to move his fingers from the outside to the inside of my panties. He didn't do that, though. Because he sensed it, the unease that was radiating off me, that was likely forming in a pinch just between my eyebrows.

"Wren's pregnant." My voice sounded weird and echoey in my own ears.

"I know," Jay replied.

I stared at him. "You *know?*" I repeated.

"Karson spoke to me." Wanted to make sure that we'd have extra cover on her now."

I gritted my teeth. "Of course he told you. Not because he's your *best friend* or anything, but because you had to discuss protecting her from *the Russian Mob.*" I couldn't contain the bitterness in my tone. The bitterness that had been brewing since dinner tonight.

It did not mix with martinis.

Jay didn't respond to this considering there wasn't much to say to my snarky tone. As silence descended between us, I moved my gaze from Jay to the writhing bodies on the dance floor below, thinking about how, a lifetime ago, I was just another writhing body unaware that Jay even existed. It was almost impossible to imagine there was a time when Jay hadn't existed in my life.

He seemed unhappy with me looking out on the dance floor, contemplating the past, because he took my chin between his thumb and forefinger and forced me to look at him once more.

In his eyes was a silent demand for more. For everything that was eating at me. And I was not one to refuse Jay.

"We haven't talked about kids," I searched his irises for a response. "Not since New Zealand. And I'm not on birth control. And I know that it's terrible of me to be thinking of myself in the midst of Wren's news, but I can't help it. I want kids. Maybe not now, but I need to know that you still want them. And I know that you have a lot going on right now, with the Russian Mob and all that." I waved my hand dismissively.

"So maybe you're not thinking about kids or you're not thinking about the fact that we've been having a lot of sex without birth control, but *I'm* thinking about it," I babbled. "Thinking both about what your feelings would be if I did get pregnant and then worrying that we've been having a lot of sex, yet I'm not pregnant. What if I'm barren? And I know that probably wouldn't be a big deal for you since you never even wanted kids in the first place, but it is a big deal for me."

I sucked in a huge breath, realizing I'd just dumped about three months' worth of worries on to Jay's shoulders. As if he didn't have enough to think about, as if we weren't meant to be easing in to the whole 'kids' thing, and I was supposed to be trying to play it cool. This totally wasn't cool.

Instead of pushing me off his lap, declaring me insane and calling off the wedding, the corners of Jay's mouth turned up, and he pulled me in to kiss me. Thoroughly.

I kissed him back. Thoroughly.

His fingers were on the insides of my panties when we were done, and I'd almost completely forgotten what we were talking about.

Almost.

On top of that, Jay was looking almost amused— turned on, too, but mostly amused. Then I remembered everything I'd just spilled and got pissed off.

"You find everything I just said *funny*?" I barked, trying to get off his lap, but his hand—the one that was not in my panties, stopped me.

"No, I do not find it funny," Jay retorted, his voice a velvet caress that did not soothe my frayed nerves.

His finger entered me, and I gritted my teeth in pleasure.

"I was just recalling the last time we were in this office and you spoke for that long without taking a breath," he explained, mouth against my neck. He put another finger inside of me, and my hand clenched onto his forearm.

"The time I thought you were going to kill me, you mean?" I asked, my voice breathy.

"The very same." He grazed my skin with his teeth, his fingers moving slowly inside of me. "It was what made me fall in love with you then, Stella. From that moment, I knew I'd move heaven and earth to make you mine. That I'd rip apart my life to make room for you to fit in it." He made the come-hither motion with his finger, the magic gesture that caused me to hiss harshly, moments from climax.

Jay stopped moving his fingers suddenly. "I've noticed you're not on birth control, pet. Noticed that you're not pregnant, too, since your body works like clockwork. It's only been six months, though, Stella. Six months full of change, of stress." He moved his finger slightly, and I groaned in pleasure. "Nothing is wrong with you, Stella. Everything about you is perfect. And when the time comes when your body isn't like clockwork, when we make something together, I'll be happy." He pressed his lips softly to mine.

"But what if we can't?" I whispered a fear that had simmered and grown these past months.

"Then, Stella, I'll move heaven and earth to make sure you get a baby," he promised against my neck, goosebumps peppering my skin. "For now, how about we practice making one? Because what I'm doing now isn't how it's done." He moved his fingers out of me, lifting them to his lips, and while keeping his eyes on mine, tasted them.

After that, he fucked me against the glass.

CHAPTER TWELVE

THREE MONTHS LATER

I woke up to Jay's mouth in between my legs on our wedding day. Wren had tried her level best to steal me away, had even booked a suite at the Waldorf Astoria for all of us. Jay had let Wren run wild on this wedding. Maybe because he was so busy. He had been distracted these past few months, tensions with his businesses. With people trying to encroach on his territory. We'd gone to Mexico last week so he could make a deal with some Mexican drug cartel. I'd asked to know it all, to be rid of the secrets, so I'd gotten it all.

I'd been pretty overwhelmed, not to mention busier than I'd ever been at work. Jay had forced me to hire an assistant, threatening to pay for it myself if I didn't. He didn't like the longer hours, the less time we spent together, the way I was running myself ragged. I didn't much like it either. I'd grudgingly held interviews, found Joseph. There had been a ton of applicants, my name having gotten rather well-known lately. I couldn't have fathomed the heights my career would reach, hadn't known how to handle everything.

Which was where Jay stepped in. He had spent an entire weekend in my office—the one he'd had renovated right beside his—going over my accounts and settling all kinds of tax and finance crap.

It had taken all weekend because I was irresponsible and had not kept organized accounts. Also because Jay was dedicated to christening every single surface in my office, which it turned out, there were many.

Jay continued to surprise and amaze me. I'd known he was intelligent; you didn't go from the streets to where he was without smarts. But he was also patient, calm and non-judgmental, speaking in soft tones, in layman's terms.

When the call went out for the assistant job, I had applicants from all the Ivy League schools, from Parsons, all with impressive resumes. But Joseph, the high school dropout wearing a vintage Tom Ford suit with sneakers and a tee underneath, caught my attention. He was quick witted, stylish and knew a lot about fashion. He had big goals, and I knew that not a lot of people would give him a chance, and if they did, he'd be working crap jobs for crap pay. Thanks to Jay, I wasn't paying any rent, barely buying any of my clothes, and thanks to myself, I was earning more than ever. Jay had me incorporated, so I was even able to offer Joseph full benefits.

I'd still been busy leading up to the wedding, and luckily, the only thing I'd really had to do was be there for the fittings. Wren had taken care of everything else. She'd tried to take care of the bill, the only other thing she'd gone head to head with Jay with. But just like getting me to the suite at the Astoria, she didn't get her way.

She'd muttered about buying us a jet or an island as a wedding present. I'd smiled, and Jay had ignored her. Karson, who was almost always present when Wren was around, displayed a little mouth twitch that was his version of a smile.

She'd also muttered about bad luck, seeing the bride on the wedding day. Jay had held firm and murmured later in my ear, "your luck was bad enough, crossing paths with me. I think we're due for a break."

That had irked me, but I'd let it slide, reminding myself that I had a lifetime to prove to Jay that he was the best thing that had ever happened to me.

And then there was his mouth in between my legs on our wedding day. His mouth, hungry, ravenous, knowing exactly how to make my toes curl, how to make me to try to rip apart the thousand thread count sheets.

"How are your feet?" I asked breathlessly when he was done giving me two orgasms on our wedding day.

Jay's finger moved around my nipple lazily. "My feet?" he repeated.

"Getting cold? You're not rethinking this whole marriage thing?"

I'd spoken in a lighthearted tone, but his face turned heavy, serious.

"Stella, I know I will not be able to erase what I did to you from your memory, I certainly can't tear it from mine." He brushed a hair from my face. "But I'm not leaving you. No matter fucking what. If

I could walk you down the aisle myself, I would. But I'll settle for standing at the end of it, waiting for you."

I blinked away the tears prompted by his tone, the intensity thrumming through it. "Okay," I whispered, not knowing how I was going to tear myself away from him to get ready for the wedding.

But Wren took care of that about five minutes later, banging on the door, shouting that she would come in and drag me out herself if I didn't get my ass up and into her car.

One did not fight with a pregnant and hormonal Wren. So I got up. And I trusted that Jay would be waiting to marry me in a few hours.

I smoothed my hands over the bodice of my dress, taking a deep breath as I looked at myself in the mirror.

The white gown was beautiful. One of a kind. Made for me. Custom Vera Wang. *Custom fucking Vera Wang.* The silk fit like a second skin, the straps crossing over at my neck, the entire back down to just above my ass bare, draping to perfection. It skimmed over every single one of my curves, and the train was long behind me. I'd always thought I'd want something more detailed. Lace imported from Italy. Intricate sleeves. Okay, pretty much Grace Kelly's dress. But the simplicity of this dress was beyond perfect for me. My hair was piled up in a messy bun, ringlets escaping here and there, showing off the teardrop diamond earrings that Jay had presented to me this morning.

I was wearing my diamond tennis bracelet and my engagement

ring, nothing else.

"Honey," my dad's voice broke. I felt it in the bottom of my stomach, that crack in my father's voice. Tears shimmered in his eyes then trailed down his cheeks. I bit the inside of my lip in order to attempt to stop my own from falling.

"Dad," I whispered, blinking rapidly at my handsome father wearing a bespoke black suit. He was freshly shaved, his salt and pepper hair slicked back to expose his slightly creased face. Still handsome. I had hope that he found a second act somewhere. A love that he found comfort in, a woman to take care of him, to retire with.

He cleared his throat loudly, wiping his tears with the back of his hands. "If there's a day a father can shed a tear in front of his child, it's the day that child, that woman, is standing in front of him looking more beautiful than she ever has." He moved forward to grasp my hands. "And happier than I've ever seen her," he added quietly, wiping away one of my rogue tears with his thumb.

"I really am," I replied honestly. Even with all the security that I knew were lurking around the perimeter of the party. Even though Jay had wound himself tighter and tighter these last two months. Karson, too, Wren complaining about how overprotective he was now that she was pregnant.

I was not complaining about that. The danger was real, I believed Jay about that, and I'd rather my friend, who I loved dearly, complained about being over protected instead of something, anything happening to her and the baby. The mere thought of it made me sick.

I'd never thought that on my wedding day I'd be worrying about the Russian Mob and my pregnant friend, but I was the one who had wanted to change my story.

"I know your mom would've been good with this," Dad added, unaware of the whole 'Russian Mob' thing. My dad was unaware of every facet of Jay's criminal life. I knew he wasn't one hundred percent convinced, no way my dad was that naïve, but he didn't know everything. Because if he'd known everything, he wouldn't be standing here with tears of happiness in his eyes.

"She would've loved this," he continued. "She loved you, sweetie. So much. More than life." He reached into his jacket as I struggled with my feelings about my mother.

I'd been struggling with them all day. Wondering what this day might've been like if she was alive. Would she be surly, vacant and medicated? Vibrant, warm, loving? Or someone else entirely?

I had Janet. Yeah, she flew all the way in from New Zealand for the wedding. She'd brought a good amount of wine, too, as a wedding present. Wine that we'd cracked open earlier with Zoe, Yasmin and Wren, while Wren moaned that she couldn't have any of it. Wren who, unsurprisingly, became fast friends with Janet.

Yes, I had my warm, slightly crazy and wonderful friend from New Zealand, I had my best girlfriends, and I had my dad, but I did not have my mother. Although her absence had pretty much been the norm for a large part of my life, it never felt more yawning than it did today.

"She would've handled this stuff better than me," Dad told me as he unwrapped something he had in a handkerchief. "I know there's something about blue, old, borrowed and new. I fucked up on the borrowed and new." He held open his hand. "But I've got something borrowed. Blue. Your mom wore this on our wedding day."

I looked down at my father's callused hand. On top of the handkerchief was an ornate hair comb. Silver with tiny, ornate flowers—daisies—glittering with diamonds and sapphires.

Dad cleared his throat. "You don't have to wear it," he stated quickly. "In case you think it's bad luck after what happened with your mom, or if it doesn't go with your dress—"

"Dad," I interrupted, putting my hand on the hair comb. "It's perfect." My voice broke slightly.

"Will you put it in for me?" I asked him, voice small.

Dad looked vaguely panicked. "I'm scared I'll mess up your hair Wren will do me, 'prison style' like I overheard her threatening her boyfriend for almost knocking over a candle earlier."

I laughed at the very serious tone to my father's voice. "Don't worry, I'll protect you. Wren wouldn't dare hurt the bride on her wedding day. It would ruin the aesthetic."

"I don't know what that means, but okay," Dad chuckled.

I turned, and my father gently slid the clip into my hair.

"You're going to have a wonderful life, sweetie," he whispered.

And because he was my dad and because the day already felt perfect, I believed him.

Jay

He should leave.

Should walk out of this place, get in a car, then on a plane and leave.

Without Stella.

Sure, it would break her. Shatter her. But she'd still be alive, breathing, albeit in pieces. Though Wren had outdone herself at making this wedding in to something spectacular, something worthy of Stella, Jay reckoned neither of them had imagined having various men with semiautomatic weapons patrolling the area to make sure no one came in armed, planning to kill the bride solely for marrying him.

Then there would be the bomb experts he'd had come in to check the place for explosives and weak spots. Everyone working the party had had to be vetted, thoroughly. Then searched for weapons.

Yes, if Stella was marrying some square jawed, all-American who worked in an office nine to five and had a semi regular upbringing with two parents who would eventually divorce and a golden retriever who would eventually die, she wouldn't have to worry about someone killing her on her wedding day.

Of course *Stella* wasn't worrying about someone killing her on her wedding day. She was far too innocent for that thought to even cross her mind. She was smart, Stella. Jay knew she understood his business, understood that he wouldn't be going so far as to have a full-time bodyguard on her if the threat wasn't real.

Stella also lived in a world where things like getting murdered by the Mob on her wedding day was a plot to a movie, not an actual, possible scenario. She trusted Jay with her life. Just by going through with this, by wearing his fucking ring, by taking his fucking name, she was trusting him with her life.

So he should've left. Because it was sick, and it was fucked up. Because Jay would be fucking ruined if something ever did happen to her on his watch. Because Stella deserved better.

But instead of walking out the door, he buttoned his jacket. He took a drink of the whisky he'd poured for himself and Richard when he'd come in for the obligatory father of the bride speech. Though he'd gone much easier on Jay than he deserved. There had been thinly veiled threats that Jay knew that Richard would make good on if he hurt his daughter. Richard loved that girl more than anything in the world, and Jay couldn't imagine it was easy to be watching someone like Jay take her in to a life that wasn't meant for her.

Richard didn't know the specifics of his life, but Jay knew the man wasn't stupid. In fact, he'd proven how wise he was when he'd come out on the balcony at dinner two nights ago, drink in hand.

"I'm not exactly a worldly man," he'd said, looking out at the ocean. "I live a simple life. But I've always know that Stella was never destined for more, that Stella would never settle for less than extraordinary. She's one of a kind, Jay, and I knew that a regular man would never be able to handle her. Never begin to appreciate her or deserve her." He'd drained his drink, looking at Jay. "And you deserve her, purely because you're convinced you don't. Because you'll work harder than any man to give her that extraordinary life. And I'm not talking about all this." Richard had waved at the house dismissively. "I'm talking about the extraordinary. I see it in her eyes. Which is why I'm looking the other way about the way you make your living. And because I know you'd do anything, hurt anyone, to protect my girl."

Richard was not a stupid man. No, he was a man who loved his daughter immensely and wouldn't hesitate to kill Jay if he fucked this up, if Stella got hurt because of him.

Draining his drink, Jay was almost ready to do one more sweep of the perimeter, check with Karson for threats and then wait for his bride when there was a knock at the door.

He'd expected it to be Karson, but he fingered the gun he was wearing underneath his suit just in case. It was not Karson, nor was it anyone he needed to use his gun on. Though it was someone Jay knew would like him out of the picture.

"Can we talk?" Zoe asked, walking into the room before he could answer.

Her black dress trailed behind her. She was not wearing it as some kind of statement, a glaring symbol of her disapproval, it was part of the 'theme.'

Black and white. Light and darkness.

Fucking Wren.

Zoe was pouring herself a drink by the time Jay closed the door behind her and turned. She was a striking woman. Beautiful, to be sure. But fierce. A woman Jay would not want to cross. Though to be fair, he would not want to cross any of Stella's friends. All of them were formidable women.

Zoe liked him the least, he knew that. Jay was good at reading people, but that was not how he knew. She'd made no efforts to hide her reservations about him, which Jay appreciated. He liked honesty and liked that Stella had a friend shrewd enough to see him for what he was.

"You're still here," she remarked.

Jay's expression didn't change. "You expected me not to be?"

She shrugged. "I expected you may have some last minute,

pretend, noble thoughts of leaving her for her own good."

Yes, this bitch was shrewd.

"I'm not going anywhere," Jay proclaimed, his words an oath.

Zoe nodded. "You'd better not. You've hurt her once, left her once. That was the only time you're going to do that. Because she's committed to you. She's like a mother fucking penguin. She mates for life. You leave, no matter what you think, there will be no one else. You may sell her short for your own piece of mind, think she'll find someone else, someone safer and be better off, but that's not how Stella works. There will be no one else."

"There sure as fuck isn't going to be anyone else," Jay replied coolly.

Zoe nodded, oblivious to the tone that had made lesser men almost piss their pants. "That was the first reason I came in here."

She took a sip of her drink, slowly, unhurried, in a way that told Jay she was making sure that he knew that she was not intimidated by him and was comfortable taking control of a situation. "I don't know the specifics of what you're into," she continued. "What your 'other' job looks like. 'Cause I'm not stupid or suicidal, which you've gotta be if you start lookin' too close at Jay Helmick. But I know that's why there are men in expensive suits packing heat, walking around this party. And I don't give a shit why they're here, as long as they're keeping Stella safe."

She put down her drink and narrowed her eyes at him. "As long as *you're* keeping Stella safe. You continue to do so, keep Stella safe and happy, we won't have problems. We're not likely to be friends because I don't forgive easy and because I see you for what you are, but we won't have problems. Anything happens to her, we will have problems."

On that note, Zoe walked out the door.

That bitch knew how to make an entrance and an exit. She also knew how to deliver a threat because Jay didn't go anywhere. Not that he was planning to in the first place.

But mostly because he loved Stella. Loved her more than he hated himself.

Stella

"You ready, honey?"

My father held out his arm for me. Soft music was playing out of the open door that Wren, Zoe and Yasmin had just left out of. There had been kisses, hand squeezing, murmurs about how stunning I looked and talk of getaway jets being fueled and ready to go if needed. That was obviously Wren, though Zoe likely would've attempted to *fly* the jet herself if I'd even hinted at having cold feet.

Wren was three months pregnant and looked amazing. Her slinky, bias cut, floor length dress skimmed over her new curves, and her boobs looked beyond good. without even the smallest swell in her lower stomach and her skin glowing radiantly, I swear the bitch was showing me up on my wedding day without even trying.

But I guessed I looked pretty darn good too.

"I'm ready," I nodded, taking my father's hand and smiling. He held me tight, his eyes glassy. We walked slowly out of the room I'd been getting ready in ... the only room I'd been able to see upon arrival.

Wren had actually put a blindfold on me when we drove up, joking that she was sure it wasn't my first time, what with Jay and all.

Heat had crept up my cheeks, and that had got her going even more. "Oh, my God. You still have the ability to be a blushing bride. Jay may be more vanilla than he seems."

I'd raised my brow at her. "Trust me, he is nowhere near vanilla."

It had gone without saying that we weren't going to be married in a church. Apart from that, the both of us had given her free reign when she'd made it very clear that she did not want either of us to be part of the planning process.

Walking in with my father, I gasped. Like a literal, dramatic, out loud gasp that I didn't think people did in real life unless Jay was fucking them. We left a hallway decorated with vases of wildflowers and freestanding candles. Overhead, lanterns hung at different levels with more flowers around them. Harps and violins were playing as we neared the huge doors where a subtle ocean wind blew through.

Somehow, the magician that she was, Wren had understood the importance, the significance of a simple sea breeze on my wedding day.

Nothing else about the wedding day was simple, though.

There was a *harpist,* for fuck's sake.

Walking out onto the biggest balcony I'd ever seen, I stepped on an explosion of flowers that trailed down the aisle and adorned the seats everyone rose from to watch my entrance. And it looked every single flower that existed was included, they were all white.

I didn't see the guests. Barely saw all the work that my incredible, kind and talented friend had done. I only saw the man at the end of the aisle. Wearing all black. His expression wasn't guarded. Wasn't cold. He was not the Jay I'd met. Not the Jay that he presented to the world. His lips were parted ever so slightly, his face soft, without any of the hard edges. He wore his love for me—his adoration—as well as he wore a Tom Ford suit.

Utterly stark and sinful against the white arch that seemed to crown him with a calm sea and a cloudless sky in the background.

My world tilted utterly and completely in that moment. So much so that I actually stopped walking. Right there in the middle of the aisle. With everyone watching me.

With *Jay* watching me.

"Uh, Stella, honey?" my dad leaned in and whispered. "I support your decision to change your mind, but people are staring. Are we going to keep going or leaving?"

I didn't take my eyes off Jay. "We're not leaving," I whispered back, not quite as quietly. "I just need to ... remember this moment."

Once I'd committed every detail to memory, I resumed walking. I would've sprinted if I'd thought my Dad would keep up with me. Instead, I settled for a brisk walk, never taking my eyes off Jay.

I was shaking by the time we reached him, standing like glorious marble in his suit. But marble he was not. Nor a monster. He was a man. One who bled, breathed and *cried*.

Which was what he did when my father handed me over to him. It was a single tear, but it may as well have been as tsunami.

His hands framed my face, holding me as if it were just the two of us, as though the world had only ever housed two people. He didn't whisper anything, didn't speak of how much he loved me or how beautiful I was. No, he just held my face in his hands and *stared*.

In a way unlike he'd ever looked at me before, and that was saying something considering Jay had a fucking PhD in intense, brooding stares. My insides jumped and moved, and my world tilted all over again.

Eventually, he let go of my face and took my hands.

I did not hear a word that the officiant said. Not a single one. I must have participated since we were married at the end, but I hadn't comprehended what I was saying beyond knowing that I was binding myself to Jay.

There was one line that stuck out.

"Till death."

Wren decided on taking out the 'do us part' bit of that since she'd decided even death wasn't bad or wicked enough to go up against Jay.

Till death it was. And beyond that.

Then there was the kiss. The kiss that was definitely not intended for public consumption. There might have been applause, I wasn't sure. Because I was Jay's wife.

Till death.

"We shouldn't be doing this," I breathed.

"You're my wife, it's my job to be doing this," Jay replied, his voice thick, my dress bunched in his fist. My *custom Vera Wang* bunched in his fist. Something that might've bothered me if Jay wasn't currently fucking me against the wall in one of the rooms of the house Wren had rented—well, hopefully rented and not bought—for the wedding. Not even in one of the rooms far away from our wedding reception. Apparently, Jay hadn't wanted to take an extra minute to gain some distance when he all but dragged me off after we were pronounced man and wife.

Man and wife.

Which was why I hadn't protested to him dragging me off, bunching up my Vera Wang and making me come loudly with all of my friends and family drinking champagne on the other side of the wall.

Jay's eyes were glued to mine, radiant intensity pouring out of them.

I clenched my hands against the lapels of his suit as my orgasm rushed over me.

"Don't you dare close your fucking eyes," he demanded the second I started to squeeze my eyes shut.

I kept my eyes open, watching as he lost himself inside of me.

"If I could've said my vows with my cock inside of you, I would've," he murmured, stroking my face.

"I think that would've made for an interesting wedding video," I snickered.

Jay didn't laugh, of course. He was too busy doing his intense, heart breaking, panty melting thing.

"I don't worship, don't believe there is a higher power, and if there is, I know I'm damned." His voice was rough against my skin, against my heart. "But you, your pussy clenching around me, that's my church. That's my fucking place of worship."

Then he kissed me.

Then, the world ceased to exist.

Eventually, he pulled out of me, set me down on an armchair while he went to the adjoining bathroom to get a washcloth. He cleaned me efficiently, gently, slowly, causing me to quiver every time the washcloth moved over me.

Somehow, magically, my dress got nary a stain. It was the magic of Vera. It was the magic of being man and wife.

Till death.

It was while I was straightening Jay's suit, I found it.

"What's this?" I wondered out loud, moving my hands around Jay's torso, brushing against something cold, hard and foreign.

Jay grabbed my wrists and pulled them back.

I glared at him and pushed his suit back to see the holster he was wearing, the kind they wore in movies, except this was very fucking real.

"You're wearing a *gun* on our *wedding day*?" I questioned, my voice low.

"Yes, Stella, I'm wearing a gun on our wedding day," he replied coldly. There was a challenge in his tone. Not an ounce of apology.

He was daring me to say more, to talk about the absurdity of the groom being armed on his wedding day. On our wedding day.

Why hadn't I expected this? I'd gone in knowing everything, the guns, the streets, the Russian fucking Mob. This was the most important day of our lives, the most special. It was pretty important that the both of us remained alive, and Jay would do anything to keep my safe. Including reciting his vows with a gun strapped to his body.

I leaned in to kiss him, tilting my head up, laying my lips on his gently at first then more passionately. He responded hungrily, despite what we'd just done. He kissed me back like we hadn't seen each other in years.

We stopped, eventually, even though I would've been happy to drown in that kiss. "We should get to our reception," I grumbled, my hands smoothing down his lapels.

Jay's eyes were green stones. "If that's what my bride wants," he conceded in a hoarse voice.

"What I want is a bed, you and to be out of this dress," I whispered. Jay's hands flexed at my hips. "But," I continued, "Wren will straight up murder us, even with your gun, if we ditched her 'reception that will make the royal family call me to plan all their future wedding, which of course I'd never fucking do after what they did to Meghan,'" I said with a pretty spot-on Wren impersonation if I did say so myself.

Jay's face was blank. "Yeah, I'm not sure I could take her on," he responded dryly.

I beamed at him, happiness spreading to my fingertips. "Later?"

His hand settled around my neck. "Later, my bride, I'll be making sure to corrupt you so much that you'll never wear white again," he murmured.

His tone and his eyes almost made me brave enough to go head to head with Wren.

Almost.

Jay moved his hand from my neck down to my hand, holding

it in a death grip, pulling me from the wall and across the room. We joined our guests, emerging during cocktail hour. A cocktail hour that almost exactly mimicked my twenty-ninth birthday party. The one Jay hadn't attended. The large room looked like nothing other than a fairy meadow. There were mini oak trees with doors inside of them scattered around the exterior of the room. Waiters and waitresses wore the wings that Wren had had made for my birthday. Wildflowers were scattered across the floor. Another fucking harpist. It was so serene, so peaceful—for about a second.

"*You!*" Wren attacked me the second Jay and I entered the reception area. "Let her go," Wren demanded, nodding to Jay's hands which were intertwined with mine.

Jay gave her an even look that communicated 'no fucking way' and contained healthy amounts of his signature, scary, badass stare.

Wren did not even blink. "You want to take me on, buddy?" she challenged. "All the hormones coursing through my body, in addition to ... just being me, I'd fucking ruin you." Hands on her hips, she leaned ever so slightly forward to communicate that she was not fucking around.

Jay let me go. But not before yanking me to his body and kissing the ever-loving shit out of me.

"We get it, you love her with a furious intensity," Wren griped, snatching my hand and dragging me away.

I was in somewhat of a daze when I found myself standing at the edge of the balcony, looking across at the ocean with my three best friends. Zoe was even doing her best to look like she was happy for me.

"What's this?" I asked, using every ounce of my willpower not to look back to see what my husband was doing.

I was a bad friend. A very, very bad friend. I adored these women more than anything.

"We're toasting to the first of us to be married," Wren raised her glass nodding to me. "He's a great first husband," she deadpanned.

I rolled my eyes.

"Joking!" she continued, holding up her glass. "But seriously. You did good, kid. I only did slightly," she held her thumb and finger together, "better." She winked. "To saucy sex arrangements turning in to love, a breakup then a beautiful reunion on the other side of the world."

"To that," I agreed, clinking my glass with each of them.

Wren had barely got the glass to her lips before a large hand snatched the crystal flute from her grasp.

"No fucking wine," Karson snapped.

I gaped at him. I was sure the last time I'd seen him, he'd been across the room. *Way* across the room. I only knew that because he'd been standing beside Jay, both of them watching our little huddle.

Jay was now watching this little huddle with the slightest twitch to his lips.

Wren's face changed so quickly, the three of us took a collective step back.

"Do you know what kind of bad luck it is to not drink after a toast?" Wren asked slowly, staring at Karson.

"Do you know how little I give a fuck?" Karson fired back in a clipped tone.

"How much of a fuck do you give about that pretty face of yours?" Wren smiled sweetly, tilting her head.

"Threaten me all you like," Karson shot back.

"Who said anything about threats?" Wren stepped forward in a way a small woman in a ball gown shouldn't have been able to. But she managed to make the motion as threatening as if a six-foot, muscular man had done it.

Karson, for his part, looked just as threatening.

The standoff was long and tense. None of us were able to look away.

Finally, Wren cursed under her breath and stormed off. Then she whirled halfway through her storm and crooked her finger at Karson. And fuck if that man didn't go running.

After all of that happened, I went back, back to Jay.

Till death.

CHAPTER THIRTEEN

"Are you going to tell me where we're going?" I asked sleepily.

We were naked. In bed. On a *jet*.

I didn't even know that people who weren't presidents or Kardashians flew in jets that had bedrooms inside of them.

Jay spirited me off in the middle of the reception, forgoing the traditional goodbyes with the throwing of the rice and the crowds. I was happy for it. As much as I loved being around all of my closest friends, celebrating our marriage, I had been greedy for Jay the entire evening. He'd been by my side the entire time, always touching me, always watching, barely engaging in conversation with those around him. Only I existed.

And as hard as I'd tried to join in with my friends, my dad, everyone at the wedding, only Jay existed for me too. Though I did not miss the way my father had lingered around Janet. That would've been something I would've focused on a lot more had my husband not purred in my ear about being hungry for my pussy.

"Do you care where we're going?" he asked, hand moving over my bare ass. The one he'd spanked then fucked. My entire body thrummed with exertion, muscles little more than jelly.

I thought about that. "Not at all, as long as I'm with you. Though you didn't have to spirit me away on some fancy jet. We could've just stayed at home for a week."

Jay cocked a brow ever so slightly. "No, we couldn't have. For the first week that you're my wife, I'm going to fuck you in a foreign country, barely let you leave bed and make sure you wear as little clothing as possible." His lips fastened over my nipple. "And I will have none of the shit lurking in L.A. even touching us."

A spike of panic shot through me.

"Is stuff in L.A. going to touch us?" I asked. Darkness and worry crept in at the edges of my perfect day. My perfect wedding.

"Nothing is going to touch you," Jay declared, flipping me so I was flat on my back, naked and thirty thousand feet in the ear. "Except me." Then he buried his head between my legs.

I learned a lot of things about Jay the first week of our honeymoon. He could speak fluent Italian, for example.

Which helped immensely considering we spent our honeymoon in Italy, one of the best countries in the world, in my humble opinion. I could do all the important things in Italian, order coffee, wine and ask where the nearest Prada store was, but I could not speak like Jay.

I was of the opinion that even the *Italians* could not speak like Jay. My *husband*. Every word flowed out of him like poetry, unhurried, lyrical and utterly sexual. And it was not just me who thought that. The woman who checked us in at our hotel in Lake Como was practically drooling despite the large diamond on my finger, attached to the arm that was wrapped around him. Despite the wedding ring on his finger and the fact that his lips were on my neck whenever he wasn't speaking to her.

The green monster reared its ugly head for a hot minute. That was until we were spirited away to our suite in Villa d'Este, one of the most opulent and romantic hotels in Lake Como, perched on the water's edge at Cernobbio.

The suite was sprawling with a huge sitting and living room, and a four-poster bed that could easily fit five people. Everything decorated in rich fabrics, chandeliers in every room, a balcony spanning along the entire suite with views of the lake. The lake had great views of us, too, since we got ample use out of the balcony. And the bed. And every other room in the suite, even though we were only there for two days.

I'm sure Lake Como was lovely, or it would've been if we'd left our room.

Venice was similar. Exquisite suite, stunning views, excellent food, more of Jay speaking Italian. We did leave the room, once, to have dinner on the canals, with music echoing across the water, tourists ambling past and wine flowing freely. As much as it was like something out of a movie, I was counting down the moments until we were back in our room. Jay's eyes and his hand on my bare thigh told me he felt the same.

We did not make it to the room that night, we barely made it to the darkened corner of one of Venice's many narrow alleys, Jay pushing me up against the wall, tearing at my underwear and taking me with people walking past mere feet away.

Then there was a short trip to Morocco.

Morocco.

To drink tea.

Because he was Jay. Because he remembered.

"I still have to see a sunset in Bali. Drink tea in Morocco. Climb a mountain in New Zealand. Do something for humanity that isn't just helping keep ateliers in Paris in business."

The first night we met. When I'd been sure he was going to kill me. When I'd blurted out all the things I'd wanted to do before I died. Tea in Morocco. The balmy breeze, the crowded alleys in the Medina. Street vendors calling out. Flaky Pastilla. My husband, sitting across from me, watching me in that way of his, sipping his tea lazily. It was tempting to ask to stay in the loud, colorful, hot and beautiful city of Marrakech for longer. To explore every corner of the Media. Buy rugs and lamps. But Jay promised we'd be back, in time. Time was what we had. Forever. So I let him spirit me back to Italy.

To Portofino.

A town perched on the rugged coastline of Italy, glittering waters stretching toward the horizon, yachts sitting in the bay looking like children's toys from great heights. We breakfasted on the terrace of our own private villa, me wearing only a tiny white string bikini—Jay had presented me with twenty new ones, varying shades of white, varying degrees of tiny—and Jay in an unbuttoned linen shirt and white linen shorts. His tanned, muscled chest was the most impressive sight, even compared to the town that graced many postcards and prints.

The air was different here, not just on the coast of Italy but between us. Nothing thickened it, apart from the unfailing desire, the hunger that we never got to sate no matter how many times he took me, how many ways. There was always the need for more.

But there was nothing else that we needed. No other pressing matters. No work. No demands from the shadows of Jay's job. No Russian Mob. No discussions about any of those things. There was just us.

I wouldn't say the magic of New Zealand was replicated, but this trip created a whole new kind of magic.

The waters of Portofino were a thousand shades of blue. Azure, turquoise, cobalt, sapphire. For as long as we'd been here, I hadn't seen them up close. Not that I was complaining, lounging about in our fabulous apartment, gazing upon them from afar, reading in my underwear, Jay's hands on my naked body while picking at fresh fruit and pastries barely clothed. No, I was not complaining in the slightest.

But Jay had proposed an outing this morning over espressos. Jay sitting on the balcony with the town of Portofino and the Italian coast behind him was not a sight that you said no to. Jay sitting in front of a plain white fucking wall was not a sight you could say no to.

I'd put on a white linen sundress with capped sleeves, buttons down the front and a tie at the waist. It hit me mid-calf, the laces of my canvas wedges snaking up my calves. I'd pinned my hair back in a claw clip, intending on putting on makeup. But then Jay had appeared behind me in the mirror, the skirt of my dress lifted to show the barely there white panties I was wearing, and well, we got busy.

I wasn't wearing any makeup on our outing, just large sunglasses and a glow from two orgasms. Jay's hand was threaded in mine as we walked down the dock. Somehow undeterred by the heat of the Italian summer, he was wearing all black. The sleeves of his linen shirt pressed up to his elbows, and his shorts showed off his muscular, lithe legs. I'd never thought legs were an attractive part of a man. But Jay's ... fuck. Especially when I knew those legs could hold my weight while holding me in the shower with his cock inside of me.

He was utter sin. And he was *mine*. People looked at us as we walked through the cobbled streets. I smiled at them, even the women shameless checking out my man. Because he didn't glance at anyone. No one existed but me.

Jay stopped to buy me a gelato because he knew I was borderline addicted to it here, and he loved to watch me eat it. He also liked to let it melt on my skin and lick it off me. I quite liked that too.

I didn't ask where we were going as I licked my gelato and clung to my husband. Why would I need to know?

Jay was not confused by the winding streets. He walked with purpose, as if he owned every single cobblestone we walked on. Soon we weren't walking on cobblestones, we were strolling down the wooden wharf that jutted out onto the ocean. The wharf wasn't busy at this time of day. Tourists were eating lunch, locals were sleeping or working. Only a few people milled about, some cleaning the boats— each more impressive than the last—some walking unhurriedly along the wharf just like us.

Then all of a sudden, we weren't walking. We stopped, almost at the end, where there were fewer boats because these were much, much larger.

"What are we doing?" I asked, taking in the vessels surrounding us.

In front of us was a large yacht. A very large yacht. It was black, sleek and seemed to dwarf every other boat anchored in the wharf. There were larger ones—the money in this single wharf was among the billions, I guessed. But something about this boat seemed larger, more imposing. It was a boat version of Jay.

"This is your wedding gift," Jay replied.

I turned to look at my husband, to gape at him. "My wedding gift?" I repeated.

Jay nodded.

"You got me a wedding gift," I reminded him. "A gorgeous pair of earrings that I could be sure were at the bottom of the ocean with the Titanic. This is not a wedding gift. This is a mini fucking cruise ship."

Jay's eyes twinkled more than the ocean before us. He grasped onto my hip and yanked my body to his, the other hand moving underneath my dress, in between my legs and right into my panties.

It was broad daylight, and we were not hidden, not in the least. Two people were meandering, looking at the boats, taking photos with their phones. Soon they would be close enough to see what was going on.

I did not stop my husband.

His finger moved inside of me, and I clutched onto his shirt.

"You have a choice, wife," he murmured, finger moving lazily. "You let the tourists get more than they bargained for." He nodded to the approaching people. "Then, of course, I'd have to kill them for gazing at the sight that is my wife coming around my fingers." He moved the aforementioned fingers, rubbing that incredibly sensitive place inside of me, and I would've collapsed if he wasn't holding me up. "Or," he continued, lips moving inches from mine. "You get on your boat and you let me feast on your pussy until you scream."

I sucked in an unsteady breath. "The second one."

He grinned wickedly.

Then he took me on board and ate my pussy until I screamed.

The boat—*my boat*, it even had Stella written on it in gold script—was even more opulent and as expensive than it had seemed on the outside. And it seemed pretty fucking opulent on the outside. The interior consisted of a full living room with plush sofas and armchairs, a wet bar, a kitchen and a bedroom suite.

Suite.

With a huge bed, chairs at the end, a balcony, a bathroom with a jacuzzi tub. There were three levels, more bedrooms, a study, various living and eating areas on deck, and a full sunbathing platform with pillows and a mattress.

It was unlike anything I'd ever seen.

And we were spending the rest of our honeymoon on it.

Sometime during Jay's feast, someone had delivered our things to the boat. Things that had been packed and ready since Jay had told me we'd be leaving this evening. Going home. I'd hid my disappointment poorly. Though I missed our home, my friends, the routine and life we'd built, I wasn't overly eager to return to it. Yes, our friends were there, my job, but so was Jay's. So were the realities of what was going on in his underworld. It had crept in to our bubble, tarnishing the golden edges, with me waking in the middle of the night to Jay staring out of a window, brows creased and jaw tense. With phone calls that Jay took in other rooms.

I knew that life would be much different when we returned. Something had been building before the wedding. Tension. Danger. Though I didn't know much, I knew well enough that the peace we were enjoying was wearing thin.

The fact that we were escaping to the Mediterranean was just fine with me.

"Just how much money do you have?" I blurted as we laid on the deck of Jay's yacht. Or what I guessed was my yacht now.

Jay looked at me over the top of his Ray Bans. Those and a pair of low hanging linen shorts were the only thing he was wearing. His skin was glossy from the sunscreen I'd put on him, his hair messy from me running my hands through it, and gaze relaxed since I'd had my lips around his cock not one hour ago. He'd reciprocated, of course. He always did.

We'd been soaking up the European sun quietly since then, the gentle splash of the water hitting the boat the only sound. Our captain—we had a freaking *captain*, along with staff—had found a secluded little cove two hours from Capri. We'd hung off the anchor for the night, and I for one, was in no hurry to get back on dry land.

"I know it's uncouth to ask such a question," I continued, moving up on my elbow and pushing my sunglasses to the top of my head. "But I figure, as your wife, I should have some sort of an idea. You can buy mini cruise ships and call them boats, fly us to Europe on a private jet, give me more shoes and purses than I know what to do with." I tilted my head. "And that, good sir, is no mean feat."

Jay's mouth lifted into what might be considered a smirk, but I classed it as a full-blown smile. "Let's put it this way... You'll be in clothes and shoes for the rest of your life."

It hit me then. Our life, my closet, our bed, our home, our future was bought with the money that Jay made off ... running the streets. Money that people had died for, killed for. My mind went to Diane, bleeding in our bathroom, talking about how much she liked *Love Actually*. People had been irreparably damaged by this business and I was sitting on a yacht in Italy as a result of it.

That should have bothered me a lot more than it did, that realization. Sure, I didn't love my husband's job, nor did I love that I needed a bodyguard, that he was in danger, that he believed that he was only worthy of existing in the dark world he'd created for himself.

But I'd gone in to this eyes wide open. I knew exactly who Jay was, and I'd fallen in love with that man.

"That isn't an answer," I objected. Something else hit me. "We didn't get a prenup."

The playful expression on Jay's face disappeared. "No, we did not."

"Why didn't we get a prenup?" I demanded. "You have *private jet money*! I make enough to *one day* buy a Birkin. That's pretty much it. You're a smart man. A very smart man. You should've made me sign a prenup."

"We're not talking about this," Jay declared.

I folded my arms over my chest. "We're not talking about this?" I repeated. "And do you get to dictate what we do and don't talk about?"

"Yes, when it's about something fucking ridiculous," he asserted.

"Ridiculous?" I scoffed. "Now you're calling me ridiculous."

"No, I'm calling the topic ridiculous," he corrected. "The topic of a prenup that doesn't exist, after we're married."

I sat all the way up so I was farther away from him, pissed off. It didn't exactly make sense that I was pissed off, considering I was not the one with the private jet money.

"But I could ruin you if things end between us," I uttered quietly.

Jay's gaze softened. For him, at least.

"Baby, things end between us, I'm ruined, with or without a prenup." He pushed his sunglasses to the top of his head then leaned in to grasp the back of my neck, yanking my body to his so our mouths were inches away.

"Beyond that," he murmured, hand at my hip, untying the side of my bikini. "I'm never letting you go."

"It will be different when we get home, won't it?" I asked that night.

We were tangled up in each other, the balcony door open, a gentle, salty breeze brushing over our naked bodies. Jay's arms, already tight around me, tightened that much more. To the point of pain. I liked that. There was a wine glass in my hand, Italian red, exquisite. We'd spent the rest of the day—after our prenup fight— drinking wine, laying in the sun, having sex.

"Yes," he answered simply.

I pursed my lips, wanting to keep them shut, wanting to leave it at that, drain the last drops of peace from this honeymoon that I could. But I didn't do that.

"Have you considered ... getting out?" I swirled my finger around the rim of my wine glass.

"Getting out?" he echoed, finger running up and down the bare skin of my thigh.

"Of the business that has you dealing with things like the Russian Mob," I clarified in a small timid voice. "Out of the business of running the streets."

Jay didn't answer me immediately. He was too busy dissecting, I knew that. Trying to figure out what was behind the question, whether I'd asked it out of curiosity or from want. I wasn't quite sure which it was either. A mixture of both, most likely.

"Up until that night at Klutch, the thought had never entered my mind, not for a moment," he eventually said. "I had never questioned my position in the world. I'd relished it, in fact. All of the ugly, dirty and horrific things that come with it suited me. I found something I was good at, something that made me a fuck of a lot of money and something that sated the dark hunger inside of me to hurt people." His finger was still gently running up and down my bare thigh. "Love hadn't entered into it because I hadn't thought I was capable of loving. And love is a liability. It was what brought down many men before me. Without my job, my title, I am no one. So I hadn't thought of leaving. Not once. Until you. Until you walked into an office you had no business in, and I knew I had no business with you unless I was an entirely different kind of man. But I can't get out, Stella. The other side of my business, the fucking charity dinners, the old money, that's a club that I will never enter in to. I'll never gain the respect of that class of people. It doesn't matter what I earn, what I own. I'll always be a gangster, a thug, a killer, a monster. There is no entry for me there, Stella."

I heard the vulnerability in his voice, the resignation. I'd already known all of this about him, of course. That there was no option of another lifestyle. He hadn't signed his soul over to the devil or any such nonsense. He'd just made choices. To survive. To thrive. The only other option for him would've been destruction. Beyond that, I didn't think one just 'retired' from being lord of the underworld or whatever he was. Jay had something inside of him that thirsted for the darkness, the violence, the power. It kept him going. And I really, really needed Jay to keep going.

"You want me to get out, Stella?" he asked softly.

My heart broke at his voice, the helplessness in it. Never had I heard Jay sound like that. I rolled over, putting my wine glass down, then I moved to straddle him, positioning him at my entrance. "No,

Jay. I want you *in*." As I guided him inside of me, we both inhaled sharply. My body was tender, delightfully so. I moved slowly. "I want inside you and your life."

He lifted up so our torsos were pressed together, forcing him deeper. "You may come to regret that, pet."

"No," I murmured, kissing him. "Never. Till death, remember?"

We made love until the sun came up and the darkness stole away the last of our perfect honeymoon.

Perfection would be lost for us for a long time after.

CHAPTER FOURTEEN

I was an idiot.

Living in Jay's dark and dangerous world, I'd thought I knew it all. Thought I understood the risks, the ugliness of it all. I'd seen enough of it, hadn't I? Yes, I knew the reality. I knew that I lived in his world, that the shadows of it fell upon me every now and then. But I thought I was ... protected. Jay certainly didn't need to protect me from himself, but he would've died before he let his world touch me. Let it mark me.

Maybe we had both been idiots.

Because there was no way for me to be married to one of the kings of the underworld without bearing some of the scars he did. This world was all sharp edges, so every single time I came in contact with it, it drew blood. Sometimes it scratched. Other times it scarred.

This was a time when it scarred. When it hit bone.

Wren and I were out shopping. Which had been the norm, even before all of this. All of this being both of us falling for very complicated, dangerous and powerful men. Before one of us got married to one while the other got impregnated by the other.

Which naturally was even more of a reason to shop.

We had bought a lot. Well, *Wren* had bought a lot. She was five months pregnant, although she barely looked it. She was wearing a skin-tight, grey tank dress, and there was only the slightest bump. If you didn't know any better, you might've thought she'd just had a big lunch. She was glowing. Her feet hadn't swelled. No morning sickness—except for a few short bouts at night. No hormonal acne. Nothing like all the books I'd read talked about. She hadn't read the books. I had because I knew she wouldn't. Because I wanted to support my friend. Because in my hopeful heart, I thought I might need to know some of this stuff soon.

Although I was happy with Jay, deliriously so, every time I got my period, my heart dropped. Disappointment was a stone in my stomach, getting heavier and heavier with each passing month.

I wanted to be a mother.

Desperately. More desperately than I'd thought I did, actually. Before I fell in love with Jay, I'd liked the idea of kids. Known I wanted one or two eventually. But there hadn't been a burning need to find the father to my children. No ticking biological clock. None of that empty uterus feeling. I hadn't even totally married the idea of procreating. Especially with my mother's past and the possibility of either turning into her or passing the trait on to my child.

Being a mother had always been at the back of my mind, but

I'd figured I'd put some serious thought in to it once I was in a relationship with a man I visualized a future with. But now it was something at the forefront of my mind, especially since I was allowed to visualize a future with Jay. Not just visualize but actively live out that future.

So now I was turning in to that woman I'd never ever thought I'd be. The slightly baby crazy, empty-wombed woman who had an entire saved—and secret—folder on her phone with nursey designs and baby clothes.

At least that secret folder had a use for Wren. She had started buying things the second she'd stopped freaking out about the pregnancy, shed away her fears and in true Wren style, had thrown herself right in to it. She hadn't waited the obligatory three months to tell anyone because that was Wren. She was happy and didn't see any reason to pause or wait. She was all in.

I liked seeing her like this. Glowing. In love. Without the complications of Karson's lifestyle bouncing off her expensively moisturized and scar-free skin. I didn't know how much Karson had told her. We didn't speak in specifics about the nature of our men's business—whether each of us didn't want to endanger the other with information we weren't supposed to have or because we didn't want to taint our relationship with the darkness that we'd let into our hearts, I didn't know.

Regardless, with everything that was changing—the wonderful and the terrible—it was nice to know that our relationship was staying exactly the same.

Whatever the reason, we were basking in the lovely day. Granted, we had a 'tail', because both Karson and Jay were overprotective, vying for the most over the top alpha male award. Then again, Wren was carrying Karson's child and hadn't changed anything about her lifestyle, apart from making her cocktails virgins and taking prenatal vitamins.

Wren was talking about names when it happened. "Striker for a boy, and Hudson for a girl," she smiled. "Karson has tried to veto these, of course, but his name is *Karson*? How can he think that he has a leg to stand on?" She shook her head as we walked out of the store.

I was smiling back at her when the world exploded.

Everything was stark. Flashing images.

Blood.

Noise.

Pain.

Screaming.

It might've been me screaming. Must've been. My hands were covered in blood. From trying to staunch the bleeding. Wren was not glowing anymore. She was pale. Lifeless.

Loud booms, loud enough for my teeth to crunch together. Glass shattering. Hearts shattering. Blood flowing through my fingers, too quickly for me to do anything.

I couldn't do anything to stop it.

Not a thing.

Then there was more noise, people trying to pull me from her, pull me from Wren. I fought them. Fought them hard. But apparently not hard enough.

Jay

He'd hoped that things would happen quietly. That he would be able sort this shit out with the Russians through discussions, with phone calls, paperwork, subtle threats. He might not have been as well established and powerful as the Mob, but he was pretty fucking powerful, and he knew there was a weakness in such long-standing power. A complacency. He was working a lot behind the scenes. Moving a lot of different parts.

Things were tense.

Dimitri's threats had gotten more and more overt, doing things that his father never would've done even on the eve of war. Jay had had occasion to deal with the Pakhan. Shrewd. Dangerous. Ruthless and old school. Though he'd killed and tortured many people, had ordered the murder of many more, he stuck to a code. He believed in honor among thieves, so to speak. Jay had appreciated that and had done some work with the man after he'd killed Heller.

But Jay had established boundaries. Getting tangled up with the Mob was the surest way to die early, and his job already gave death close proximity.

Then he got the phone call.

Death was not just in close proximity. It was reaching in to his fucking chest and ripping his heart out.

Stella

No one was telling me anything.

I'd screamed at first. When the hands were on me, trying to take Wren from me. I'd screamed and screamed, then it was blank. Not black like everybody seemed to describe unconsciousness. It wasn't dark, murky. If anything, it was pure white, stark bright nothingness. Just a blank space. After that, I was here, inhaling the sterile smell of the hospital. Cleaning products and decay. The sheets scratched against me, sounds echoing through my ears as if through water. It took me too long to get my bearings, to make sense of what had happened, to come to the horrific realization that what had happened had actually happened. It was not some gruesome dream. Not some hallucination. I wished harder than I ever had that it was the thing I'd been most afraid of. That my mother's illness had suddenly rushed forward, that it was madness that had put me here instead of reality.

It was laughable really, how quickly, how hard I wished for my worst fear to be true, how much I longed for it.

My mouth tasted dry and cottony. My limbs screamed in pain, and my heart was in shreds in my chest. Plus, the man in front of me with the combover and ten-thousand-dollar watch was ignoring me. He'd come in after I woke up, the nurse checking my vitals, rubbing my hand with warmth and sorrow, whispering that the doctor was on his way.

If I had been able to get my bearings, I wouldn't have even waited for this manicured and superior looking doctor to enter the room. I would've gotten out of this bed and torn the fucking hospital apart to get some answers.

But the sounds, the smells, the pain, most of all the scattered memories of what had happened, had me stuck to the shitty, thin mattress, unable to hold on to a clear thought and unable to get up from the bed.

"Ma'am, you need to rest," the doctor uttered gently but almost dismissively when I'd started asking questions. There was a distance in his eyes, a distance I assumed that he needed to get through each day. There were countless sick, dead and dying.

I sat up in my bed, a small twinge radiating through my body as I did so.

They'd given me something. Something that made the ride here blurry and dreamlike. Something that filled my mouth with bitterness and turned my insides to cotton wool. It was wearing off now, and the pain was creeping back in.

I was glad for the pain because I needed it right now.

"I need someone to give me some fucking answers," I ground out, my voice rough, scratchy and too weak for my liking.

The doctor's eyes flickered up from where they'd been focused on his chart. "I cannot give you answers, Mrs. Helmick. As I said, you must rest."

It was then he turned his back on me. To go off to heal the wounds of whoever else was next on the list. Or to pronounce a time of death.

Horrid memories of blood and my friend's lifeless face assaulted me with such force, I was surprised I could breathe through it. It was the pain from those memories that got me out of the bed, that helped me rip the IV from my arm so I could cross the distance between myself and the doctor to get right up in his face.

My feet were bare. It was unnerving because I lived my life in heels, was used to being six inches higher, which usually put me at eye level with most men—apart from Jay—and gave me a sense of confidence. Beyond that, it was unnerving because I hadn't taken off my shoes. Someone else had done that for me. In the gaps. Someone had unstrapped my sandals, removed my clothes—including my bra— and put me in a hospital gown. It was by no means the most important fact at this juncture, but it was a strangely intimate and unexpected.

Not unexpected enough for me to stop what I was doing.

"You're not going to walk away," I seethed. "You're not going to call me ma'am in that vague, cold and professional tone. I'm a *human being*. I'm a human being whose last memory of her friend, her friend who is five months pregnant—" my voice broke here, but I managed to carry on despite the splinters in my insides. "My last memory of her is blood pouring out of her, trying to make it stop."

I looked down at my hands. They were shaking. Clean. Someone had cleaned them in the gaps too. But not well enough. They were stained pink with flecks of red. My stomach roiled, and I swayed slightly.

The doctor put his hand on my arm, steadying me. "Mrs. Helmick, you have a serious concussion, twelve stitches in your arm, not to mention the shock your body is going through right now. You need to get back into bed." He began to try to direct me back to the bed I'd gotten out of. The one I hadn't put myself in.

I tore my arm from his grasp. "You need to tell me where *the fuck* my pregnant friend is!" I screamed in his face.

He blinked once, not in surprise. I'm sure he was jaded to his patients losing it at him by now, but he must have realized that I was not going to let him leave this room without information.

He sighed. "She is in critical condition." His voice was sober. But not gentle. "She lost a lot of blood, but it looks like she will recover." Then he paused. My heart broke apart during that pause. The flesh shredding inside of my chest in a sensation that was horrific, grotesque and inescapable.

"Unfortunately, she lost the baby."

I heard him even through the dull roar in my ears. Although I'd known he was going to say it, the words out loud solidified the ugly, horrid truth. The ground moved up, and blank spots danced in my vision.

"Are you sure?" I demanded. "There was a lot going on, Wren is strong. Are you sure you didn't make some kind of mistake?" My words were a plea. Even though my brain already knew the truth, my heart was aching for it to be a lie.

"I'm sorry," he replied with finality in his tone. His eyes went to my arm. "You need to get back into bed so we can reattach your IV."

I glanced down in that direction. Blood was trailing down my arm and dripping on the floor. It sickened me, the sight of it. How little there was. Wren had lost so much more, yet I only had scratches and stitches.

"I need to see her."

"You can't see her right now—"

"You don't take me to see her right now, I'll make sure that you're fired from this hospital, that you're evicted from whatever bachelor pad in the Hills you're living in. I'll make sure your wife finds out about your mistress and that you default on all your loans," I hissed, sounding hysterical and crazy.

"And then I'll kill you," another voice chimed in, not sounding hysterical or crazy. Smooth. Cold. Sure.

I was barely holding myself up at this point. There was a man at my side, taking my weight, smelling of home, his entire body so tense it was like marble.

"Who are you?" the doctor asked, pale and starting to look more than a little afraid.

"I'm her husband," Jay answered, focusing his stare on the doctor, arm at my waist.

"Well, as her husband, I'm sure you're concerned about your wife's condition. She needs to get back in that bed so our nurses can see to her." The doctor was trying his level best to keep authority in his tone, to act like Jay wasn't intimidating the fuck out of him. He was failing miserably.

Jay's hand tightened around my waist. I used it as an anchor, even though he was likely moments away from placing me in the bed bodily.

"My wife told you what she needs," Jay told him. "I'd appreciate it if you'd direct us to her room."

"Mr. Helmick, your wife is bleeding."

Jay's jaw hardened, and his eyes turned stormy. The energy in the room changed. "I'm more than aware that my wife is bleeding. It isn't life threatening, is it? No. So she will get what she wants because she's made it clear that she's more than willing to bleed for her friend."

I might've collapsed at Jay's feet right then and there if my need to see Wren hadn't been so strong.

The doctor, knowing when he was beat, led us to her room. My steps were hurried, and every movement was agony. But I leaned on Jay. And he carried me there. In more ways than one.

Wren was asleep. Thankfully. It was cowardice that had me relieved. Karson was sitting beside the bed, face drawn and pale, his large form drawn in on itself. He was holding Wren's small, limp hand in his large one like you might hold a baby bird, cradling it with the lightest of touches.

He didn't even glance at us as we walked in, me leaning heavily on Jay, my blood dripping onto his shirtsleeve.

I didn't get close to her. Didn't move away from where I'd stopped in the middle of the room. Jay didn't ask what I was doing standing there or how long I planned on doing it. He didn't do anything but let me bleed on him. Eventually, he carried me back to the bed.

It wasn't until I was back in my hospital bed with a new IV attached that realized that Jay had not spoken directly to me since he'd arrived. Not once. He'd been touching me constantly. But no words. He'd barely even met my eyes.

The energy thrummed between us as the nurse finished with me, my gaze hard on my husband, his eyes watching the nurse's slow and careful movements. His face was blank, ice cold, but his eyes burned, standing beside the bed, stroking my hair.

I longed for the nurse to finish so Jay would be forced to speak to me, to talk to me, to somehow suck up all of the pain vibrating inside of me.

The nurse took so long I almost screamed at her to get out, which wasn't fair since she had kind eyes and looked utterly exhausted. But my best friend being shot on the street and losing her baby wasn't fucking fair.

Then when the nurse left, I wished for her to come back because I couldn't handle Jay's reaction. He fell to his knees at my bedside.

To. His. Knees.

He grabbed my hand, grasped it, clutched it like it was the only thing tethering him to this earth.

Jay's face was as pale as I'd ever seen it, his eyes running over my body, focusing on the bandage on my arm, then the IV in my arm, and finally to the tight, hot area on my cheekbone. He stood then, moving as if his entire body was made of stone, eyes burning like emerald infernos.

He was building up to say something. Likely something that laid the blame firmly and squarely at his own feet. This had happened because of our connection to him, after all. Jay was already torturing himself, I could see it in his eyes.

"Stop," I whispered, unable to speak louder, firmer. "I see you're about to add this to whatever tally of marks you've decided go against your soul. But I need you to stop. This was not your fault."

"You're laying in a hospital bed, Stella," he uttered, voice cold faraway. "A bullet grazed your arm. A bullet." His hand squeezed mine tighter. "One that could've ended your fucking life. And there was another one that did end a life…"

His voice cracked then. Split apart into a thousand little pieces of sorrow, each sharper than the other, cutting me in a thousand little places even though I'd been sure I didn't have any unbroken places left.

Jay lowered his head to my hand, pressing his lips against it. My hand was wet from his tears. They were like acid on my skin.

When he lifted his head, his eyes were devoid of whatever sorrow and regret had been living there before. Now they were full of only one thing: death.

"They will all die." He vowed through his teeth, each word ripped from a dark and ugly place. His tone made my skin crawl.

I thought of the blood still staining my hands, how small and empty Wren looked in that bed. I thought of what her life would look like when she woke up, about what had been stolen from her.

"They will all die," I agreed.

CHAPTER FIFTEEN

I was kept overnight. Jay slept in the armchair beside me. That was after he had me moved to a different room. A private suite. The rich person hospital room. As if it made a difference.

Wren was in one of the suites too. Her parents had arrived, her father making sure she got the best of the best, calling surgeons, doctors, specialists. Her mother ordering flowers, candles, fresh fruit, silk nightgowns. Anything to stop and let the reality of what happened to their daughter hit. Avoiding the knowledge that all the money in the world could not change what had happened, could not buy back the life that had been lost.

Wren had been in and out of consciousness, eventually lucid enough to be told what had happened. I was there when the doctors told her the news because her parents couldn't handle it. They gave their daughter the world but did not know how to witness it being taken away from her.

Jay had left this morning. After my interview with the police, after they'd discharged me, murmuring about things that needed to be done with violence and death in his eyes. He'd stroked my swollen cheek, wincing as his finger trailed the discolored skin. Then he'd kissed me. Not gently. Not with the hesitation and regret that he'd been touching me with since he'd arrived at the hospital. With something hungry, desperate and dark. I kissed him back with all of my hungry, desperate darkness too.

There were orders not to leave the hospital, to stay in sight of one of the men who were stationed at the doors to our rooms. Wren's parents hadn't asked about them, which made me wonder how much they knew about Karson and the business he was in.

My father hadn't been told about what happened. Not yet. I'd eventually tell him about Wren and the baby because he considered her a second daughter. Because he was as excited as a grandfather might've been, which meant he'd also be as heartbroken as a grandfather.

Truly, it was fear that stopped me from telling my father. And because I knew that he'd fly up here to try to help, to try to suck up the hurt and sorrow like men did. Because I couldn't let him see my face. I was going to wait until I healed to tell him. I didn't know whether that was the right decision, didn't know what lies I was going to tell in order to inform my father of what happened.

The lies had already been told to the police. I'd been interviewed with Jay at my side. He hadn't coached me to say anything, but the familiar way he shook the hand of the detective in charge told me that they were acquainted.

I didn't tell any lies to the police, obviously, but I did withhold some truths. About whom my enemies might be. I didn't have any, that was correct. But Jay did. And we were married, what's his was mine now.

Then the detective left, and Jay did too.

Jay's absence was a yawning chasm in this horrible nightmare. There were things to be done, I knew.

People who had to die. Wars that had to be planned. It was interesting to me. War had always been a far-off concept, either it was images on the news, explosions, guns, men and women fighting for our country. Or it was swords, knights and fucking dragons in Game of Thrones. Either way, war was something that happened away from my world. It was something that existed on screens, in books, still images. Not in my life. And it was nothing like the books, the news stories, the fucking television shows.

Jay and Karson would seek blood for this. More than blood. They would seek utter destruction. And as much I hadn't considered myself a bloodthirsty person, I was glad about it. Because I had to sit beside my friend's hospital bed, my hand in hers and help her navigate a loss like this. Watch the grief overtake her with absolutely no power over it. I had thought I was a make love not war kind of gal, but it was love that made me thirst for war.

Wren was strangely calm. No, calm was not the word for it. Empty. That was it. She was *empty*. I was sitting beside her bed, where I'd been nonstop aside from bathroom breaks. Zoe and Yasmin were coming and going in shifts. Her parents hovered, coming in and out, talking about things that needed to be done, not looking at their delicate, broken daughter. Wren was not alone for a moment.

"There was another reason I didn't want to have children." Although Wren spoke softly, the tenor of her voice tore at the air around us. I held in my flinch at the defeat in my friend's voice. Just barely.

"I didn't talk about it because it sounded ridiculous to say out loud and because saying it out loud ..." she trailed off to look out the window. "Because saying it out loud gave it more power. Made it possible."

Wren looked tiny in the bed. Like she'd shrunk down to half of her usual self. Wren was larger than life, despite her stature. She lit up a room. Now she was barely a glimmer. I had to press my fingernails into my palms to stop from crying.

"I went to a psychic when I was backpacking around Europe," she continued. "One in Romania. The real deal. Didn't speak English, lived up in the hills, an hour away from the closest village." Wren's gaze was faraway. "The guy with me translated as she told my fortune. She told me I'd be loved many times by many men. But I'd only ever love one man. And that man would be my destruction." Wren paused, her fingers fisting the fabric of her blankets. "That I'd love that man until my death, but I may not share my life with him." Now she looked toward the door. The one that Karson was standing outside of. He wouldn't move. Not until Wren told him to come in. And if she didn't, if she couldn't, he'd stand there. All night.

"She told me I'd be a mother for only a short time. That my child would not breathe air, and that I'd never have another."

When Wren's hands went to her stomach, I clenched my fists harder, seeking something more painful than watching my friend cradle the stomach that used to hold her baby.

Wren squeezed her eyes shut then opened them. "It was a girl." Her voice sounded stronger than it should've. "I thought it was bullshit. Or, at least, that's what I told myself. But I knew. Even before the boy I was with translated what she was saying. I knew that woman spoke the truth. And she did."

I moved across the room because I couldn't sit there watching my friend sink into the bed, shrink into nothingness.

I grabbed her hand. "*No*," I whispered. "The Wren I know doesn't let anyone, not even an old Romanian woman who lives in the hills, tell her her future is already decided. The Wren I know makes her own future." I stroked her face. "This is not the end for you. You will remember her. You will love her. She will live in many different ways, and you will heal. I promise."

Wren smiled weakly and nodded, pretending to agree with me. I knew she'd already convinced herself of that truth, of a future that held only emptiness and pain.

I was leaning against the door outside Wren's room, phone pressed to my ear, eyes directed toward Eric who had let me cry on his shoulder ten minutes ago. I didn't know much death and violence the man had experienced before this. Working for Jay, I figured it was a lot, but he was wearing the reality of this on his handsome face, seemingly unable to grasp on to the badass mask that had been his norm before all of this.

Although I was sure their job was meant to let any and all humanity rebound from their strong exteriors, Wren had an effect on everyone. They were meant to be monsters, so the horrors of this monstrous world didn't claim them. But the problem with Wren was she turned even the most horrific of monsters into men, made them feel, made them hurt.

"I'm leaving the office in five minutes. Does she need anything?" Zoe asked, voice strained. She was doing her level best to be strong, steadfast and unwavering for Wren, for all of us, but I knew she was struggling. Zoe was an alpha female in all of the best ways. She protected and loved her friends with a ferocity that was unbeatable, unyielding. She spoke the truth, even when it hurt. She celebrated every victory we had as if it were her own and felt the pain of every sorrow.

"No, she doesn't need anything," I replied, my voice low and scratchy. "Nothing that we can give her anyway."

"I hope they die slowly," Zoe seethed after a moment.

That shocked me into silence. Zoe was not ignorant to the violence of this world. She was realistic, cynical, living her life with one hand up as a shield because this world had yet to prove that it wasn't out to hurt her.

But she'd never been violent herself. She'd had to deal with a lot in her life despite her parents working their asses off to give her a peaceful one. Zoe had had a choice, when faced with the realities of how cruel this world was. To take injustice and let it turn her bitter and angry, or to hold her head up high, not let a single person force her to bow down, to shrink. She'd chosen the latter. And she was the most regal person I knew.

Yet now she was out for blood.

"Me too," I whispered.

I hung up, my world shaking, tilting. I knew that nothing was going to look the same after this was all settled, and I struggled against how powerless and small that made me feel.

When I looked up, Eric wasn't in front of me. Karson was.

He was still wearing the same black tee and jeans he had been in when all of this happened. His eyes were bloodshot, heavy, showing that he hadn't slept. I glanced down to his hands. Though he'd washed them, I didn't miss the slightly pinkish hue to them. Blood.

He was staring at the door to Wren's room, standing in the hallway as if he was a statue and not a man.

"It's my fault." His voice wasn't flat, empty, harsh as I'd become used to with Karson. Even when he was with Wren it was like that. He wasn't like Jay. He didn't let even a whisper of his heart, his true feelings, slip out.

But his eyes, the ones that were dead and dangerous the night I'd met Jay, danced with life and love whenever he looked at Wren. Whenever Wren was in the vicinity.

To say those eyes were dead now wasn't accurate. They weren't just dead. They were decimated, ruined, obliterated. I saw something else too. Resignation. That alpha male glint that had been in Jay's eyes when he'd walked out on me, thinking it was for the best.

"You're leaving her?" I asked, sharpness in my tone despite

looking at the naked pain on his face. I didn't need him to say it out loud to know it was true. Fuck, if Jay hadn't been married to me, if our lives weren't coiled up the way they were, I was sure he would've attempted to leave me. As it was, I still couldn't be sure he wouldn't.

It was the way of these men, trying to protect us with more pain because they thought their absence was some kind of gift, some kind of mercy.

Karson rubbed at the back of his neck. "She's better off without me," he glanced to the closed door then looked back to me. "If she hadn't met me, none of this would've happened. I need to go now. She'll only know pain with me."

I stared at this man. This ruined man. The one who I knew struck fear into the blood of whoever crossed him, whoever encountered him. The one capable of doing terrible, violent things to other humans. The man who my best friend loved with all of her heart. Her mangled, broken and bleeding heart after losing a baby she hadn't known she wanted.

"You're a coward," I spat with all of my anger and sorrow. I leaned forward when I spoke, to make sure he knew I was not afraid of him. Not impressed by whatever sacrifice he thought he was making. Not one bit.

"Not just a coward but a narcissistic one at that," I continued. "You know, if I hadn't gone into Klutch that night, I never would've met Jay, never would've met you and therefore Wren never would've met *you*. That doesn't mean this is my fault." I looked at that door again, swallowing against the pain in my throat, the pain in my heart before meeting Karson's eyes. "There is no one to blame for this except the people who did this. You took care of them, didn't you?"

Karson nodded once, brusquely.

Yes. Taken care of. Dead.

I was happy. Glad that whoever tore my best friend's life apart, who'd made it so she'd be scarred for life, broken for life, who killed her fucking *baby* was dead. I hoped it was long and painful.

"They've been punished. The people who are truly responsible," I sighed. "You walking away now is not punishing anyone but Wren. Not hurting anyone but Wren. And that woman, that fabulous, kind, open hearted woman has been torn apart." My voice broke ever so slightly at the end, but I soldiered on. "And so help me God, if you even think about leaving her at a time when she needs you most, I will hunt you down, and I will end you."

It seemed rather ridiculous to me that I would be threatening someone like Karson who probably knew at least fifty ways to kill a person. In other circumstances it would be. But not this one. I was being completely fucking sincere.

I pointed to the door. "You march your ass in there. You show her all that pain you're feeling. Don't you dare fucking hide it because she needs to see it. She doesn't need you to be the big, strong man without a heart. She needs your heart. Your broken heart. To know she's not in this alone." My hand was shaking as I pointed toward the door.

Karson stared at me for a beat longer, heartbreak glittering in his eyes, defeat saturating his every pore. Then he turned and walked to the door, disappearing inside.

My entire body sagged in relief and exhaustion. In sorrow.

I jumped when something moved out of the corner of my eye.

A black shadow. A shadow that turned out to be a man. I should've known better. I was here, holding myself together only so my best friend could fall apart. I could collect all of her broken pieces and keep them safe until she was ready to put herself together again.

He didn't come to me immediately. He stood there, watching me, the silence in the hallway a roar in my ears. My hands started shaking first. Then my entire body, to the point where I wasn't sure how I was still standing.

Then I knew why I was still standing because Jay was holding me up.

CHAPTER SIXTEEN

Things had changed drastically in two short months. For the worse except for one magnificent, extraordinary thing that I'd been keeping to myself for the past week because I'd had no idea how to be happy out loud when everything around me was so dark and uncertain.

Wren had been discharged from the hospital after two weeks. She'd broken up with Karson. Or had tried to. He'd tried his best to fight for her. His very best. And the very best of a badass, deadly alpha male was pretty fucking good.

Wren was better.

On a good day, Wren was better.

But this was not a good day. These had been the absolute worst days of Wren's life. She was not at her absolute best. Therefore, the breakup stuck. No matter how hard we all tried to talk her out of it, reminding her that she loved him, that he fiercely loved her and that they'd lost something ... together. That they could heal together.

But sometimes, when you lose something so precious, so all-encompassing and so brutally, it doesn't matter how much love there was. The pain was too great; it scooped out everything that came before.

Karson still followed her practically everywhere. She ignored him. She pasted on fake smiles, threw on heels, lip gloss and couture and strutted herself back in to her old life. The one that no longer fit her anymore. It was much too small. The trauma had made her expand, forcing open all new places to fit her pain. Sure, she could put on the same heels, follow her old patterns, but she'd never be the same woman.

We were all holding our breath for the moment when that realization hit her. For the inevitable breakdown. Because despite a few bouts of tears in the hospital, Wren had held tight to her grief, with a death grip. She was not in denial, but she was *something*. The closest she'd come to truly losing it was at the bonfire she had in her backyard, burning every piece of baby memorabilia she had collected the past five months. She'd watched the flames with dry eyes and a full glass then flirted with the firemen when they came.

Karson, despite following Wren around every spare moment he got—including sleeping in his car outside the gates to her house—had turned near mute. I found it physically hard to look at the man now. If you could call what he was a man.

Despite the yawning chasm of my friend's pain, my life had returned to what could be called a semblance of normal. Albeit with a serious increase in security and Jay refusing to 'let' me take jobs he could not vet first. Before all of this, I would've put up a hefty fight, but I was wearing a small scar on my right arm to prove that that was not a fight worth having. I let Jay 'vet' my jobs. Didn't say a word about the increased security or the guns. Plus, I now had something else I was trying to figure out how to tell him.

Tonight was meant to be the night when I told Jay the news. The extraordinary—though incredibly bittersweet given what Wren was going through right now—thing that scared the shit out of me but also filled me up with a unique kind of warmth, a kind of hope.

A feeling that I really wanted to share with Jay. Something I wanted to give him. More than anything. Especially now, with all of the stress of this conflict on his shoulders. He'd been more tense than usual. More inside his head. And the way he fucked me was with more urgency, more desperate intensity than ever before. Like he feared that each time might be the last.

This news would give him something different. Something positive. Hopeful.

So I got home earlier than I'd told him I'd be home. I put on music. I even cooked. His favorite. Osso Bucco. Which I did despite the smell of the cooking meat turning my stomach, despite the fatigue that was dragging down my body and the fear of what this news might bring.

I didn't hope for any joy at this news. Not at first, at least. Whatever vague vestiges of happiness I had roused within Jay were nowhere to be seen these past months. He kept the majority of what was happening from me. And I hadn't pushed because I truthfully couldn't handle it. The specifics. I trusted Jay. Trusted him to take care of whatever he needed to take care of, keep me safe.

It was selfish, not pushing him, not giving him somewhere to turn, to be the place he could vent, offload. But the only way I could do that was to fight him, corner him and yank it out of him. I didn't have the strength for that. I was hoping that this news would do something, help him somehow.

But the second he walked through the door, I knew this was not the night. A black cloud followed him. Engulfed him. His face was drawn, cold, eyes shuttered.

Instead of going to me in the kitchen like he normally did, he went straight for the bar. I watched his back move, biting my lip, switching the stove off.

My movements were unsteady, unsure, as I walked toward him.

Jay didn't look at me, instead going to one of the white chairs in the living room. One of the chairs, a lifetime ago, we'd often be curled up in, talking about the wedding and our future like it was something to look forward to.

He'd brought the bottle of whisky with him, settling it on the side table. Not a good sign.

Everything radiating from my husband was prickly and dangerous, so despite the urge I had to touch him, I settled gingerly on the arm of the chair.

Then he looked at me. My gorgeous, cold and deadly husband. His eyes were an abyss, yawning yet not empty. Full of things that brushed up against every exposed nerve I had, pain radiating to my fingertips.

I pursed my lips, shaking, unsure of what to say to him, the man I'd married.

"I know how to handle pain," he spoke before I could, draining his drink. "I'm not immune to it but used to it. Being used to it means I can withstand it." He lifted a hand to brush my hair from my face. "There was a time when I longed to hurt you. Because you didn't know it. I wanted you to be hurt so you'd never forget me. So I'd always own a part of you." He leaned over to pour more whisky into his glass. "This was back when I was trying to keep a part of me good, with intentions of letting you go. Of course now, I'm utterly and entirely wicked by keeping you here, with me. In this life. Now you are getting used to pain that isn't mine. That's a result of my life. And I cannot find a way to get right with that."

My blood turned cold, my stomach lurching at his words. At what threaded through them. A finality.

A goodbye.

I snatched the glass from his hand and placed it on the side table. I climbed onto his lap, straddling him and grasping his neck, forcing his gaze to mine.

"You get right with it," I demanded. "Because you have no other choice. I am your *wife*. You made vows, Jay. No matter how wicked you are, you stick to your words, Jay. Your promises. And you promised to stay with me forever. So you get right with all this."

I didn't tell him that night.

Or the one after that.

THREE WEEKS LATER

He hadn't noticed.

They were small, miniscule things in the grand scheme, but Jay usually noticed everything. Even the miniscule. Especially the miniscule.

But he hadn't noticed that I didn't come home and pour myself a glass of wine, which was a routine I held almost sacred. When he poured me wine, which he always did, I would sip it daintily, wait for him to leave the room so I could pour it down the drain. I realized that was pretty much sacrilege, considering how much the bottles were worth and how scarce and coveted they were, but I wasn't taking risks. Not with something this precious, something that I was convinced I would lose at any moment.

He did not notice that the slightest touch to my breasts caused me to flinch in pain, because whenever he was touching me, it was with an animalistic hunger that was *meant* to cause pain.

Nor did he notice that I nibbled on dry toast and sugary tea in the mornings instead of a triple shot latte and whatever it was I felt like eating at the time.

He didn't notice any of that. Because his mind was elsewhere. On the growing tension with the Russians, if *tension* was even the word for it. They'd ordered the attack on me and Wren which, of course, they'd denied and Jay could find no proof. Which meant things were more complicated than declaring outright war.

Jay had explained all of this to me over the course of many

nights, his words clipped, his expression drawn and his hand—the one that wasn't touching me—clenched into a fist. He was coiled tight, braced, ready for something. I couldn't get to him, not to the soft core I'd found. He'd closed it back up because he was scared.

Not for himself. I knew that Jay had faced much worse in his life, that he was not scared for himself, his business or even for his employees. He was scared for me. I had only truly begun to understand why he was the way he was. Why he structured his life so carefully, making sure that no one got close, no one became important to him.

Because in his business, the people who he did business with— like the Russian fucking Mob—picked off those people, the ones who were important, the ones who they would wound until there weren't any soft places left to wound, without any blood left to bleed.

I was ruminating over all of this one afternoon at home, some stupid reality show playing on the television, nibbling on pork rinds because they were the only things I could stomach right now.

Joseph had just left. He was handling things well didn't ask a single question about the bodyguards who trailed me now or all of the changes to my schedule. He just did the work, in addition to brining me herbal tea instead of coffee, without saying a word.

If Joseph were straight and if I were not his employer and if I was not madly and irrevocably in love with—and married to—another man, I totally would've married him.

While I was nibbling on my pork rinds, watching a Real Housewife catfight and worrying about the future, Wren walked in.

Strutted in.

In six-inch heels, wearing tailored white pants and a Balmain blazer. Long, bouncy curls tumbled around her flawless face. Her makeup was expertly applied, and she was sun kissed everywhere. The smile on her face was utterly fake, and her eyes glowed with pain.

"Oh, my God, I love this episode. You're making me totally tempted to stay change into some sweats, Postmates a margarita and get drunk as hell to watch television gold," she chirped, eyes flickering from the TV to me. Then to the pork rinds in my hands.

"You on Keto or something?" she smirked with a glint to her eye.

I stared at her, heart hurting in the same way it always did when I looked at my sweet friend. "You're not staying?" I asked.

Her smile faltered. "I'm on my way to the airport."

I blinked at her, putting down my pork rinds. "The airport?" I repeated.

She nodded. "I leave for Nepal in..." she glanced at her phone. "Two hours. And flying commercial means I actually should have to leave twenty minutes ago." She reached out to grab my hand. "But I had to say goodbye."

My mind struggled to catch up with the words coming out of her mouth. Pregnancy brain had a lot to do with it. And the fact that Wren had not mentioned, not once, going to Nepal.

"Why are you going to Nepal?" I finally asked.

She sighed. "I'm going to hike into the mountains and stay in a monastery. Try to get some monks to forget their vows." She waggled her eyebrows, but she wasn't fooling either of us. "I just need to ... *go*."

"You can't leave," I whined, holding onto her hand as if I could do so forever, to keep her here.

She squeezed my hand, smiling sadly. It broke my heart that my stunning friend smiled with sadness now. "I have to."

"What about Karson?" I asked. "He needs you. You need each other."

Wren's eyes turned glassy. "I can't look at him without seeing..." she sucked in a ragged breath. Literally ragged. As if the very air she was breathing was sharp.

"I can't look at him without seeing what we lost," she admitted. "I can barely look at myself. And I know he lost something too. I know he's hurting. But *I can't*. It's ugly and it's weak, but I'm not strong enough to be with him, Stella. I'm barely strong enough to look at myself in the mirror." She cupped my cheek with watery eyes. "My amazing friend, I'm barely strong enough to look at *you*."

Something in her words gave me pause. There was a knowing there. A knowing about a secret I hadn't uttered to anyone because I was terrified.

But before I could say anything about her knowing, Wren stepped back, sucking in a heavy breath, straightening her spine and plastering on a smile so fake that it hurt my insides.

"You're coming back right?" My voice was shaky, dreading her answer.

"Of course, I'm fucking coming back," she scoffed. "It's Nepal. Not exactly my natural habitat. I'm going for a vision quest. For an Eat, Pray find some fucking peace type experiment. Then I'll come back. I'll get more Botox. Plan a party. I'll be me again." She smiled, a more genuine one now but still saturated in sadness. "Even if I'm not me again, I'll come back. For you, mon chéri. I'll definitely be back within six months." She winked once, leaned in to kiss my cheek once more and then she walked out the door.

I stood there, staring at the door, crying for a long time.

In the movies, underworld wars happened quickly. With explosions, blood and the good guy coming out on top. There were no good guys here, this was not a movie. Things didn't happen like that, apparently. It was much slower but with no less blood.

Thankfully, none of it belonged to my husband.

Yet.

Jay was home late. He was always home late these days. Though I wasn't alone. He ensured that there was always someone with me. Multiple someones. Multiple armed someones. Our home was like a fortress now. All of my movements were documented, all of my locations were tracked. It was stifling. Suffocating. But I knew there was no possibility of me trying to argue this. Not after what happened. I wasn't stupid enough to argue. No, not now. Not with everything I had to protect.

Zoe and Yasmin came over often. Both were good enough friends not to mention the multiple, black clad, serious and dangerous looking men—and two women, thank God for female badasses, though I made a mental note to require that Jay have more female badasses in his employ—guarding the gate and constantly walking the perimeter. They didn't ask questions either. They didn't agree with this life, did not approve, but they were my girlfriends, the kind of friends who were like an old oak tree, unwavering, unyielding and with deep roots.

I was sure Zoe knew my secret, likely Yasmin, too, but they didn't mention that either. Not with their words, at least. I did not miss the knowing looks, the raised eyebrows. I knew they were waiting for me to tell them. But there was no way I could until I told Jay. And there was no way I could tell *him* right now. Not when he was coming home late, immediately showering then fucking me into oblivion every night.

Tonight was different, though. I was sitting out on the balcony despite the chill in the air, staring out into the darkness, letting the salt settle on my cheeks.

He didn't touch me when he came outside. He wasn't doing that as often as he used to either. The casual, playful touches that I'd taken for granted before were dwindling, all the ground we'd gained was crumbling at our feet.

"Wren is gone," I told him in a small voice. The waves almost drowned it out, but I knew Jay had heard me. A lot of things might've changed these past months—for the worse—but Jay still listened to me with a fervent intensity.

"I know," he murmured.

Of course he knew.

He knew she'd left. Knew that it would've had this effect on me, knew I would be sitting here hurt and worried about my friend, yet he'd still come home late. I wondered how much of it was because of the blame he carried around with him over what happened to Wren and how much of it was the actual war he was having with the Russian Mob.

Jay stood behind me silently, both of us staring into the darkness. I waited for him to touch me, offer me more. I hungered for it. But he didn't.

"Stella, come to bed," he ordered, voice cold, commanding. I felt it between my legs despite my sorrow.

And, like always, I obeyed him.

It was after he'd fucked me in that way I loved. In that way that I hated. It was cold, hot, detached and too close all at the same time. It was Jay how he'd been before we truly became us yet a version of him that I'd never seen before.

Though my muscles burned and my body thrummed with satisfaction, parts of me were chilled with fear, worry. When he pulled out of me and rolled off the bed, he moved farther away. He didn't even pull me into his chest afterward. In the past, he'd go into the bathroom to get a warm washcloth and clean me up gently, with reverence. By that point I was usually barely awake despite my fears.

My body was growing life in addition to working practically round-the-clock. All the nonstop worrying I was doing about Jay, the future of our marriage and Wren's state of mind. Then there was all the end of the world sex I was having. Which was what it felt like every night. Like we were the only two people left at the end of the world, moments away from certain death, clinging onto each other for dear life. For one last time.

It was mind blowing but terrifying. Yet despite that, I sank into oblivion. I couldn't be sure he came directly back to bed, but I knew he'd slept at some point because my bladder always woke me in the night, and he'd be clinging to my body with an iron grip.

This night I fought sleep because even hormones couldn't battle against the fear that Jay was slipping away from me.

I spoke as he stood up, naked, his silhouette carved out of the moonlight.

"I can survive this," I spoke to his scarred back. "I can handle all of this. Your life. What comes with it. Although I didn't think I could, I can." Jay hadn't turned. "Despite what you likely tell yourself daily, I chose this. I chose *you*. So I can survive this part of your life. This part of our lives. Because I made vows. I made promises about lifetimes and forevers." I sucked in an unsteady breath, tears welling up in my eyes. "Those aren't just promises, they're oaths, Jay. For better or for worse. And as long as I have you, I can survive the worst that life may throw at us, even if you doubt that. Even if you hate yourself for it. I can and will survive. For us. For you. I'm not going anywhere. What I can't survive, what I won't survive, is losing you. Losing the parts of you that were only mine. I don't blame you. For any of this. I don't hate you, Jay. I love you."

I was crying now. Tears silently trailing down my cheek, Jay's back still to me.

Jay was silent for a long time. Too long.

"You should hate me," he replied finally. "I deserve it. I don't deserve your love, Stella."

And then he walked into the bathroom. Got the washcloth, cleaned me up, then left me in bed alone to quietly cry myself to sleep.

CHAPTER SEVENTEEN

They shot Eric. In the face. In broad daylight.

I might've screamed. Or maybe I had been in too much shock to do so. Everything had been normal, I was sipping my coffee—decaf—Eric was talking about how Kieran wanted him to move in, but he personally thought it was too soon. I was urging him to go for it, nothing was too soon when it came to love and all that. Then I was teasing the big, bad, hulking badass for being absolutely terrified in the face of love.

I was teasing him while thinking about how I was going to tell my husband that I was pregnant, punishing myself for keeping this secret locked inside me. It was hypocritical, me holding this in while I'd demanded that we have no more secrets. But I was afraid. Not afraid of the man Jay was currently, the man who'd had to embrace the darkest parts of himself in order to fight this war. No, I knew that he was scared, scared of what might happen to me, what had already happened to Wren.

There was barely any time to have the life altering kind of conversation that I knew it would be. What had happened to Wren had altered things. Had thrust his dangerous and wicked life out of the shadows and into the daylight. The danger had gone from being some faceless, foreign entity to something real, something tangible enough to live as a scar on my arm and a wound in my heart. The reality of what Jay's life entailed—what he'd been trying to protect me from by leaving—had hit. Had stolen my husband away from me. Yes, he was still in our bed every night, except when he left in the dark hours then came back. He always showered first. Once, I'd gotten up to shower with him. The water was light pink, diluted with the blood he was covered in. I helped him wash it off.

Jay still fucked me, with urgency, hunger and violence. But he was mentally gone, and I hoped that when this was over, I'd get him back.

Jay was doing everything and anything he could do to end this, to win this war. Meanwhile, he was letting blood stain our home.

Oh, the things men did to show they cared.

He could not say it. He could barely speak to me. It didn't anger me, though it frustrated me, broke my heart, I did not blame him for it. I understood it. Jay had fought many of these kinds of wars in his time, covered himself in plenty of blood. I figured that in order to get to the top of the criminal hierarchy, you had to get comfortable with death and violence.

But Jay was not comfortable with having something to lose.

Having something that could hurt and destroy him.

Me.

And what he didn't know that there was something else, someone else who could destroy him further. I'd decided that the news would not bring him back to me. No, it would only push him away, give him something else to be afraid of losing.

It was better to wait, or so I'd thought until Eric was shot in the face in front of me. Until I had his brains on my cheek. Until the men who did that bundled me into a black sedan.

Then I'd wished that I had told Jay that I was carrying his child. Because I couldn't be sure I'd see him again to give him the news. I couldn't be sure there would be a baby to tell him about after all.

Jay

Something was going on with Stella. Jay should've noticed it sooner. But he was distracted, to say the least. He was planning on taking down one of the oldest criminal institutions to exist. It was not something that could be done quickly. Not something that could done out in the open. Neither side wanted news headlines nor did they want the attention from federal law enforcement agencies. The Pakhan—Mikhail Kuznetsov, the head of the Russian Mafia—did not want a war, Jay knew. They were still vying for a partnership, even *after* what they'd done.

The old man knew that Jay was of more value to them alive. He had loyal soldiers, had steadfast connections and had plans in place for his entire organization to self-destruct upon his death.

So no, they did not want war, because Jay had made the act of killing him incredibly risky and stupid. The Pakhan was a lot of things, stupid was not one of them. A worthy adversary if not for his trigger-happy son. The one who Jay was planning on taking out in reparations. Karson had not demanded it, he was too loyal for that, but Jay knew he thirsted for his blood. As did Jay. They'd killed many men, including the ones who'd fired the guns. They'd killed every single person they'd traced to the shooting, which of course, led nowhere near the family. Because the Pakhan was smart.

What was done was unforgiveable, even in his business. What was taken could not be given back, no reparations could be made. It was all Jay could do to not track down Mikhail Kuznetsov and cut him with a thousand tiny cuts, leaving him to bleed to death in unimaginable pain. Though when the time finally came for that, it was Karson's right, not Jay's.

The man was quieter now, if that was possible. Nothing human lingered beyond his eyes anymore. Only a quiet rage burning inside him, the need for vengeance keeping him going. Those were the only things keeping him going now that Wren was gone. Jay was all too aware that he would be like Karson if Stella had suffered that same fate. If she had lost something that he could not get back for her, if she had been cut in a way that would never heal. Jay did not know if he would be able to have Karson's self-control, though.

He was consumed with it. He knew he'd damn near reverted back to the state he'd been in when they'd first met, the cold, emotionless, cruel man he was forced to be in order to survive.

His perfect wife loved him. Had taught him how to be a man with her smile, her jokes, her rambling, her snow globes, her cat and her mere presence. Jay had all of that now and more. But the possibility of losing it was strong enough for him to taste a rancid, empty life on his tongue. He couldn't shake it. Couldn't rid himself of that taste no matter how often he filled his mouth with Stella's sweetness.

She mourned for her friend, for herself, for the life that had been torn from them that day. She struggled with her own demons, too, Jay knew this. Her fears about her mother, about the possibility of the same fate befalling her. And above all, he knew his magnificent wife worried about him. Fretted about the nights he left her, about the demons he himself fought with.

And something else, something else beyond all that, something that made her almost skittish around him, something that lurked behind her eyes. Something that Jay might've figured out before now had he not been so distracted, had he not purposefully distanced himself from Stella because he feared what he might do to her. How tight he might hold her.

No, it was better to get this finished, end this before he tried to fix what was wrong with his marriage. Stella had told him she wasn't going anywhere. And she'd meant it.

His thoughts were interrupted by Karson walking into his office. His downtown office. His legitimate one. The one that Karson had never set foot in because Jay made sure to keep those two areas of his life very separate.

There was no reason for Karson to be walking through that door except the end of the fucking world. The end of Jay's world.

Jay moved his hands from the desk to the tops of his thighs

because they were shaking.

"Is she dead?" he asked, voice flat, his insides shriveling up, dying.

Karson shook his head once. "No." Eric is. Shot

Nothing inside of Jay relaxed. He stopped planning his own imminent death, pushing those plans in the back of his mind. Because there were many, many things that could be happening to Stella right now that would take her from him. That would set fire to his fucking life.

His hands were still shaking.

"Eric's dead," Karson repeated in a clipped tone, face cold and empty eyes flickering with minute flashes of emotion. Jay knew that Stella meant something to Karson, because Stella meant something to Wren, and Wren was everything to Karson.

Jay nodded away the death of one of his men. One of his friends. Or as close as he could've been to one. Eric had stood next to him at his wedding. Eric was Stella's friend, he knew that because she talked about him and her friend Kieran all the time, talking about how perfectly they matched and what great style Eric had. Jay's heart clenched remembering Stella like she was already gone.

"Shot on the street," Karson continued. "They left him there. Took her."

"We know it was the Kuznetsovs?" Jay asked, voice even.

"Not explicitly," Karson replied. "But we got lucky. They were walking to their car, the car has a camera, front and rear. Got everything, managed to ID one of the Vors. They weren't trying to hide it like..." Karson cleared his throat. "Not like last time."

Jay did not have the fucking energy to think about Karson right now. "Go to every single one of the known locations, find people who matter. Not fucking mules or anyone expendable. They won't know anything. Because they planned this. It'll take longer to find people who know shit." Jay took a breath and lifted his hands, setting them back on his desk. They weren't shaking anymore. "Kill all of them."

Karson's eyes flickered ever so slightly. "Are you sure?"

Jay stared at the man in front of him. "They have my wife," he stated in little more than a whisper.

"I know, and we're—"

"They have my WIFE!" he roared, sweeping his hands across the desk, sending everything clattering to the floor including his computer. "You don't get me a location on her or bring in someone who knows her location, I will rip you apart piece by piece." Jay knew he was talking to his friend. One who had remained by his side through the years, had come up the ranks with him and had helped him take over this whole empire.

Jay knew that, somewhere inside of him. Jay also knew that he was speaking the truth. In the midst of this, there were no friends, only foes. He would rip apart anyone and everyone on this fucking earth to get to her.

Or he would die trying.

Because if anything happened to Stella, he was dead already.

FOUR HOURS LATER

Karson was out, killing while Jay was at Klutch having a meeting with one of his top lieutenants, Hector. Hector had been with him almost as long as Karson had. He'd stood up at his wedding, purely because of that.

"We have the location of the warehouses where the Russians store their coke for distribution?" Jay asked calmly.

Hector nodded.

"Take them over," Jay commanded. "Kill every single man working in them. Once that is done, burn them to the ground. Product and all."

Hector blinked. "Sir. That is millions of dollars' worth of cocaine. Tens of millions of dollars' worth."

Jay nodded.

Hector gaped. "You will start a war if you do this."

Jay's hands were flat on his desk. He ached to clench them together into fists, itching to beat them against flesh, pummel it down to nothing, to grind bone down to dust. But that was not how he got things done. That was not how he got Stella back. Getting Stella back—for now, at least—meant sitting behind this desk, giving orders.

"So what?" Jay asked.

Hector swallowed visibly. Jay knew that other men in his employ were intimidated by him at the best of times, and this was far from the best of times. Everyone was downright terrified—as they should've been. No one else, save Karson, would even think to question an order.

"So what? A war with the Russian Mafia, right now?" Hector pressed.

Because it was Hector, and the man had saved his life countless times, had bled for him and had helped him take control, Jay did not scream at him, fire him or beat him bloody.

"Yes, for Stella we will start a war," Jay replied. "To get her back, I'd go to war with the whole damn world. I'd burn everything down. Kill every last man, woman and child. Do you have a problem with that?"

Hector met Jay's gaze evenly. Hector was married. With one kid. Had as far as Jay knew—and Jay knew almost everything—never stepped out on his woman, though he was an attractive motherfucker and had some of the finest women in the city coming on to him.

"No, sir, I do not have a problem with that."

Jay nodded curtly. "Then go and burn down the fucking warehouses."

TWO HOURS LATER

Jay took off his jacket and laid it carefully on a chair. He squeezed his left sleeve where Stella had sewn a heart made of ruby.

She had done it to every single one of his suits, of which he had many. She'd sewn them all herself. He'd found her in their closet, her fingers bleeding. Of course, he'd pulled her up, grabbed her by the wrist and forbade her to make herself bleed for him every again.

She smiled. A soft, open and loving smile that was a punch to the stomach. He'd squeezed her hands so hard they'd bruise later. She didn't make a sound of protest. "I'll bleed for you, Jay," she whispered. "I'll bleed for you endlessly to show you that you wear my heart on your sleeve. That you have it with you always. I'll bleed for you so you know that you don't have to walk alone in this world thinking that there is nothing but darkness and hurt for you there."

The memory of that almost brought him to his knees.

Jay steeled himself, finding the part of him that wasn't human. It was smaller now, felt foreign, but that was what he needed. To be with Stella, he needed to hold on to his humanity. To find her, he had to abandon it all together.

But something stopped him.

Some people.

They came in threes.

The women.

First, Wren called.

Jay had no idea how she'd found out what happened, being in Nepal of all places, not speaking with Karson and—as far as he knew—not being a part of a criminal organization. What mattered is that she found out and that she was on the phone. Jay did not want to talk to Wren. He did not need to hear the ghost of what had been killed inside her that day. It filled him with too much regret and terror. Terror that he might find Stella distorted and empty like Wren was now, if he found her at all.

But he couldn't bring himself to hang up on Wren either.

"I'm getting her back," he said firmly when Wren made it known she was aware of Stella's kidnapping.

"Of course you're getting her back," she agreed.

That stunned him. Stunned him mute. The blind faith in her voice. The confidence. The trust. Wren actually trusted him to get her back. After everything he'd done to Wren, she still trusted him.

Fuck.

"She's pregnant, Jay," Wren's voice was small, but it was roar in Jay's ears. He couldn't hear a single thing beyond his ruined heart beating, thundering, cracking at his bones.

"She didn't tell me because she didn't want to hurt me. Didn't want to share her joy in the face of my sorrow," Wren sucked in a breath, and Jay marveled that he could still hear her since it seemed his entire body was shutting down.

"But I knew. A good girlfriend knows. We all knew."

Jay still didn't speak. He couldn't fucking speak.

"Okay, I'm guessing you're in some kind of waking coma because despite your badass alpha male skills, you didn't notice that she was pregnant," Wren continued. "But you've had shit going on, so don't be too hard on yourself. Our girl is strong. She's going to be okay. Until you find her, she'll be okay. I'm on the next flight home. If she's not back in your house eating pork rinds by the time I get home, I swear to fuck, I'll go and get her myself."

And then she hung up, leaving him with all of that.

Leaving him paralyzed.

The second came not long after the phone call. After he'd stared at the walls of his office in shock and fury, trying to digest what Wren had told him.

Pregnant.

Stella was fucking *pregnant.*

Jay went over every moment of the past three months. Then he cursed himself. Would've found a whip and fucking flagellated himself if he'd had the ability to move. Almost *three months*. And she hadn't had her period. And he hadn't fucking noticed. One month, perhaps, considering what had been going on.

No.

Even one month was unacceptable. There was no excuse for him losing focus, for him not noticing every single thing about his wife. He'd let himself become so consumed with losing her that he'd begun losing her in an entirely different way.

She hadn't been drinking. He'd poured her wine, she'd sipped it gingerly, never pouring herself more, yet her glass was always completely empty when he came back into a room, even if he was gone for less than five minutes.

The coffees too. She wasn't constantly carrying around a coffee cup. Herbal tea. She drank more of that. In the mornings she nibbled on dry toast, looking more pale than usual. Her nipples. Her fucking breasts. Swollen. Tender.

What in the *fuck* was wrong with him?

He'd made it his business to notice every single fucking thing about his wife since the moment he met her, savoring the way she smiled, knowing she was nervous when she tucked her hair behind her ear or turned on when she bit her lip and pressed her nails into her palms.

Pregnant.

With his child.

In the hands of one of the deadliest organizations in the world. In the hands of that animal, Dimitri. Jay would've torn his office apart with his bare hands had the elevator doors not dinged open.

"What are you doing?" Zoe demanded, eyes on Jay. They were full of blame and anger, but most of all fear.

"Everything in my power," Jay replied, surprised he was able to speak right now. His voice sounded strange and faraway, though Zoe was in stark focus.

She was wearing a bright red suit. Jay didn't like that. It reminded him of the fact his wife could be bleeding right now. His pregnant fucking wife.

Zoe shook her head rapidly, her curls moving as she did so. "No, you aren't. Because if you were doing everything in your power then my girl would be sitting here, breathing, unharmed," she spat. "*She is not*. Therefore you are not doing everything you can."

Jay wondered vaguely how Zoe even knew what was going on, though that was a stupid fucking thing to wonder with Wren in the picture. Even without Wren, Zoe would've found out. Yasmin too. These women were smart, connected and they loved their friend. They might not know what exactly what was going on, but they knew she was in danger, therefore they kept a close eye on her, calling her often, texting her more, coming around to the house at least twice a week.

"I knew. *I knew*," Zoe continued, her voice thick with blame. Blame that he deserved. "I knew that you would hurt her. And you did. First you hurt her heart. You changed her world. You dragged her in to your dark, dangerous and depraved one. I didn't like it, but she was happy, and I found peace in the fact that you're one bad motherfucker. The baddest, which meant you would move heaven, hell and everything in between to make sure that nothing happened to her. And if something did, I felt that you would make it right. Because there is no right in you except her." Her eyes were a black inferno.

"Except your love for her," she added, voice lower now but no less menacing. "That's the only right thing in a very *wrong* man. And that's very fucking dangerous for anyone who has even thought about harming her. So get some blood on your fucking hands. Make it happen."

She stared at him for a long time, daring Jay to argue, daring him to do anything, say anything. And when he didn't, she turned and walked off.

Then came the third.

On the heels of an angry, bloodthirsty woman, came another kind of woman all together. One who carried warmth, light, peace and was trailed by a stiff jawed man who had likely attempted to forbid the woman from coming here.

Polly hugged him before she spoke, not even hesitating at the energy Jay knew was surrounding him, the kind of energy that made all of his men hesitate before entering the room. The kind of energy that Heath—Polly's husband—was skilled at recognizing and the reason for the tight and dangerous look on the man's face.

"We're here to help," she told him when she finally let him go. She looked at her husband who did not at all seem like a man wanting to help Jay whatsoever.

The Greenstone Security men operated within the gray but were mostly good men with morals. The heroes. The only reason they were consorting with the villain was for love.

Polly did not see the distinction between the gray and the black, between the heroes and the wicked. She somehow saw the human within. That was her magic. That and getting her husband here, offering his help.

Her husband had had to live through what was killing Jay. He'd had to survive seeing his woman broken by the same kind of men that had Stella.

Polly had somehow survived. Somehow had emerged resembling the person she was before, managed to hold on to herself and her husband. The probability of that happening had been one in a billion. It would not likely be the case if something happened to Stella. Not because Stella wasn't extraordinary, but because of Jay. He was not a man like Heath, he didn't have anything inside him to help his wife heal. All he had was the ability to kill everyone who hurt her, show her their fucking corpses.

Jay swallowed acid.

"I appreciate you coming, but I don't need help," Jay balked tightly. He needed Polly to leave. The woman may be a certain kind of magic, but there was a limit to that. A limit to how long Jay could control himself.

Polly cocked her head and observed him. "Though I can't understand what you're going through, I know a man who does." Polly paused to look at her husband, Jay hating what passed between them because he'd had it once, and he was facing the prospect of never having it again.

"I know you'd tear down the walls of this city with your bare hands if that's what it took. Ripping them apart, bloodying them. I'm asking you to try it another way." Though Polly was nothing like Zoe—she wasn't wearing the same hatred in her gaze that the other woman had—she was just as determined. A worthy adversary. She would not leave his office without getting what she came for, without giving him what she came for.

Help.

So Jay relented.

And Greenstone Security joined the search for Stella. Jay hoped that the heroes and the villains were able to create some kind of magic.

But then Jay remembered who he was.

There was no fucking magic here.

Only ruin.

Jay wondered when he was supposed to call Richard, to tell him his daughter had been kidnapped. While carrying his grandchild.

No, he didn't call him to tell him she'd been kidnapped. He either called him when she had been returned safely with news of his grandchild or he called him when he found her, with news of his daughter's death.

ONE HOUR LATER

He had five men lined up on their knees. They had been rounded up by his own men and were now bound. Each of them had connections to the Russian mob, two were 'Vors'—the equivalent of made men, the title only given to men who worked for it, proved their loyalty. Those two were at the end of the line farthest from Jay, chins tilted upward, stoic and accepting of their fate. The other three were in various degrees of panic. Sweating, shaking, pleading.

Jay didn't waste time with words. He moved his gun to the forehead of the first man, fired then moved on to the next before the first hit the ground. He killed three in as many seconds.

Now the Vors were looking a little uncomfortable.

"I understand that you're accustomed to a certain kind of protection, given your position," Jay told them. "That there is a code, even between us villains, regarding who can and cannot be touched. Who deserves respect because they've earned it." Jay pressed the barrel of his gun to the forehead of the first Vor. "But there is no code here. Not now. Because you have touched who should never have been fucking gazed upon. I have no code. I will have no mercy. Your deaths will not burden me. Not in the slightest."

He pulled the trigger.

"So," he paused, moving the gun to the one remaining man. "Will you tell me something, or will you die?"

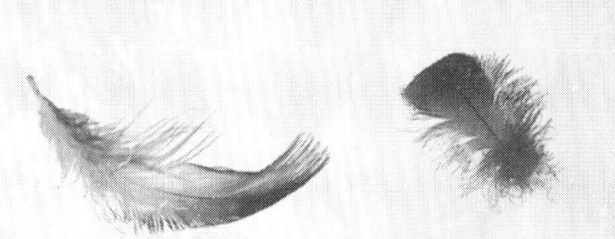

CHAPTER EIGHTEEN
Stella

N o one had hurt me.

At least not yet.

Well, the one called Dimitri with the square jaw and cruel eyes had backhanded me when I told him to go and fuck himself.

There was an older man with him, one with the same eyes as Dimitri only slightly less cruel. He had white hair, what I suspected was a square jaw underneath his gray beard and an air about him that told me he was in charge. He'd grabbed Dimitri's wrist when Dimitri raised his hand to hit me again.

"You do not touch her, *moy syn*," he hissed. He had an accent. Russian, of course, since I'd gathered that the Russian Mafia were the ones who had kidnapped me. I'd realized this without a calm, detached mind, with the fear that most likely should be paralyzing me right now.

Maybe I was in shock. I'd just seen my friend shot in the face. I'd brushed parts of his brain off my shirt. I didn't even vomit, I'd started doing that the past few days. That scared me. What if something was wrong with the baby? What if the shock had done something? I kept moving in my seat, looking for any kind of wetness in my underwear or stain on my pants.

Nothing.

Yet.

Dimitri's eyes flared. "Why the fuck not? Was that not why we brought her here? To punish that *mudak*?"

The man's eyes were even and calm in his son's fury. "She is here as our guest, to persuade Mr. Helmick in to accepting our partnership. If he cannot be persuaded then she shall be dispatched. With civility."

I tasted bile at the firmness of his words. The finality. There was no threat there. He did not need to threaten me. I was a pawn in all of this. This was the Russian fucking Mafia. If I didn't serve my purpose, they'd kill me. That was for certain.

I steeled myself not to cry, not to beg, cradling my stomach. No, I wouldn't cry or beg, I'd watch. I'd trust Jay was going to come. And I'd fight. For me. For our child. And for Jay. Because if anything happened to me, to our unborn child, he would be gone. All trace of humanity would drain from him like water draining in a bath.

He wouldn't do anything like hurt himself. No. He'd hurt other people. He'd hurt everyone and anyone without remorse. He'd hurt himself most of all. Torture himself with guilt, and he would live every single moment of his remaining life in agony.

There was no way that was happening.

I wasn't tied up. There was no need for it. We were in an

obscenely decorated living room. Gaudy, full of gold, stiff couches and fifty thousand-dollar rugs. I was sitting on an ornate armchair, digging my fingernails into the fabric, watching father and son fight about my fate.

"Why are we bothering with this bitch anyway?" Dimitri demanded, yanking his hand from his father's grip to pace the room.

His father stayed in one place, watching him.

"We have the manpower to take him over, with force," Dimitri continued.

"What? And let the blood stain the sidewalks of this city?" his father asked coolly.

Dimitri's eyes went wide. "Yes, Father, that's exactly what we do. That's what we *used* to do."

His father shook his head. "And fighting like that almost ended us," he countered softly. "The world has changed, and to survive, so must we. We do not fight like animals in the streets, drawing attention to ourselves. We work in the shadows, the darkest of which even the most penetrative eyes cannot see. We wear our suits, we look civilized in the daylight. We cultivate relationships. That is the way forward."

Dimitri stared at his father. "Cultivate fucking relationships?" He threw up his hands. "You have gotten soft, old man."

The man moved in a blur to even my eyes, and I was watching them very closely. His hands were around Dimitri's throat before the man could blink. He wasn't using the action to send a message either. Dimitri's eyes bulged, and his face reddened as he let out spluttering, choking noises. He pawed at his father's wrinkled but strong hands, but it was no use.

"You have gotten stupid, *moy syn*," the old man retorted softly. "You were in diapers when we fought wars on the street. You are spoiled, weak and only playing pretend. You are insolent."

Dimitri's face was so red it was turning purple, his hands weaker now as they pawed at the wrinkled hands. The father still held fast, choking, killing his son.

"You forget that your blood may protect you from many things, but it does not protect you from me," he continued, speaking slowly, elegantly. His accent was thick, but his English was impeccable. "I am still the head of this family. I am the reason this family still exists."

Finally, he let Dimitri go, to collapse on the floor, gasping, coughing and clawing at his throat.

He looked down at his son with contempt. "You see only the surface. Jay Helmick is a lot more than his surface. He is smart. He is powerful. He is utterly ruthless. It would've been stupid and suicidal to approach him earlier. He was strong and had no weaknesses."

The man speaking had ignored me since I'd entered the room, expect to stop his son from hitting me. Now his attention was focused on me, and my bones chilled underneath his gaze, my skin crawling.

"Now the man has a weakness. A way in. He will sit down with us and be forced to listen to our proposal. Jay Helmick is a smart man, he will not turn us down."

I jutted my chin upward. "You're wrong," I contradicted him in a firm voice. Being the weak, vulnerable woman right now would not serve me. I remembered the conversation with Wren that seemed like a lifetime ago where I'd been certain I couldn't be that type of woman. The wife of a man who dealt with the Russian Mob.

But in this moment, I found out that I could.

"Wrong about what, *milyy?*" Though the endearment was in another language, I recognized it, the patronizing tone, the way he barely even focused on me. To him, I was not worth focusing on. I was not a threat. Little did he know, that if he gave me the chance, I would be.

"Him sitting down with you," I replied, straightening in my seat. I needed to stop cradling my stomach, calling attention to it. The second they knew I was pregnant, things got more dangerous for me, for Jay. For our baby.

It was a good thing that Jay didn't know. It would've made him more dangerous and unpredictable.

"You've taken something from him," I continued. "You," I nodded to Dimitri, still wheezing on the floor, "put your hands on me. There is no going back from that." I smiled, wide and seething. "He's going to kill you all."

The man observed me, and it made me sick. Because his gaze was not dissimilar to the way Jay used to look at me, trying to pull me apart so he could use me.

"You have no idea who we are, *milyy,*" he said finally. "Your husband, he is powerful. He is ruthless. But so are we."

"I have an idea who you are," I disputed, maintaining eye contact. "And you think you know how ruthless my husband is. How powerful. But you've just pushed him over the edge. It doesn't matter who the fuck you are now. He will show you no mercy, he will destroy you all."

Jay

Jay got no intel out of the Vors. No satisfaction from their deaths either. He could not save her. He could not save his fucking wife. Jay was sitting in his office at Klutch, looking out onto the empty dance floor, wondering if he'd ever see Stella again. If he'd ever be human again.

It was the most unlikely person who saved Stella.

Though Jay couldn't be sure that she was saved since he didn't know if she was still alive.

But it was the most unlikely person to *maybe* save her life. Maybe save Jay.

When Felicity walked through the door of his office, he was ready to hurt her. It didn't matter that he had a code about hurting women. He had no code anymore because he had no religion, no place of worship, no fucking Stella.

Jay was a dangerous man to be around, and Felicity knew that. Because she knew him. Or she knew who he used to be, when he was younger, weaker, when he wasn't ready to burn the whole world down to smell his wife's hair again, to feel his child growing in her stomach.

"I know where she is," Felicity stated as he stood, rounding his desk to do fuck knows what.

That stopped Jay in his tracks. "You better tell me more, and tell me why you know this if you want to leave this room."

Felicity didn't look afraid. She was not a woman who was afraid of threats from men, even when those men were willing to follow through on them. Felicity was the daughter of a very powerful man, a very old family, one that was not friends of the Kuznetsovs.

"My father has been surveilling them, waiting to strike," she offered, eyes never leaving his. "He knew they'd be distracted, weak, being preoccupied with you. I didn't know she was gone until now, or I would've come sooner."

"Where the fuck is she?" Jay demanded, a tremor in his voice.

Jay left the second Felicity uttered Stella's location. He knew she'd expected more, had expected him to hear her say whatever she had to say, whatever goodbyes, but he didn't have time.

He needed to get to his wife.

His child.

He needed to wear the blood of everyone who had thought they could take her from him.

THIRTY MINUTES LATER

He was covered in blood. Some of it might've been his. He hoped it was, he deserved to bleed for this. Whatever Stella had gone through, he needed it tenfold. If he found her hurt, if he found her dead, all he could hope for was that his wounds killed him too.

Even if she was untouched, if this was some kind of perfect fucking world where his wife—his pregnant wife—was kidnapped by the Russian Mafia, and they hadn't laid a hand on her, she would not come out unscathed. There would be scars. There would be the knowledge that he had been unable to protect her. She wouldn't blame him. But he'd spend a lifetime blaming himself. Hating himself. If he was somehow lucky enough to be given a lifetime with his wife.

With their child.

He didn't think anymore.

Couldn't think anymore.

He had to focusing on killing. He was good at that. Magnificent at that. Being a husband, being a father, being a human—that's where he failed.

The mansion on the coast had been guarded well. Though they were arrogant enough to think he wouldn't find them, they weren't stupid enough to rule it out. Jay had not brought as many men because he hadn't needed to. They'd killed quietly because they did not want the old man to know they were there. The second he knew of their presence, he'd kill Stella.

The Greenstone Security men were on the perimeter because Jay had told them to stay at the fucking perimeter. He knew they'd have thoughts about mercy once they took over the house.

There was no room for mercy here. No room for heroes.

They weren't leaving any alive. Not a single one. Karson was at his side when they entered the living room. The room that had been guarded heavily. The room that contained Stella.

Stella was the only thing on his mind as he slit the throat of the very last man standing in his way. He'd go to her, drenched in the blood of his enemies, eyes full of death and violence, he'd go to her as a monster.

Because that's all he was now.

Stella

I'd just finished eating.

They'd served me steak, rare, and potatoes. Though my stomach was roiling at the sight of meat, I'd eaten it because I knew I needed my strength. And because I needed the steak knife I was cutting up the bloody meat with.

The old man watched me eat, sitting across from me eating his own steak. It was a predictable move, the hostage pocketing the silverware, so I knew that I'd never get away with it without a distraction.

And we were kind of running short on distractions. Being a hostage was actually a lot more boring than I'd thought it would be. Of course there was the undercurrent that I could die at any moment. But I knew that they'd taken me for a reason, they wouldn't kill me until they sat down with Jay.

Jay would do anything to keep me alive. Us alive.

So I waited.

There was a lot of waiting.

No more hitting me in the face. Dimitri had come and gone from the room, finally settling himself in the corner, drinking vodka, muttering to himself like a surly teenager.

My cheek felt tight and hot. I knew I'd have a black eye. The first time in my life I'd ever been hit by a man. I knew he wasn't long for this world.

"I did not think Jay Helmick was stupid enough to fall in love," the old man commented to me, inclining his head with interest. "I figured him much too smart for that." His eyes ran over me, making it an effort to keep my steak down. "But I understand it. You are a beautiful woman."

"You ordered the shooting that killed my best friend's unborn child," I spat. "Therefore, you are an evil, despicable piece of dirt, and I can't wait to know you're rotting in hell."

He grinned, showing all of his teeth. "Fiery too," he nodded. "No one who speaks to me like that is long for this world."

I gripped my steak knife, longing to sink it into his wrinkly neck. "This is not your world, buddy," I snapped. "It my husband's."

And like I'd fucking timed it, the doors crashed open.

The first man through it was covered in blood, wearing a black suit and a wedding ring. A gun in one hand, knife in the other. Jade eyes focused on me. Dimitri stumbled out of his chair, knocking over his bottle of vodka as he did so. I figured he was going for his gun, but Karson was quicker. It was a beautiful sight to see, Karson holding a knife to the man's throat.

I moved quickly, without thinking, pushing out of my seat and sprinting toward Jay, still gripping my steak knife.

Jay moved quickly, too, toward me. But he didn't give me what I wanted, he didn't pull me into his arms, didn't let me smell him, touch him. He moved to the place he'd promised me he'd stand ... in front of me.

He had to do that. We were still kind of in the middle of something right now, we couldn't exactly have a romantic union. So I made do with pressing myself to his back, breathing easily for the first time in hours. I did not smell the blood, the death, if such things had a smell. I only smelled Jay.

The old man had stood from the table casually, looking far too calm for someone who was severely outnumbered by a lot of men and women with knives and guns. I recognized most of them.

Not Eric, though. Eric was dead.

"Your men are dead," Jay declared, speaking to the old man.

His voice was music. Poetry. It was a glass of ice-cold lemonade on a blissful summer day.

For his part, the old man nodded once, without grief or loss.

"Take her away," Jay ordered, eyes not on me but on Dimitri and his father. His voice was ice cold. It was coated in death.

Though it scored my skin, that voice, that void space where my husband should've been, I held fast, staring at his profile.

"I'm not going anywhere," I declared, yanking my arm from Karson's hand.

When Jay's eyes flickered to me, I hid my flinch well. He stared at me like I was a stranger.

He nodded once, then turned back to father and son.

"You overstepped," Jay stated. "By a long fucking way. You overestimated your power, underestimated mine. You lost the second you went after women." His eyes flickered to Karson then my stomach. "And children."

My stomach dropped, and my mouth went dry. He knew. Somehow he knew. Whether he'd figured it out himself or someone—likely Zoe or Wren—had told him, it didn't matter. He knew. This was not the way I wanted to share that news with my husband, not at all. Then again, I hadn't planned on doing some kind of cutesy surprise with a pregnancy test in a box with some booties or whatever people did on social media these days.

No, I hadn't. But I certainly hadn't expected this either.

"What are your terms?" the old man asked, chin lifted up, eyes not simmering with the fear that should've been living there.

"You will kill your son," Jay said.

The old man stared at Jay without emotion, without surprise. "Very well."

Dimitri gaped at his father, face turning various shades of red and purple as he struggled in the arms of the man who held him. "You cannot be serious! I am your son, I am the heir—"

"You are *nothing*!" Dimitri's father roared, crossing the distance between them. "You are the reason I am standing here, with my men, my friends and brothers killed because you had to swing your dick around. Because you saw the most powerful man in town and wanted to prove you were stronger than him." He stepped forward, almost nose to nose with his son. "What I have been trying to teach you all of these years, is that the second you need to prove your strength, you no longer have any."

Dimitri was breathing heavily now, fear transforming his face into something small, weak, pathetic. "Father," he whispered.

He cupped his son's cheek. "I love you."

Then he lifted a gun and shot his son in the temple.

I didn't scream, though I did on the inside, unable to look away, the second man I'd seen die tonight. This one I was much, much gladder to see.

The old man stared down at his son's corpse without emotion, though he stared at it for a long time. No one else spoke. We just waited.

Then the man lifted his head, face scrunched in fury and hatred. "It is done. You have your vengeance."

Jay nodded to the man who had been holding Dimitri. He jerked forward and snatched the gun the old man had been limply holding. It wasn't very impressive; I would've thought the commander of a Russian crime syndicate would fight to avoid being defeated so easily and without any kind of resistance.

He looked very much like an old man now.

Jay stepped forward, holding his own gun.

The old man didn't retreat. "Men like you think they can hurt us," he spat. "Think you can bring down my family. You want to show the old family what strength you have. What power you wield. You—"

"There are no men like me," Jay interrupted him. "There is only me." He raised his gun to the forehead of the old man. Then he pulled the trigger.

The shot echoed. The body fell to the floor with a thud.

CHAPTER TWENTY

I didn't get a second alone with Jay.

I wasn't quite sure how that had happened, but it did. Karson drove the SUV that we left the mansion in. Jay barely looked at me except to run his hands over my body, checking for injury. His hands paused over my stomach for less than a second then moved over my swollen cheek. His face was inscrutable, eyes dead.

Not one word was spoken. No heartfelt reunions, no declarations of love, absolutely nothing. Then again, I'd known Jay was not a man for heartfelt reunions, though I had expected *something*. I didn't speak because I was afraid. Not of the blood that covered him, not because I'd just seen him kill a man. That mattered surprisingly little. I was afraid of the anger that was humming through him, that was a physical thing, brushing against me the entire ride home. I ached to at least take his hand in mine, initiate some kind of contact between us, but something stopped me. He stopped me.

I settled for his body next to mine on the ride home, settled for his mere presence, albeit a furious one, my heart beating in my throat.

Once we got home, things didn't exactly get better. Jay did not speak, though he opened the door for me, helped me out of the SUV. I cherished the fleeting brush of his hand against mine, but it was quickly gone.

When we got home, there was a strange woman in our living room wearing a white coat and a kind smile. A doctor. There was also a makeshift bed made from the sofas in the living room. And an ultrasound machine. Or I was pretty sure that's what it was. There mere sight of it stopped me in my tracks.

I wasn't sure how Jay had managed to get an ultrasound machine delivered to our house by the time we got home. But then again, I didn't quite understand how he and an unknown amount of his men and women seemingly defeated the Russian Mafia. It shouldn't have been surprising.

I hadn't had an ultrasound yet. Hadn't even seen a doctor about the baby. There was no way I could do that without feeling like I had truly betrayed Jay. Being faced with the machine, I was suddenly overcome with terror. What if something was wrong? What if that screen showed nothing? Or even worse, what if it showed something, something that had been created with love yet had died somewhere in the midst of all of this?

My mouth turned dry, my stomach full of knots. My hands started shaking, and I had an overwhelming urge to run. To run where, I did not know. There was no running from this. Either the news was good, or it wasn't. Either our baby was okay, or it wasn't. Fear wouldn't change fate. I'd continue breathing regardless.

"Stella," Jay's voice was still cold, detached.

I blinked, staring at him. He'd wiped off some of the blood that covered his face at some point, so his face was mostly free of it, but there were still splatters here and there. It remained on his hands.

If the kind looking doctor thought it odd that a blood-spattered man in a suit had ordered an ultrasound machine be brought to his house, she didn't act like it.

"Mrs. Helmick," she greeted me softy. "If you'll lie down, I can check you over. Then we'll take a peek at your baby. Get some photos for you and your husband." She spoke in a calm, warm tone, much unlike that doctor who I'd screamed at all those months ago.

When Wren lost her baby.

My blood went cold, and the room tilted slightly. Jay was at my side in an instant, holding me up, face no longer a mask of cold granite. Worry, terror flickered there.

I was up in his arms in an instant, him carrying me the short distance to the makeshift bed. He brushed the hair gently from my forehead, eyes burning into mine before he stepped away. He didn't go far while the doctor—Abagail—checked me over. First, she took my blood pressure, asked some questions. I answered them on autopilot, convincing myself that my baby was gone. Our baby was gone.

"Now, this will be a little cold," Abagail warned before squirting something on my stomach.

I felt nothing. I was already numb, already bracing for impact.

Jay stood close, staring at me. I couldn't look at him. Instead, my eyes went to the monitor connected to the ultrasound machine. If things weren't different, I might've asked how the fuck Jay had managed all this.

Things weren't different.

I just stared blankly at the screen as it lit up.

Her wand moved against my stomach. "Now," she murmured, staring at the screen.

I would've fallen down if I wasn't already laying down, because right there, make no mistake, was a baby.

A noise thumped through the speakers, fast, quiet, but it vibrated through my bones.

"That's the heartbeat," Abagail announced, smiling at me. "Your baby looks to be measuring perfectly for thirteen weeks."

Perfectly.

Our baby.

Though it was hard to tear my eyes from the screen, I managed to look at Jay, tears streaming down my face.

He was staring at the screen in awe.

Too quickly, Abagail moved the wand and wiped the jelly from my stomach. As soon as she stopped, there was a hand there, on my stomach. A large, masculine hand, covered in blood, cradling my stomach. Cradling our baby.

For an instant. Then he pulled down my shirt and helped me up to a sitting position. "Stay there," he ordered.

I frowned at him, but he was already looking at Abagail who was packing up her things.

"The baby is perfect, healthy," the doctor assured us, looking to me then to Jay, tensing when she met his eyes.

I couldn't blame her, there was something about Jay right now. Even in the best of circumstances, he had a 'do not fuck with me' vibe.

"And Stella?" Jay demanded.

"Your wife is healthy too," she replied, meeting his eyes. It was exceptionally brave of her. Not that Jay would do anything. "She is a little dehydrated, and obviously her eye will be swollen for a time, but she is young. She'll be fine."

I wondered what this woman thought. If she thought Jay was the reason for my eye. I wondered if she was doing this for money or for some other reason. She seemed kind, strong. But there wasn't exactly time for me to invite her to stay for coffee and tell me her life story. She was gone once Jay was assured of my health, but not before giving me her card, urging me to use it day or night.

Then it was just us. Me and Jay. Alone.

I thought that's what I'd been waiting for since the second he stormed through those doors. Since I'd watched a friend of mine die in front of me.

Now it was here, now it was just the two of us, and I didn't know what to do. How to be, what to say. Jay was across the room from me, staring. My skin burned underneath his stare, the harsh lights overhead illuminating the blood that stained his neck, his suit. Magnifying his beauty.

"You're pregnant." Jay's voice was empty. Scarily so. Eyes too. I'd felt a considerable amount of fear these past few days. A lot, actually. But never had I been so terrified as I was now.

I swallowed, my throat dry and scratchy, nodding because I didn't trust myself to speak.

He stared at me with that chasm behind his eyes, the shape of the man I loved but with no substance. This was the monster.

"You're pregnant, and *you didn't fucking tell me!*" He roared the last part.

Roared.

I'd never heard Jay raise his voice like this. Never. And it was in the face of the news of his unborn child growing inside of me. My stomach lurched with the need to be sick.

Jay was pacing now, like a caged animal, not looking at me, eyes darting around the room as if he was searching for something that he could destroy. There were many expensive, breakable and rare things in this room. Things that would shatter easily, beyond repair. But none them more delicate than me right now.

I steeled myself for the hurt, for the rejection, for the emotional blow, even though he'd promised he wouldn't do it again. He had promised he wouldn't break me again. But that was my fault, wasn't it? For believing the lies of a sinner.

Jay didn't break anything. Not yet, anyway. He stopped in the middle of the room.

"You kept it from me." It was an accusation. A sentence.

"I didn't keep it from you," I rasped, my throat still dry and scratchy. "I was looking for the right time, with—"

"The right time, Stella, would've been the second you found out. The moment you knew that you were growing our child. *That* was the right time."

Then he did something that I didn't think Jay would ever do to me again. Not after everything we'd been through, not after I'd just been kidnapped by the Russian Mob or told him about the baby.

He walked away from me.

Although I felt alone, terrified and heartbroken, I did not follow Jay. It wasn't a smart decision. I needed him. I'd gone a whole day thinking I'd never see him again, then thinking that I'd lost our baby. My hand went to my lower stomach, still flat. My other hand fingered the black and white picture sitting on our kitchen counter, the one the doctor had printed out before she left.

Of our baby. Our healthy baby.

As happy, as deliriously grateful as that made me, I was afraid. There had been no joy on Jay's face. Not an ounce. I worried that I'd pushed him with my lies. Pushed him too far. Away.

It was eating me, that worry. Causing my hands to shake and my vision to blur. So I moved to the kitchen, made myself a very sweet cup of tea, one that was meant to cure all things. I sat on a bar stool and drank it, staring at the black and white picture of our baby, waiting to find the strength to go to Jay.

It was dark in our bedroom when I found the strength to go there. Jay was not in bed. He was sitting in an armchair, facing the window, nothing but a shadow.

I was a coward. I didn't know how to exist around this version of the man that I loved. I went to the shower because I was still wearing the same clothes that were stained with Eric's blood. The grime of this day. I stayed there for a long time, letting the hot water wash over the knots in my shoulders, mixing with the tears that I finally let fell. Parts of me, tiny, hopeful, foolish parts thought Jay might come to me then. Might step into the shower, fully clothed, take me into his arms, hold me. Whisper his love and devotion then fuck me slowly, filling me up utterly and completely.

But he didn't do that. That was not my husband.

I got out of the shower, drying myself with the lush, expensive towels I'd washed myself earlier that week—I did those things now. We'd bought everything in the fridge together, only last week, a lifetime ago. Slowly, I lathered lotion over every inch of my body. Once that was done, I took a breath and stared at myself in the mirror. My face was rounder than it used to be. Fuller. Even my lips. My breasts were larger, much larger with every day it seemed, the veins going to my nipples bright and dark against my pale skin.

I turned to the side, running my hand down my stomach, feeling the place where our child was growing. Standing like this, under the harsh light of our bathroom, I could see the swell in my stomach, barely visible but there.

"I see you, little baby," I whispered.

Then I met my own eyes, took a long and deep breath then went to our bedroom. Went to my husband.

He was still sitting in the same place he'd been when I'd entered. If I didn't do anything, I knew he'd sit there all night. I knew he'd retreat further and further into himself where I couldn't reach him.

I didn't turn on any lights, we needed the night. My footfalls made no sound as I moved toward him then knelt at his feet. My palms went to his thighs as they opened ever so slightly for me. He was naked.

Even that simple touch sent relief to my bones. Need to my blood. It was slight, the tension leaving his granite body, but I noticed it.

"You once told me that you lied as easily as your breathed," I whispered, tilting my head up to him, knowing he was looking at me. "I do not know how to lie. Not to anyone, but especially not to you."

"But you did," he hissed into the darkness, anger saturating his tone. "You lied to me for *months*."

"Did I?" I asked, clenching my hands around the bare skin of his thighs, rubbing them gently. I ached to go higher, to grasp his cock in my hands then take it into my mouth, but I knew it wasn't time for that.

Yet.

"I told you in a thousand little ways, without words," I explained, still rubbing his thighs.

He let out a harsh breath, not touching me. "But I needed the fucking words, Stella."

I bit my lip. "I know. I know you did. I owed you them. And I will torture myself with what might've been different if I had told you." Maybe Eric might not have died. Maybe Jay wouldn't be so far from me right now.

Maybe.

"But I did. I lied, in my own way. And I'm sorry. But our baby is healthy, Jay. And we are here. Together. Safe."

Jay didn't say anything, and it hurt. Killed. But I understood it.

"Did you end the entire Russian Mafia?" I asked on a whisper when he'd been silent for some time.

He chuckled without humor. It was the first time I'd heard such a sound, and I hated it. "A snake does not only have one head, pet. There will be more. There will always be more. This is not over. This will always be your life." A pause. Thick. Ugly. "If you want it."

At that, I moved, standing only long enough so I could climb on his lap. He was hard already. I was wet already. Therefore, I did not torture either of us. I lowered myself onto him. My swift intake of breath was dwarfed by the animalistic sound that came out of the back of Jay's throat.

I leaned forward, moving slowly, savoring the way he felt inside me. My hands settled on his neck, pressing our foreheads together. "There he is," I moaned. "There is my man. My husband. My whole heart."

He didn't speak, but I hadn't expected him to. His hands settled on my hips, squeezing tightly, with the perfect amount of pain, the perfect amount of Jay.

"Nothing in this world will tear me from your side," I continued, my voice breathy, orgasm building. "No battle, no blood, no wars. Nothing, Jay. I love you, including your entire wretched and wicked heart."

Finally, he kissed me, deep, angry, loving. It was then I exploded around him, crying out into his mouth, breaking apart on top of him. His hands gripped even tighter around my hips, moving me against him.

"I love you," he rasped. "With all of me. Till death."

"Till death," I whispered back.

ONE MONTH LATER

Recovery from what happened did not come swiftly. Jay had been struck with his greatest fear: losing me. Not only losing me but the child that I hadn't told him about. He'd had to honor the most wicked part of himself in order to get me back. I understood that. I understood he could not rebound to who he once was. I knew he was fighting his way back to me.

And I did everything in my power to bring him back. I played Debussy. I framed every new sonogram photo we got—and he made sure that we got one per week, our doctor not even bothering to argue with him anymore.

I started designing our nursery—gender neutral because surprisingly, Jay did not want to know the gender. Jay. The man who loved control above all else. Who needed control above all else.

He wanted a *surprise*.

I gave him that too.

He wanted me working less. I didn't love that but considering my morning sickness was making itself known the entire day, it wasn't exactly a hardship. I set to redesigning our house, turning it into a home.

Wren, Zoe and Yasmin were around often, and they helped with decorating, their laughter bouncing off the walls. Even if Wren's was forced. She had barely left my side since she got back and had pointedly ignored Karson when he was around, which was often.

It was hard to watch. They'd had so much together, they'd had everything, and in one stroke, there was nothing. It haunted me, the sorrow for my friend and fear for myself. At how close Jay and I could've been to such a fate.

I did not get out of what happened unscathed.

I woke in a cold sweat often, and tonight was no different. Jay was always there.

"A nightmare," Jay told me, his hands holding my wrists above my head. I must've been fighting him in my sleep. It was something I did now.

"You're safe," he murmured into my neck, transferring his grip of my wrists to one hand, the other cradling the swell of my stomach. Which he was doing more often now. Cradling my growing stomach. Laying his lips gently against it. Murmuring things to our baby when he thought I was sleeping.

"You are both safe," he promised.

Then his hand moved lower. Low enough that I gasped.

"You are mine," he moved his finger inside of me. "Till death."

Then he removed his finger and fucked me until I passed out. I had no more nightmares that night.

Eventually, I had none at all.

FIVE MONTHS LATER

Ruby Grace Helmick came into the world with purpose. The first person she saw, with her wide blue gaze, was her father, since he was the one who delivered her.

We didn't have time to get to the hospital, the best one in the city. The one that Jay had made sure always had a birthing suite available one week on either side of my due date. Our doctor had assured us that first children always come late. Our doctor had not taken in to account that Ruby took after her father and was not going to let anyone tell her what to do.

At three in the morning, two weeks before my due date, I woke up to contractions. I'd felt off the entire day before that, so I'd dismissed them as Braxton Hicks. Jay, who was hyperaware of my every movement these days, woke immediately. I'd told him all I needed was a cup of tea and maybe some pork rinds—I was a fucking fiend for them—but then my water broke.

Jay, for his part, did not panic. Not even the slightest. Not even when it became very apparent that we would not make it to the hospital to deliver our daughter. Jay, of course, acted like he delivered babies every day, not commanding the criminal underworld. He played Debussy. He coached me through the contractions, let me scream and try to break his fingers in my grip, let me curse him to high hell. He did that all with an aura of control, one that made me feel safe, comfortable, protected. When I wasn't telling him what a fucking asshole he was for not knowing how to administer an epidural, that was.

And then Ruby came.

Jay cradled her in his arms, cutting the cord and cleaning her with the upmost care and tenderness. "A girl," he rasped, tearing his eyes from her to me. Tears ran down his cheeks. "We have a daughter."

"Ruby," I whispered weakly as he placed her on my chest. The whole world on my chest.

"Ruby," he agreed, holding us both close.

Ruby had a lot of people ready to welcome her into the world on her birthday. My father, who I'd called at four in the morning, exhausted in my bed, holding our baby girl—once my doctor had made a house call, checking the both of us over thoroughly. We were both fine. Well, I was not fine. I had given birth in my bathroom, with my husband seeing the entire process without drugs. I was in a lot of fucking pain, though it didn't much matter with my daughter in my husband's arms, sleeping soundly against his bare chest, looking like she didn't have a care in the world.

Jay was gazing down at her like he had all the cares in the world. All the love, devotion and *worship* in the world. It seemed he had a new church. And I was totally fucking okay with that. Because he was back. Entirely. The moment our daughter fell into his arms—even in my pain drenched haze—I saw him, the last piece of him, come back to me.

Once my father had heard about it all, he decided to get in his car, at four in the morning, and drive all the way to L.A. No way was he waiting for a flight to meet his granddaughter. He hadn't needed to since Jay had already sent the jet for him. It said something that my father didn't even argue or grumble over it. He just got on. He wanted to see his grandchild.

Everyone wanted to see our Ruby.

Wren, Zoe and Yasmin were permanent fixtures, of course, showering their niece with gifts, making it so she was barely in her crib, always in someone's arms. Though they were mostly Jay's. He was loath to let his daughter go and scowled at anyone who had her in their arms a moment too long. Except me, of course.

Janet arrived the same day as my father, within only a few hours of him, which made no sense since I'd only texted her the night before to tell her that Ruby had entered the world safe and sound. I was sleep deprived and full of hormones, but I was pretty sure that math did not compute. Though I figured it out quickly when we were sharing a cup of tea while I was feeding Ruby.

"You *moved* here? To America?" I gaped.

Janet smiled, nodding with her hand lightly brushing Ruby's head. "I did."

I stared at her. "Why?"

She looked over to where my father and Jay were smoking cigars on the balcony. "Because, my girl, love makes you do some crazy shit."

I blinked.

My heart bloomed. "My dad? You *love* him?"

She turned back to me with her brows raised. "Of course I fucking love the man. I'd be mad if I didn't."

Janet. And my father. How had I not seen it?

Oh, because I was busy being pregnant, kidnapped and helping my husband find his way back to me, that's why.

But still.

I hadn't seen the most wonderful thing in the world. Well, second to my daughter. And my husband.

My father finding love.

So yeah, Ruby's birthday was pretty fucking eventful.

And me, just having given birth and all, found everyone being around a lot. Jay, being Jay, noticed that I was overwhelmed and kicked every single person out without apology. He was greedy for us to be alone, that much I knew. And I was too.

Leaning on Jay heavily, I watched Ruby sleep peacefully in her bassinet beside our bed. I'd never seen anything more beautiful in my life. There was a smattering of dark hair on her tiny head. I already knew that she was going to take after her father.

"If it was a boy, I'd know what to do better," Jay commented, speaking low, being careful not to wake her.

Our daughter.

"I'd teach him how to be strong, how to defend himself, his mother, how to be the man I wasn't." He looked down at the little scrunched up, chubby, perfect face of our daughter. My heart cracked with the love and fear injected in his gaze.

I moved my hand to cradle his jaw, the one that seemed so strong, like granite, but was as fragile as an eggshell in my hands.

"You will teach her how she deserves to be loved," I whispered. "You will teach her that there will be never a person on this earth who loves her as much as her father. You will teach her how to throw a punch. How to make a mean fettucine. To appreciate classical music. To love poetry. You will teach her a thousand and one things."

Jay looked up at me. "Just like her mother taught me. A thousand and one things."

My eyes filled as the sea breeze filtered in the windows.

EPILOGUE

My father got married in New Zealand.

To Janet.

Obviously.

Though she was quite happy to live in Missouri with my father, she was intent on getting married on the beach in New Zealand. Since my father utterly adored her—he worshipped her—he, of course, agreed.

They got married on the beach, the one I'd once considered as mine, the one that turned out to be theirs. I was more than happy about that.

Ruby was their flower girl. She walked down the aisle with her father because she didn't like to be far from him. And because she was unsteady on her little feet. He did not like to be far from her either.

Ruby was a daddy's girl. Which I didn't mind since she was also a mommy's girl. Our beautiful, dark haired, emerald eyed girl had more than enough love for the both of us. For everyone. She was a happy baby. Peaceful. Barely even cried.

At the beginning, I was on the phone to the doctor constantly, freaking out that there was something wrong with her. There had to be something wrong with her.

But she was perfect.

Jay was perfect with her. Calm. Patient. Adoring. The same way he was with me. His hands were always on me, his lips, too, waiting for the day that the doctor gave us approval to have sex again. Although we didn't do that well at waiting since I'd seemed to heal quickly, and the hunger for my husband was impossible to deny.

Though becoming parents was something that wholeheartedly changed the landscape of our world, it somehow did not change us. Did not change who we were. It didn't fix us either. We still had our problems, Jay still had his demons.

But we battled. For each other.

For our daughter.

The one who flew across the world at just one year old without a fucking *peep*. She lounged happily in her father's arms the entire trip. And then she never left the side of the grandfather she adored, the one who adored her right back.

We all stayed at the cottage that had been my escape. The cottage that had brought Jay and I back together. In the days before the wedding, he put us in the car, not telling us where we were going. Both Ruby and I were content in Jay's company and more than happy to let him lead the way. We drove, marveling at the scenery I hadn't had the chance to see the first time we were here. Ruby was happy too, looking at the window, playing with her toys, giggling at her father. We ended up at Tongariro National Park, to hike the crossing. To climb a mountain in New Zealand. The last thing on the list, since we'd stopped off in Bali for a week before coming here, watching the sun set, drinking cocktails and eating some of the most wonderful food in the world. Ruby loved our adventures. She was happy to be strapped into a backpack and hike six hours. I was less than happy since my fitness level wasn't exactly at its peak. But it was worth it. Totally fucking worth it.

"I'm going to have to make a new list," I whispered, leaning against Jay, staring at the breath-taking scenery around us.

"Make as many lists as you like," Jay replied, kissing Ruby's head. "I'll spend my life crossing off each and everything thing."

So yeah, things were fucking great.

We made it back to the cottage for the wedding, my cup already overflowing.

I was my father's best man, standing happily beside him, wearing a black, tailored YSL suit, though I was a little over dressed for a wedding where the bride went barefoot.

Wren, Yasmin and Zoe were also in attendance, also wearing couture so I didn't care. As I stood and watched my father find his happily ever after with my husband in the front row, our daughter sitting contently on his knee, her little hand curled in his large one, there was not a thing wrong in the world. Not at this moment, at least. I knew that Jay's life—our life—meant that it would not always be like this. We would not always have peace. There were still nights when Jay came home with blood on his hands and death in his gaze. His demons still clawed at his throat, trying to convince him that he was not worthy, that he was too wicked for us.

He still hated himself.

But he did all of that less often. A lot less.

We had plenty of things to celebrate. And celebrate we did. With a ceremony and a party on the beach, huge tents erected right in the sand, bursting with people, music and food. Though there was one person noticeably absent from the party.

"Hey, you," I handed Wren a glass of wine before I sat beside her in the sand.

She took it with a smile. A sad one. Still so sad. My marvelous friend had yet to let the light back in to her life. She had yet to let Karson back in to her life. He had not stopped trying.

Wren didn't speak of it, what was going on with her and Karson. Not one single word. Not to me, not to Zoe, not to Yasmin, not to Jay. The two of them had become close. Something I liked since neither Zoe nor Yasmin enjoyed that kind of relationship with him. Though Zoe had warmed considerably since my kidnapping. Something had changed between the two of them, and I was happy for it.

"Hey back," Wren clinked her wine glass with mine.

We looked out upon the sunset as the music from the party filtered along the beach.

"I'm happy for your dad," she remarked. "He's a total DILF, and I would've married him myself if he hadn't stopped babbling on about me being young enough to be his daughter."

I laughed, looking at my friend's profile for a beat before turning back to the sunset.

"He deserves it," I agreed. "Happiness. Just like my friend does."

Wren kept staring at the ocean, taking a large sip of her drink. "I'm trying, Stells. I promise, I'm trying."

I blinked away tears. This was the closest Wren had come to letting me in for a long time. She'd been stateside since my kidnapping, coming and going throughout the months of my pregnancy. I knew it had been hard for her, for her to see me grow more and more pregnant, to see what she had lost. She'd been happy for me. She showered me with love and gifts, but I knew it killed her to do so. I knew that she was a walking wound. But somehow, she soldiered on. She utterly adored Ruby, spoiling her rotten and never tiring of whatever game Ruby was obsessed with at the time.

"I know you are, sweetheart," I whispered, reaching for her free hand and squeezing it. "You will get there."

She looked at me, her eyes twinkling with unshed tears. It looked like she might've been ready to talk to me, finally, if not for someone calling my name. Well, one of my names.

"Mommy!"

We both looked toward the sound.

Ruby ran through the sand, her father holding her small hand, walking slowly beside her. She'd probably refused to be carried because she was strong-willed and independent. And Jay would not have argued with his daughter because Jay always let his little princess call the shots. Oh, we were going to have fun in her teenage years.

"I am happy," Wren said, watching them. "Seeing you like this, babe. Seeing you get everything you deserve. And more."

I squeezed her hand. "You will get it too, I promise." I silently vowed to make sure I figured out a way to keep that promise.

Wren stood, not saying anything, just kissing my cheek and running to Ruby, lifting her into the air and kissing her cheek before putting her down and whispering in her ear. Ruby giggled, the sound carrying over the ocean.

She then ran from her Aunt Wren into my arms. I lifted her high and cuddled her close. Jay's arms were around the both of us in the next second.

He kissed Ruby's cheek, then mine. I inhaled. The smell of my daughter, of my husband and the smell of the ocean. The sweetest smells in the world.

Jay

Both of them slept.

Both of his girls.

He leaned in to kiss his daughter's head, inhaling the sweetest smell in the world, tied with the smell of his wife's hair.

Jay brushed her chubby cheek then went back to bed, back to his wife. She curled up against him immediately, sleeping deeply, clinging to him, trusting him. After everything, his warm, pure and kind wife still trusted him with everything. With the whole world.

He did not deserve that trust. He did not deserve either of them. But he had them. And God help anyone who tried to take them from him, for he world wear their blood.

ACKNOWLEDGEMENTS

This is the first book I've written since being home in New
Zealand. It definitely won't be the last. After the absolute chaos and
heartbreak of last year, writing this was a breeze. I think my muse lives
here, between the mountains, the rocks, the lakes. I am so so proud of
this story. I know that book one was hard. That Jay was cold, cruel,
unlikeable. I hope you love him by the time you're reading this. I hope
your heart feels full.

I know mine does.

I'm so lucky to come out of the other side after the year we've
had. I'm so lucky that I have the solace of writing. That I have
wonderful people in my life that make all of this possible.

Taylor. My partner, my best friend, my soulmate. You endure my
moods, my ups and downs, my demons. Thank you for keeping me
safe. For making me laugh. For letting me cry. For holding us together
these past few months. For going on any adventure with me.

Dad. You can't read this. But nonetheless, you are the reason I'm
here. You taught me how to be a badass, how to believe in myself,
how to leave my manners on the side of the court when I was playing
netball. To be kind. And you're the reason I have such expensive taste.

Mum. You are my hero. My best friend. I am always so surprised
when everyone doesn't list their mother as one of their best friends.
Because not everyone is lucky like me. Thank you for taking my calls,
for never judging me for buying shoes that I don't need, for urging
me to get the matching bag. I know what a strong woman looks like

because of you.

Polly, Emma, Harriet. My girls. You're still over on the other side of the world, but you're always there if I need an opinion on a selfie, or to have some form of breakdown.

Jessica Gadziala. My #sisterqueen. You are the reason I get through many of my writing blocks and general anxieties. You are a selfless friend, a kickass author and an all around queen.

Amo Jones. My ride or die. You tell me when I'm being crazy, you support me no matter what.

Michelle Clay. I am so lucky that you came into my life. You are such a special human. You're so precious to me. In short, you're family.

Annette Brignac. I'm so glad my books brought us together. I honestly don't know where I'd be without you. My books would not be the same. My life would not be the same. Thank you for being you.

Ginny. You are so important to my books. To my life. You know my characters almost as well as you know me. You know when I need a kick up the butt or some kind words. Thank you for being there for me always.

Kim. Thank you not only for being an amazing editor, but being there as a friend too. You are such a special human and I'm so so lucky to have found you.

You. The reader. I would not be typing this without you. Without your support. You are the reason I get to live my dream. Why I get to write stories and call it a job. Thank you for making my dreams come true.

ABOUT THE AUTHOR

ANNE MALCOM has been an avid reader since before she can remember, her mother responsible for her love of reading. It started with magical journeys into the world of Hogwarts and Middle Earth, then as she grew up her reading tastes grew with her. Her love of reading doesn't discriminate, she reads across many genres, although classics like Little Women and Gone with the Wind will hold special places in her heart. She also can't get enough romance, especially when some possessive alpha males throw their weight around.

One day, in a reading slump, Cade and Gwen's story came to her and started taking up space in her head until she put their story into words. Now that she has started, it doesn't look like she's going to stop anytime soon, with many more characters demanding their story be told as well.

Raised in small town New Zealand, Anne had a truly special childhood, growing up in one of the most beautiful countries in the world. She has backpacked across Europe, ridden camels in the Sahara and eaten her way through Italy, loving every moment. She has settled down with her fiancé, their dogs and happy to be in one place…for a while at least.

Want to get in touch with Anne? She loves to hear from her readers.
You can email her: annemalcomauthor@hotmail.com
Or join her reader group on Facebook.

ALSO BY ANNE MALCOM

Resonance of Stars

VEIN CHRONICLES
Fatal Harmony
Deathless
Faults in Fate
Eternity's Awakening
Buried Destiny

RETIRED SINNERS
Splinters of You

STANDALONES
Birds of Paradise
Doyenne
Hush (Co-Written with BT Urruela)

Printed in Great Britain
by Amazon

11234875R00198